Moon Dance

CHRISTINE POPE

DARK VALENTINE PRESS

MOON DANCE

ISBN: 978-0-9883348-8-5
Copyright © 2016 by Christine Pope
Published by Dark Valentine Press

Cover design by Ravven
Book layout by Indie Author Services

To learn more about this author, go to
www.christinepope.com.

Moon Dance

Chapter One

"Goodness, Iselda," my Aunt Lyselle called out to me just as I passed the small salon where she sat with her embroidery, "I would think you have had enough sunshine for one day!"

The sunshine was not the real reason why I had decided to flee the castle once again, but I did not wish to enter into that particular conversation with my aunt. Also, I wondered whether anyone could truly get "enough" sunshine, but all I said was, "Don't worry, Auntie—I am bringing my hat." And a basket with a book to keep me amused and a small flask of cool water to prevent me from becoming too warm, although I did not bother to tell her that.

My reply seemed to reassure her that I would not return at the end of the afternoon looking browned and quite unlady-like, for she lifted her shoulders and returned to her attention to the piece of fine linen, half-covered in delicate blue forget-me-nots, which covered her lap. "Dinner is at seven," she said as she raised her needle once again.

I offered a smile, although I did not bother to reply. Dinner had always been at seven ever since I came to live here some six years earlier, but I supposed she found it reassuring to remind me of the household's routine, especially because I had a tendency to lose myself in a book and quite forget what time it actually was.

Of my cousins there was no sign. I assumed they must all be up in my eldest cousin Adalynn's suite, for my aunt's maid, who had been overseeing the construction of the wedding wardrobe, had just this morning brought up the last of the dresses she'd created, including the all-important wedding gown. Adalynn was to be married to the only son of the Earl of Delmayne, a very great triumph for the daughter of a simple baron. That wedding would take place in less than a week, which meant the household had been thrown into quite the uproar during the past few days as the preparations for that all-important event grew more and more frenzied.

It also meant that I had begun to find whatever excuses I could to flee the chaos as often as was possible. My aunt, I feared, knew very well why I had made myself so scarce, but as she was a kind-hearted soul, she did not bother to remonstrate with me, for she knew I was not entirely happy about my current circumstances. Adalynn was only a year older than I, twenty to my nineteen, and yet I had no betrothed, and few prospects for one.

The reasons for my regrettably single state were well known to nigh everyone in the kingdom. Not because of anything I had done, or because of any particular objections to my person, for, as my aunt always hastened to say—"no one could deny that you have grown into a very lovely young woman, Iselda!"

No, the reason for my fairly ineligible status was that my sister had fallen into a terrible trap through no fault of her own. Our father, I fear, was a most intemperate man, and one night while he was in his cups, boasted that she had the ability to spin straw into gold. While Annora was an accomplished needle-woman, even she did not possess that particular talent. Her life would have been forfeit at the old king's whim, were it not that a man of singular talents had stepped in to save her.

But magic, even of the sort that could create gold from nothing and the finest of precious stones from thin air, had been forbidden for centuries in our kingdom of Purth, and once the lovers were found out, both their lives were once more at risk. Tobyn—the man who loved my sister, and was now my brother-in-law—could do nothing except kill the mad king to save the woman of his heart, and as a result, both of them were forced to flee our homeland, never to return. The scandal, I was told by my cousins, did not die down for many months, and still was resurrected from time to time, even so many years after my sister and Tobyn had gone into exile.

I, being a mere thirteen at the time, had nothing to do with any of those goings-on, although my younger self had thought the whole affair tremendously exciting. Unfortunately, merely to be a member of the Kelsden family was enough to taint my prospects, and so, even though I had been spirited away to live with my unreproachable aunt and her daughters, I still had had no offers of marriage.

Most of the time I found myself reasonably resigned to my situation. Perhaps I could remain and be a companion to my aunt as my cousins were married off one by one. Adalynn was the lucky bride now, but the eldest son of Count Bellender was staying with us for a few weeks, mainly to see if he and my cousin Carella would suit. Lord Mayson had been engaged to be married from the time he was a very small boy, but his betrothed had died of a fever several months earlier, and now his father was eager to get him engaged again.

It was a good plan, save for one unfortunate thing—Lord Mayson showed very little interest in Carella, although he had been quite friendly with me. Too friendly, some might think, and yet there was little I could do about the situation.

Was it any wonder that I tried to escape the confines of my aunt and uncle's castle as often as I could without seeming too irresponsible?

The day was bright and windy, and I tied the ribbons of my hat securely under my chin as I made my way to my favorite spot on the estate, down near the edge of a stream that wandered lazily along between green banks dotted with forget-me-nots and daisies. A great willow overhung the water there, and I could be guaranteed of shade so as not to darken my pale skin.

However, I had not sat there for so very long before I heard the rustle of footsteps in the green grass. A moment later, Lord Mayson appeared, his own dark head bare to the sun and the wind. He smiled when he spotted me sitting under the willow, and approached.

"Good day, Lady Iselda."

To be truthful, I had no actual claim to that title. It was my three cousins, or Lady Janessa, another of my aunt's wards, who should be addressed thus. But I supposed that the young lord thought it rude to simply call me Iselda, or to refer to me as "mistress," which would indicate that I was of lower birth than he.

"Good afternoon, Lord Mayson," I replied as I set down my book. "How do you fare this day?"

"Well enough," he said, then sat down on a fallen log not too far from the one I currently occupied. "But I will confess that I was beginning to feel somewhat...confined."

Meaning, I supposed, that my uncle the baron had been giving him more not-so-subtle hints. I loved my Uncle Danly far more than I loved my own father, for he possessed a kind heart equal to my aunt's, but subtle he was not.

"I am sorry," I said, holding out my flask of water. "Something to wet your throat?"

Lord Mayson took the water from me and allowed himself one carefully measured swallow. That was like him; he would not wish to leave me without enough to quench my own thirst on the walk back to the house.

"I do not think my uncle will be pleased to learn that you have sought me out, however," I went on.

"No, I suppose not," Mayson agreed. He returned the flask to me, and I set it down on the hollow log where I sat.

An uncomfortable little silence fell, only partially obscured by the chatter of the stream a few yards away. This was not like us, for we had found one another easy to talk to almost from the time his lordship had come to stay at my uncle and aunt's castle. We had read many of the same books, enjoyed walking outdoors, and had little use for court intrigue.

Not that I'd had much of an opportunity to experience court life myself, exiled here in the hinterlands as I was, but from what I'd heard, it did seem to be a place of gossip and backstabbing, even under the rule of our good King Harlin.

Then Mayson said abruptly, "You and I have become good friends, have we not, Iselda?"

I agreed that we had.

Another pause. He was a tall, handsome man, well built and with a generally amiable aspect. Now, however, his dark eyes were stormy, his mouth a twist of dissatisfaction. This expression was so unlike him that I almost commented on it, but then decided to hold my tongue. Clearly, he had come out here to say something to me, and I thought it best for him to come to it in his own time.

And what if he wishes to make you his wife? I thought then. *Uncle Danly and Aunt Lyselle will be dreadfully cross, even if they will do their best to hide it. And I fear that Carella will never speak to me again.*

I tried to tell myself that I was ranging far ahead of anything that had actually occurred. Lord Mayson had spoken no words of love to me, had paid me no flowery compliments to win my heart. But perhaps that was simply not his way...or perhaps he thought there was no real reason for him to do so, not when he was the son of an earl and I merely the daughter of a disgraced merchant who seemed intent on drinking himself to death.

"So I believe that means we will suit very well," Mayson went on.

My eyes widened. "Are you saying what I think you are saying, my lord?"

He flushed then, and looked away from me, toward the creek. I could see the muscles in his throat tighten as he swallowed. Then a bitter smile touched his mouth. "I am not sure what I myself am saying." Shifting on the log where he sat, he turned back in my direction. "I thought—" He stopped there, anguish clear in his friendly features, so ill-suited to such a look of torment.

"Please, my lord," I said, troubled by his obvious distress. "We just agreed that we were friends, did we not? And so friends can say anything they like to one another." Or at least, I believed that to be the truth, even though I had no close friends. My cousins were the only real family I had here in Purth, and I loved them, but even after spending years together, they did not confide in me, nor I in them. They knew they would move on and leave me behind, because no one seemed to want me.

"Yes, you are my friend, Iselda," Lord Mayson said, his expression clearing somewhat. "What would you say if I told you that I did not wish to marry at all?"

"You don't?" I was rather pleased with the manner in which I asked the question, for I thought I had managed to sound curious, but not discouraged. And, to tell the truth, I wasn't disappointed. I liked Lord Mayson very much, but I knew my attachment did not go any deeper than that.

Or at least I did not think that it did.

"No." He stopped there, as if he'd intended to say something else but decided against it.

"But...." I, too, paused as I searched for the right words. "But you were betrothed."

"An engagement arranged when I was not yet five years old," Mayson said. "You know that is how it is done."

I could only nod. Younger siblings sometimes were allowed the luxury of waiting longer to find their matches, as was the case with my cousins Carella and Theranne, but Adalynn, the eldest, had been betrothed since almost the time she was born. And Mayson, being the heir to a title and a large estate, would also have had his matrimonial future decided before he was old enough to even really comprehend what marriage was.

"However," he continued, his voice heavy, "I know that is what is expected of me. I will do my duty. But I would find it much easier if the woman at my side was a friend, rather than simply someone my father thought suitable."

While I was glad to know Lord Mayson viewed me as a friend, I could not help but wince inwardly at his use of the word "suitable." My cousin Carella was suitable; I, most assuredly, was not. Even if my family had not had the blot on its reputation because of what had happened to the former king, I was still only the youngest daughter of a merchant, and Mayson should be marrying someone with a far grander pedigree. "Perhaps you should merely tell your father that you need more time," I ventured. "While I understand his wish to see you married, it is not so terribly urgent, is it? I had heard that his lordship is in good health."

At my comment, Lord Mayson actually laughed, although his laughter had a grim edge to it, as if he knew something more about the matter than he was letting on. "Yes," he said, "my father is in excellent health, and very robust for a man in his late forties. But I fear that is not enough to prevent him from reminding me of how I should be fulfilling my duties as the heir to the earldom."

"If that is his desire, then I doubt very much he would be happy to learn that you had set your sights on someone as lowly as myself." Mayson frowned then, and I added hastily, "That is, if such a thing is even your intention. I must confess that I find myself somewhat confused by what you have been trying to say to me."

"You and I both, Iselda." He went silent for a moment, his fingers tugging restlessly at the loose lacings of his shirt. It was quite a warm day, warmer than usual for early June, and he had undone the ties that held together the high collar of the shirt he wore. Underneath, I could catch a glimpse of smoothly tanned skin, and I swallowed. There was something strangely enticing about the sight, even though I had told myself I did not really think of Mayson in such a way. "I came down here thinking I could speak to you honestly, but now...now I am not so certain."

"I think you have been very honest with me."

"Have I?" A short laugh with very little humor in it. He ceased playing with the laces on his shirt and instead shifted on the log where he sat so he could once again face toward the stream. It glittered and danced in the bright sunlight, enticing.

If I had been there alone, I would have taken off my shoes and stockings, and hitched up my skirts so I might go wading in the creek and cool my feet, but of course I would never do something so unladylike in front of Lord Mayson. As it was, I pushed the heavy hair off the back of my neck and wished I had thought to pull it back with a ribbon. That hair, long and golden and reaching nearly to my waist, had won me a number of compliments, but it was also extremely warm.

As a young woman of nineteen summers, I should have begun to put it up, for girls my age only wore their hair down at grand events, but my Aunt Lyselle could be quite lax about such things when we did not have company. I supposed she did not think of Mayson as "company," since she had known him since he was born, and because he was staying with us for such an extended period of time.

He rose to his feet and walked down to the water, then paused there. For a few seconds, I thought perhaps he was going to do the very thing I had dreamed of—take off his boots and stockings and go wading to cool his feet. Instead, he squatted on the bank and trailed his fingers in the water, staring down at the creek as if it were the most important thing in his world.

Then he turned and looked back at me, an unspoken plea in his eyes. "Would it be so very bad, to be the Countess of Bellender Rise?"

As far as I could tell, there was no guile in that question. He truly wished to know my answer. I stood as well and came down toward him, then gazed up into his face. I did not have my sister's height, and so even though he was not overly tall, I still could not look at him completely eye to eye. "It would be if you did not love me."

His eyebrows lifted, and his mouth twisted slightly. "I had no idea you were so romantic, Iselda."

"I—"

Was I romantic? True, I did spend a good deal of my time reading stories of places and people from far away and long ago, and perhaps their tales had made me slightly less inclined to appreciate the here and now. But I knew that was not the real reason why I had given him the answer I did.

No, I supposed I could blame my sister and her husband for that. Of course they had not done anything to mislead me, or tell me the world was different from the place it truly appeared to be.

No, it was more that I had seen the way they gazed at one another. Poor Tobyn had been terribly disfigured when the former king tried to burn him at the stake because of his magical abilities, but those scars seemed to disappear when Tobyn looked at my sister, his face transformed by his devotion. True love had blazed from his eyes, just as that same passion had warmed hers when she looked back at him. She did not care what the fire had done to his face, for she loved his heart and soul and mind.

I hadn't realized it at the time, but when I saw them looking at each other in such a way, it was as if I had made a silent vow somewhere deep within my soul. If I could not be with a man who could also gaze at me with all the strength and beauty of his heart and know me to be his—and if I could not experience the same feelings as I gazed back at him—then I would rather spend my life alone.

"Perhaps I am romantic," I said, forcing a carelessness into my words that I did not quite feel. "But, even though I was a young girl when my mother passed away, I saw how she and my father fared together. They were not content, I fear, for theirs was a marriage arranged with no thought for their future happiness. It is better to be alone, I think, than to be with someone who cannot give you all of his heart."

For a long moment, Mayson said nothing. Once again I saw how his mouth tightened, and a certain anguish entered his dark eyes. I could not say whence that anguish had come, only that I sensed it did not have anything to do with me.

When he spoke, however, he sounded calm enough, with no trace of anger in his tone. Rather, there was resignation, as if he had finally faced an unpleasant truth he'd been avoiding for too long and decided there was nothing else he could do.

"You are a wise young woman, Iselda Kelsden. I hope that one day I may find happiness with someone even half as wise."

If his father and my aunt and uncle had their way, I rather feared he would not. I loved my cousin, but Carella was certainly not what anyone might call wise. Lighthearted and sweet enough, but no tragedies had ever touched her, nor anything untoward which might bar her from breezing happily through her life. She had no appreciation of the lessons learned from pain, and so, I thought, would not be able to provide any true comfort to someone in need of such a thing.

I said nothing of that, however. Mayson would have to make his own choices, whatever those might turn out to be. In the meantime, I would only try to be his friend, and hope that he might someday be able to tell me what troubled him so.

Because the air was so taut between us, I essayed a smile and said, as carelessly as I could, "As for that, I doubt my Aunt Lyselle would think me wise for venturing out of doors on a day when the sun is so fierce. No doubt I will be as brown as a hawthorn branch by the end of the summer."

Mayson did not return my smile. "I think not. For you take care to keep in the shade, and besides, your skin is like milk. It is not the type to brown easily."

That assessment was true enough. I had given myself a burn once or twice when I was careless, but after it faded, I was as pale as ever. Whereas my cousins had inherited their father's somewhat deeper complexion, and did have to take care to avoid looking like a gaggle of farmer's daughters, tanned from working in the fields all day.

"I suppose you are right," I said. Because I knew that my aunt and uncle would be displeased if Mayson and I spent much more time alone together, I thought it best that I go back to the castle. He did not seem inclined to end the conversation, and I certainly was not rude enough to pick up my book and begin reading in front of him. "But I still think it is probably time for me to return."

So I bent down and gathered up my basket, only to have Mayson hurry to take it from me. When I began to protest, he only shook his head and gave me the first real smile I had yet seen from him that day.

"You have quite enough work to do managing that hat, I think."

Well, I couldn't argue with that observation. My aunt had returned from a trip to our capital of Bodenskell a month earlier armed with all sorts of insights as to the state of fashion in our fair country of Purth. Skirts were becoming more voluminous, necklines lower—although she would not allow such a trend to take hold in her household—and many of the court ladies had donned large straw hats to protect themselves from the sun.

She'd been so taken with the hats that she'd brought back several for each of her daughters, and one each for me and Janessa as well. While I did appreciate the way the hat shielded my face from the sun, it was unwieldy enough that if I didn't keep one hand free at all times, the broad-brimmed straw would take it into its head to go sailing off if the wind was strong enough.

"Thank you, my lord," I said sincerely.

In silence, we headed away from the stream and back toward the castle, which did not look quite so dreary in the bright sunlight as it did at most other times. The structure had been built many centuries earlier, and while I supposed it must have been formidable enough when it came to resisting a siege, it was certainly not the sort of edifice to elicit admiration because of its architectural grace.

When we were almost to the gates—which always stood open in these times of peace—Mayson gave me a quick bow and an even hastier farewell as he handed me my basket, and headed off toward the stables. It was true that he did love to ride, but in that moment I guessed he was more interested in making sure neither my aunt, nor my uncle, nor any of my cousins saw us walking together, rather than in a brisk after-noon gallop.

Or perhaps he had decided that a long ride outside the castle's gates was what he needed to clear his head. In that moment, I wished I could go with him. It would be good to ride away, wild and free. But I sensed he wanted to be alone, and I knew I did not have the luxury of indulging in a solitary ride without a chaperone. A walk down to the creek was one thing, and indeed the farthest I was allowed to go unless accompanied by a servant or one of my cousins.

So I made no protest, and watched Mayson walk away, dark hair catching glints of warm copper and mahogany in the bright sunlight.

And I wondered if he would ever tell me the real truth behind his desire to marry me.

Chapter Two

As I had expected—and rather feared—all was chaos in the wing that had been given over to "the girls," as my somewhat beleaguered uncle liked to refer to the gaggle of young women who lived under his roof. Adalynn, being the eldest, had a room of her own, while her sisters shared the chamber next to that one, and Janessa and I occupied the room across the hall from Carella and Theranne.

But my chamber was empty as I went there to drop off my hat and my basket, although I didn't have to look very hard to see where everyone was. No, one of the maids went scurrying past me as I poked my head out into the hallway, and from the open door just beyond, I heard the clamor of feminine voices, apparently all talking at once.

My first instinct was to quietly close the door to my bed-chamber and retrieve my book, and hope that no one would realize where I was hiding. Unfortunately, I knew that particular stratagem would probably not work, or at least not for very long. Sooner or later, someone would come looking for me.

So after I had taken off my hat and done my best to smooth my windblown curls, I took a deep breath and went out to Adalynn's room. The door stood open, and I could hear Carella's rather high-pitched voice, saying,

"Oh, Addie! You will be the most splendid bride in all of Purth!"

As I entered, I thought Carella's assessment might not be that much of an exaggeration. Adalynn had inherited her mother's beauty, and, with her chestnut hair and green eyes, actually resembled my own sister far more than I did. Now Adalynn stood in front of a tall mirror that had been brought up from her mother's chambers, and turned this way and that as she inspected the gown of deep rose-colored watered silk she wore. Pearls had been stitched around the neckline and on the slashed sleeves, along with fine embroidery in pale gold.

Clearly, my aunt and uncle were sparing no expense to ensure their eldest would be wed in a style that befitted both her station and the rank of the man she was marrying. I did not begrudge her the gown, or her future happiness, but at the same time, I could not help but feel a small stab of jealousy as she stood there in her gleaming gown. I doubted very much I would ever have anything so fine...even if I was lucky enough to find someone who would overlook my family's sullied reputation.

"It is very beautiful, and so are you," I said, and everyone looked over in my direction, Janessa and Theranne apparently surprised by my sudden appearance, Carella obviously pleased that I agreed with her.

But Adalynn's full mouth thinned slightly. She and I had never gotten along that well. Or rather, I had done my best to be friendly with her, for I knew I was living on her parents' sufferance and must do all I could to keep the peace, but she seemed to have none of it. I still wasn't entirely certain as to the reasons for her antipathy. Certainly she could not see me as a rival. Our looks were very different, but I thought she was quite as pretty as I—if not prettier—and so there should not be any jealousy on that point. As for the rest, well, she was the eldest daughter of a baron and engaged to the son of an earl. Whereas I....

Well, no reason to belabor that point.

"Yes, I do think Delanis has done well with the gown," Adalynn said, after giving me a dismissive glance before turning back to the mirror. "I am still not certain of the color, though."

The other girls gave a collective gasp and began vigorously shaking their heads. "Oh, no, Addie," Carella said at once. "That color makes your skin look like rose petals."

"Yes, it's just lovely," Janessa put in. Normally, she was quite shy and retiring, as one might expect of someone living in the household as a ward of the baron and baroness. Janessa's mother had died of a terrible wasting sickness, and her father had announced himself quite incapable of looking after a young girl on his own—although he didn't seem to experience that same deficiency when it came to raising his son—and so she had been living with us for the past three years.

She and I had that one thing in common, anyway. Neither of our fathers wanted anything to do with us.

Adalynn honored Janessa's comment with a faint nod and then went back to the inspection of her appearance. Looking past my cousin, I saw that the bed and several of the room's chairs were piled high with various high-waisted gowns and chemises, seeming to indicate that she had been trying on her wardrobe all afternoon and had decided to have the wedding dress be the climax of the activity.

Logically, I knew this all made sense. The ceremony was now only a few days away, and so if any further alterations were required, then best she find out now while there was still some time to do something about it. On the other hand, I couldn't prevent the uncharitable thought that Adalynn was indulging in this frenzy of peacocking about in her gowns so her sisters could see everything she had and they did not.

No wonder that all of Carella's interactions with Mayson lately had had a definite air of desperation about them. Adalynn would not be quite so high and mighty if her younger sister also managed to betroth herself to the son of an earl.

And no wonder that Mayson himself was beginning to feel a bit desperate. It was clear enough to me that he felt no real attraction to her, although she was nearly as lovely as her older sister.

Well, he was a grown man of twenty-two. He was not bound to stay here, could make his excuses at any time and leave. Such a departure might lead to some recriminations from his father, but after all, Carella was not the only unmarried woman of good birth in the kingdom. My uncle was quite wealthy, apart from his title, because of the tin mines located on his lands, and so I supposed that made Carella somewhat more of a catch. Still....

My aunt appeared then, pausing in the doorway so she could take a look at Adalynn. Her expression was generally one of amiability, but it softened even more than usual as she took in the sight of her daughter resplendent in rose and pearls. In the next instant, however, she became all briskness and business, and strode toward the bed with an air of exasperation.

"Look at these gowns!" she cried. "All thrown willy-nilly! Where is Delanis, and why has she allowed things to be left in such a state?"

"I wanted her to take in the bodice slightly, and she had left her sewing basket in her room," Adalynn said carelessly. "She will set all this to rights when she returns."

Aunt Lyselle did not appear mollified by this reply. She gave her daughter a more critical look this time, then shook her head. "My dear, if you take in the seams of that bodice any more, you will not be able to breathe. That, or you may find yourself exposing more of yourself than you would like if you do take a deep breath."

Her sisters and even Janessa giggled at this remark, but Adalynn did not seem at all pleased by her mother's observation. "It will be fine," she said. "I do not plan to take it in much, as that would disturb the embroidery at the neckline. But the side seams could do with an extra half inch."

"Hmm." Lyselle went closer to her daughter and inspected the seams in question, then gave a sigh. "If you must. But if Delanis is going to be occupied with tearing out those seams for the tenth time, then perhaps the rest of us should tidy up this mess. Come girls," she added briskly, "let us do what we can to make order from chaos."

For the barest second, Carella's lower lip stuck out in mutiny, but then she did as she was bidden, and went over to the bed and began gathering up the discarded gowns. Likewise, Theranne and Janessa put themselves to work picking up chemises and stockings. I made a move to help, but my aunt shook her head at me. Adalynn and I were of an age, and for that reason my aunt was careful to avoid asking me to do much in her service, of doing anything that might make it seem as if I were her inferior.

So I stayed where I was, in my post not too far away from the door, while Aunt Lyselle busied herself with tidying up the rather dizzying array of slippers that lay scattered on the floor. She put away several pairs, then picked up the next and let out a sound of dismay.

"Goodness, Adalynn! Whatever have you been doing with your shoes? They look as if you've been sweeping the stable yard in them!"

"What?" Adalynn demanded in annoyance, finally turning away from the mirror so she could inspect the shoes in question. At once her expression altered to one of consternation. "The new embroidered ones you brought me back from Bodenskell?"

"The very ones," my aunt said, looking none too pleased. The slippers she held were very pretty indeed, or at least had been once upon a time. Now I could see that the soles had been shredded almost to nonexistence, and the delicate embroidery in shades of blush and ivory and pale green had been torn, with loose threads hanging everywhere.

"But I have only worn them twice!" Adalynn protested. She left the mirror and went to her mother so she could take one of the shoes and inspect it for herself. "And both times only indoors. I wanted to make sure that they stayed pretty so I might wear them with my new green gown."

Her mother frowned as she turned the shoe she held over in her hands. "Are you sure, my dear? For I have slippers that I've owned for five years which are in far better condition than these."

"Of course I'm sure." Now Adalynn wore a frown to match her mother's, her full mouth pursed in irritation. "It must be shoddy workmanship. You should complain to the shoemaker the next time you are in town."

"But he's made all your other fancy shoes," Aunt Lyselle pointed out. She went to the wardrobe and withdrew another pair, these ones in fine pale blue kid hand-painted in delicate swirls and arabesques. "These ones look as if they've never even been worn."

A shrug, the fine silk covering Adalynn's shoulders glinting with the movement. "Perhaps he has a new apprentice, one who is not so skilled as he. All I can say is that I only wore those slippers twice, and so nothing *I* have done could have possibly put them in that state."

For a few seconds, my aunt appeared as if she wanted to pursue the topic. Then she, too, shrugged, and put the shoes she held back into the wardrobe. "Very well. I will take the matter up with him the next time I am in town." She glanced over at her daughters and at Janessa, who had finished their tidying-up and stood all in a row beside the bed, looking rather like cadets awaiting a military review. "Thank you very much, girls. Run along to the solarium and attend to your own needlework, for it will be supper soon enough."

They ducked their heads and rushed out, giggling and whispering amongst themselves. Although I had not been specifically included in that command, I thought I should follow them as well. My sister was fabulously talented with her needle; I, on the other hand, possessed neither the skill nor the will to sit and make flowers bloom on cloth, or even manage the far more prosaic task of darning socks. But I was treated as a daughter of this household, and so I was expected to put in my daily hours at the activity, much as I might loathe it.

Now, though, my aunt put her hand on my sleeve as I went past and said in low tones, so Adalynn might not overhear, "Go to your room, Iselda. I would have conversation with you there."

My heart sank. Perhaps the feeling of foreboding which came over me then was only my conscience, somewhat burdened already because of what had passed between Lord Mayson and myself. It had to have been perhaps the most oblique marriage proposal ever delivered, but if my aunt inquired, I knew I could not lie and tell her that his lordship and I had spoken only of inconsequentials.

As I knew it would be useless to protest, I bowed my head slightly and said, perhaps in a louder tone than was required, "Oh, I must go and fetch that chemise with the torn lace from my chamber."

The other girls did not appear terribly interested by my pronouncement, since they cared little which project would occupy my next hour. But my aunt gave the barest of approving nods, obviously glad that I had come up with an excuse not to head immediately to the solar, where the abundant light provided a good space for working on embroidery or mending.

I headed toward my room, and, once inside, began to make rather a show of rummaging through the chest of drawers there, just in case any of the girls should lag behind and take a peek inside to see what I was up to. A moment later, though, I heard the last of their giggling and whispering recede as they descended the stairs. Soon after, my aunt came into my chamber and closed the door.

"So Lord Mayson met you down by the stream?"

Resisting the urge to sigh, I turned away from the dresser and nodded. My aunt might have given the impression of one who was light-headed in the extreme, concerned only with fashion and gossip and the marital futures of her daughters, but six years of sharing the same household with her had taught me something quite different. She missed very little, especially when it came to the young man everyone hoped would marry her middle daughter.

"It is a good place to escape the heat of the day," I said, my tone noncommittal. Yes, I knew that I would have to tell her the truth eventually, but her possible reaction worried me. I thought I might as well put it off for as long as possible.

"That it is," she returned, her tone equally neutral. "One might argue that the arcade on the north side of the castle is equally cool, and perhaps better for catching the breeze."

"I suppose."

Aunt Lyselle put her hands on her brocade-covered hips and watched me carefully for a moment. "And I suppose you think that I am going to be angry with you."

Her remark made me blink. Certainly nothing in her voice indicated she was angry at all, but I'd also learned over the years that she was quite good at hiding what she was thinking, of putting on the façade of the even-tempered, always good-natured lady of the house. Her outward mien did not always indicate what might be occurring inside.

"I-I am not sure," I said honestly. "I would hope not, for Lord Mayson has his own free will, and may walk where he wishes. I certainly did not invite him to come see me there."

"No, I did not think you had, for you are far more circum-spect than that." She paused, hazel eyes searching my face. As I often did, I found myself examining her features, seeing in them an echo of my own mother's countenance, although it had been ten years since we lost her, and some of the details of her appearance had begun to slip from my memory. And I also tried to see something of myself in her, and again found myself failing. My mother had told me once when I was very young that I had inherited my golden curls from her mother's mother, but I had never met my great-grandmother, nor my grandmother, either, as they had both passed away before I was even born.

True, I possessed the greenish-hazel eyes of my mother's family, but in shape they were quite different from my aunt's, or my sister's. To anyone who had not known us, we would not have appeared to be related at all.

"But," Aunt Lyselle went on briskly, "I would have to be blind to see that Lord Mayson has very little interest in Carella, whereas he seems to make some effort to seek out your company, Iselda."

"I am very sorry," I began. "I have never encouraged—"

"No, I know you have not," she broke in. "I did not mean to imply such a thing. But if he has taken you into his confidence—if he has said anything—" A pause, as if she was steeling herself to face an unpleasant truth. "If Lord Mayson has spoken with you, then you must tell me, my dear. I do not want Carella to make a fool of herself by chasing him if there is no possibility of a marriage between them."

I swallowed. "Dear Aunt Lyselle, I must confess that he did say something, but his entire manner was so strange, his demeanor so agitated, that I am not sure what to make of it."

My reply seemed to flummox my aunt. She crossed her arms, head tilted as she surveyed me. "What on earth do you mean, Iselda? Did he offer for you or did he not?"

"He—" Oh, how I wished I might be anywhere but here confronting Aunt Lyselle, who looked as if she couldn't decide whether to be worried or confused. "He spoke of how he didn't wish to be married at all, but if he must, that he would rather it were with me, as he seems to regard me as a friend. I must confess that I did not understand him at all, and told him that if I were to marry, it would be to a man who loved me and did not merely regard me as a friend."

"You told him that?" For some odd reason, she did not seem angry. Rather, her lips quirked, as if she was attempting to hold back a smile.

"Yes," I replied. "Was that wrong of me?"

"Oh, no, my dear," she said. "It's just that I see your sister's influence, even though she is many miles away and has not spoken to you in years."

As to that—I did not reply, but only lifted my shoulders. What Aunt Lyselle did not know was that my sister had perfected a system whereupon she contacted me via letters written by a scribe, so her writing would not be recognized, and using language so oblique that her missives could have come from almost anyone. These letters appeared at random intervals, sometimes only a month or two apart, sometimes with almost a year between them, and were slipped between the pages of the latest book I had ordered from the shop in the village, or folded around the bill from the dressmaker, or any of a number of clever means she'd devised to keep in touch with me in a way that would prevent anyone else from knowing. Poor Tobyn still had a price on his head, and although King Harlin did not seem overly consumed by a need to avenge his father's death, neither could he pardon my brother-in-law. Since there were agents in the land who would gladly track down even a purported mage in exchange for a hefty bounty, such secrecy was necessary.

It was in this way that I knew Annora had borne a son two years earlier, and that, far from being outcast, Tobyn was well-regarded by the Mark of Eredor himself, a man who did not believe magic was solely evil. Whether or not our own King Harlin's agents knew of Tobyn's position in that far-off land, I couldn't be sure, but it seemed that Tobyn and my sister and their young family were all prospering in their exile.

Whereas I....

"Oh, I suppose I was romantic and impressionable when Annora went away with Master Slade," I said, my tone as blithe as I could make it. "So I will not lie and tell you that her happiness had no bearing on what I might have said to Lord Mayson. But that is not the whole of the matter, dear Aunt Lyselle. I saw how unhappy my parents were, and I have no desire to repeat their history."

At this mention of her sister's marriage, my aunt winced slightly. "No, I can see why you would want to avoid such a situation. But my dear, if Lord Mayson truly wishes to make you his wife, then I think you should consider well whether it would be wise to refuse his offer. Perhaps there is not the sort of wild, romantic love you saw in your sister and Master Slade, but if you and Lord Mayson are friends, then you already have the foundation of a happy marriage. There are many couples who cannot say they were so lucky."

I did not bother to argue with that remark, for I could see the wisdom in her words. From such friendship could come lasting affection—if I would but allow such a thing to happen.

But then I recalled the wild, tormented look in Mayson's eyes as he told me that he had no wish to marry, and I somehow knew that the happiness my aunt had spoken of would very likely be nothing more than a dream, something his lordship and I could never really share. I still understood very little of why he should feel so violently opposed to marriage, but if that was the truth of his heart, I did not see the wisdom in attempting to change it.

"I understand your point, Aunt Lyselle," I said slowly. "But I also know that his lordship and I would not be happy. I am not saying he would treat me ill, for I have seen nothing in his manner to suggest such a thing. But I also know that we would both want something the other person could not give, and in the end we would grow to resent one another."

For a long moment, my aunt said nothing, only gazed at me with an unreadable expression in her eyes. Then she allowed herself a sigh before saying, "You have grown into a wise young woman, Iselda. I wish my daughters had even half your sense among them."

It was the first time I had ever heard her utter a word of criticism about her daughters. Oh, she would rebuke them from time to time when they did not seem overly inclined to do their needlework, or, in Carella and Theranne's case, spend adequate time on their studies, for they were still young enough that a tutor came to see them four days each week. But never once had I heard my aunt say anything to make me believe she thought them deficient in any way. That she had uttered such a statement now seemed to indicate how much she had been moved by my words.

"Oh, they are sensible enough, I think," I replied. "And indeed, I believe Annora would smile to hear you call me wise, for I know she often thought me quite foolish, always with my nose in a storybook, dreaming of princes and knights errant and days of magic gone by."

"Only they are not so long gone as we once thought," my aunt said. "Indeed, I certainly never thought magic would touch my family, and yet here is your sister married to a great mage."

"I don't think he believes himself to be a great mage."

"Perhaps he does not, but I know of no one else who could have achieved the things that he did. Indeed, I would not have believed such exploits were even possible, were it not that there were so many witnesses to his deeds."

I could not argue with her assessment. Indeed, while I had read of the great feats of magic performed by sorcerers of those long-ago days, in my mind I had always thought of those stories as nothing more than that—stories. But stories often had their basis in fact, as I had come to learn.

"That is only because there are so few mages left, I suppose," I said. "When there are probably fewer than fifty on the entire continent, it would make sense that any of their exploits would be cause for comment."

"Goodness!" my aunt exclaimed. "As many as fifty?" She both looked and sounded quite horrified, although I knew she had never blamed my brother-in-law for any of his actions. He had been forced to violence; it was not something he had sought out. But as open-minded as she appeared to be on the subject of magic, I knew the very notion of it still discomfited her somewhat, for it had been forbidden in our land ever since the conclusion of the mage wars, nearly a thousand years before.

"Only a guess, dear aunt," I replied. "For there is Tobyn, and the Markess of North Eredor, and no doubt others who have kept their talents a secret. But still, that is not so many when you consider how widely scattered they must be."

"Ah." She said nothing else just then, and I thought I guessed the reason why. Although she chided her daughters to attend to their studies, she herself was no great scholar. I imagined that she had only a very hazy idea of how great the continent where our homeland of Purth lay actually was. Then her manner became brisk, and she went on, "Well, if you will not accept Lord Mayson's suit, then I suppose that is the end of the matter. Go along to the solar, and then down to dinner at seven."

I took these words for the dismissal they were, and nodded before hurrying off to the sunlit chamber. A sense of relief filled me, for it seemed she was content to let the matter go.

For the time being, at any rate.

None of my cousins appeared all that puzzled by my delay in joining them. Or rather, they were busy enough with their own conversations that my absence had barely been noted. They were chattering about which of the young men in the area would be attending Adalynn's wedding, and whether there would be any appealing candidates among them.

I was rather surprised to see Carella so engaged in this discussion. Perhaps she had already decided that Lord Mayson was not as likely a prospect as he had once appeared, and so she must set her sights elsewhere. If that was the case, she did not appear overly upset by the notion, for she seemed quite lively as she debated the qualities of one young lord over another.

Or perhaps she was merely doing her best to hide her disappointment. My cousin had always reminded me of the stream that flowed across my uncle's lands—bright and chattering and not overly deep. Perhaps it was simply not in her nature to feel a hurt all that deeply, especially when nothing formal had been arranged.

Whatever her true feelings, I found myself relieved that no one attempted to engage me in the conversation, and that I was able to pick up my needle and apply myself as best I could to repairing the damaged lace at the neckline of my good chemise. Nothing could induce me to like needlework, but at least when I was mending something, I could tell myself I was doing some good by extending the life of a garment.

At length, the dinner bell sounded from somewhere below, and we all happily set aside our projects—which would be brought to our rooms later by one of the maids—and headed down to dinner. Lord Mayson was nowhere in evidence, and my aunt explained that he had gone to have his dinner at the estate of Sir Locksen, a neighbor whose lands bordered those of my uncle.

I had not known that Mayson and Sir Locksen were good friends, for our houseguest had never shown any particular interest in the elderly knight and his family before. But I guessed that Lord Mayson had decided to absent himself from our company for the evening because he had not quite regained his composure after his little confrontation with me down by the creek.

For the barest moment, I wondered if I had made the wrong decision, whether I should have accepted his suit as my aunt had wished me to. But no. It did trouble me to have upset Mayson, but even my worry over his well-being did not serve to change my mind.

And so our dinner was a quiet enough meal, with Adalynn, as usual, dominating the conversation. My uncle was a kindly man, still obviously besotted with his wife even after so many years of marriage, and so he did not do much to guide the discussion, but only listened and nodded, and from time to time signaled for one of the servants to refill his plate. He was one of those lucky men who could consume whatever he wished and still remain as lean as he had been when he was younger, and so, while I was now more or less used to the prodigious amounts he could eat, I still could not help but be astonished by the feat.

At length it was time to go upstairs. We all bade the lord and lady of the castle good night, then went up to our rooms.

Janessa was also quiet as she got ready for bed, although I noted a speculative gleam in her eyes as she looked over at me. Just as we were slipping beneath the covers of our narrow beds, placed up against opposite walls, she said, "So it is true that Lord Mayson has asked for you."

"Not at all," I lied. I did not see the point in telling her the truth, for then I would have to explain why I had refused him... and I was not sure I could even explain that to myself. Not convincingly, anyway.

"That is what Carella was saying."

I wondered if Carella had somehow managed to hang back and eavesdrop on my conversation with her mother. "Well, Carella can sometimes have incorrect impressions about things. I can assure you that I am definitely *not* engaged to Lord Mayson."

"Hmm." Janessa wriggled about under her bedclothes, but she said nothing else, and so I prayed that would be the end of her questions.

Apparently it was, for a few short minutes later, I heard her breathing deepen and become more regular. I let out a small sigh of relief, and hoped I would slip into slumber just as easily. It had been an odd and long and rather tiring day.

My wish was granted, it seemed, for the darkened room blurred around me and then slipped into blackness.

I cannot say if I dreamed. All I do know is that something woke me much later, something that made me sit up in my bed with a start, although I could not recall hearing any sound in particular. I sat there for a moment, blinking into the dimness of the chamber, although it was somewhat lighter than when I had first gone to sleep. A gibbous moon was now perfectly framed in the arched window across the room, a window whose curtains had been left drawn so as to let in the cool night breeze.

The moonlight revealed that Janessa's bed was quite empty.

Her absence puzzled me for a few seconds, but then I realized she must have gotten up to use the garderobe, which was located in a little alcove behind a wooden screen. I settled myself back down in bed, sure that I would hear her quiet footsteps at any moment.

Only...I didn't. I lay there and waited, and yet she still did not return to her own bed. Worry flickered within me, although I tried to tell myself there must be a reasonable explanation for her absence. Perhaps she had slipped out to have a midnight gossip with Carella and Theranne.

That did seem rather odd, but it would be easy enough to find out. I pushed back my bedclothes and slipped onto the floor, the silkiness of the rug soft against my bare feet. Moving quietly, I went to the door, then opened it and peered out.

Nothing stirred, save the faintest of drafts along the hallway, a draft that made the candles in the sconces flicker gently.

I padded over to the room that Carella and Theranne shared, certain I would hear muffled giggles and whispers from within. But all was quiet, so silent that I fancied I could hear the hooting of an owl as it sat in the large oak tree just outside their window.

Well, I would just have to go in. If they were awake, then I thought I would offer the excuse that I had heard a sound and had come to investigate. They might have a good giggle at that, but I did not think they would question my explanation.

So I pushed open the door.

Chapter Three

And found...nothing. Oh, the beds belonging to my two cousins were there, but they were just as empty as Janessa's. None of them were to be found—not that they had anywhere much they could have gone, since the room was merely a large rectangle, with no alcoves or cubbyholes to speak of, except the screened-off area which hid the garderobe and the bathtub.

They simply weren't there.

Fear began to rise in my breast, although I told myself that I must keep calm, that of course there had to be a logical reason as to why three girls had vanished from their beds in the middle of the night. Although I certainly did not wish to be subjected to her mocking, I knew I must go to Adalynn and tell her that her sisters and Janessa had disappeared.

Or perhaps they are all in Adalynn's chamber, I thought then. *I have no idea why she would allow them to disturb her sleep, but that certainly makes more sense than any of the rest of this.*

I went back out into the corridor and down the hall to Adalynn's room. There was always the possibility that she could have locked the door, but I did not think so. Certainly she had never locked it before.

To my relief, the door was not latched. It swung open easily enough, even as I opened my mouth to explain to an annoyed Adalynn why I was bursting into her chamber in the dead of night.

Only...she was not there, either. The moonlight pouring through the window revealed her bed to be as empty as those of her sisters, and of Janessa.

Something was terribly wrong here. My hands began to shake, but I knew I must do my best to stay calm, to try to discover a logical reason for why all the girls were missing from their beds. Had they all been kidnapped as they slept? But it would have taken more than a few armed men to steal away four grown young women, and how could so many strangers have entered the castle in the first place? Our kingdom was at peace and had been so for many years, but that did not prevent my uncle from having armed guards at every entrance to the castle. Perhaps he did so more out of habit than need, but that still didn't change the fact that several men guarded every door which led to the outdoors. Even if they had been challenged, the noise would have been enough to wake up everyone who slept within the building.

Frowning, I went over to Adalynn's bed and stared down at it. The bedclothes had been folded back neatly. There was certainly no sign that anyone had taken her forcibly. In fact, as I looked around, I realized that the embroidered slippers she had worn earlier that day, and which she usually took off and kept at the foot of the bed, were missing, as was her chamber robe of deep blue Keshiaari silk.

This discovery led me back to Carella and Theranne's room. Now I realized that their slippers were missing as well, along with their dressing gowns. And I had no doubt that if I went back to the chamber I shared with Janessa, I would find her slippers and robe gone, too.

Sleepwalking? Such a thing had always seemed to me an invention of storytellers, and not something that happened to people in actuality. Certainly I had never walked in my sleep. And I had shared a chamber with Janessa for more than a year now. If she had a predilection for rising from her bed and wandering the castle in the middle of the night, I would have encountered it before now. At any rate, even if one of my missing companions actually did sleepwalk, it would strain the bounds of credulity for me to believe all four of them suffered from the same affliction.

I knew I should not waste any more time in speculation. I must go downstairs and wake my uncle and aunt, and tell them that their daughters were missing, along with the ward whose person they had sworn to protect. Enough time had already been wasted.

But as I turned toward the door of Adalynn's chamber, a strange lassitude came over me. Although I had been alert—even nervous—but a moment before, now it seemed as if I could barely keep my eyes open. Nothing was so terribly wrong, after all. I only needed to return to my bed, and all this would be as if something from a dream.

Without consciously realizing what I was doing, I moved down the hallway and went into my room. I did not glance at Janessa's empty bed, but only climbed into my own and pulled the covers up nearly to my chin. Within the next instant, I was fast asleep.

An ear-cracking yawn woke me. I blinked, and realized the yawn had come from Janessa, who was sitting up in her bed and rubbing at her eyes. Her rich brown hair tumbled over her shoulders, rather than being confined to its usual nighttime plait, and I frowned. I could have sworn I had seen her braiding it right before bed, just as she always did.

She must have caught me staring, because she mumbled, "Good morning."

"Good morning," I replied. Something about this felt dreadfully wrong, as if there was something I knew I should be remembering but which appeared to have eluded me for the moment. All I could recall was lying down and putting my head on my pillow, just as I did every night, and yet it seemed as if I had forgotten something of vital importance

Another yawn, and Janessa stretched, then grimaced. "I cannot think what I did yesterday to make me so weary! It feels as if every muscle in my body aches."

Truly, I could not think of what ailed her, either, for, as far as I knew, she had spent the day sedately within the confines of the castle, and hadn't even taken a walk down to the stream, as I had. Again, I experienced that nagging sensation, as though a lost memory tickled at the back of my mind but wouldn't quite surface.

Oh, well, if it was truly that important, then it would reappear at some point. I said, "Well, I am sure that a warm bath will cure most of those aches, whatever it is that caused them."

"I suppose you are right," she replied. "But it is most curious."

I could not argue with that. Nor did I have time to, for soon thereafter the maids appeared with the hot water for our baths, and the greater part of the next hour and a half was spent in the two of us getting ready for our day. By the time we had bathed and dressed and had our hair arranged by our maids, the sun was quite high, and we knew we must hurry, or be late for breakfast.

As Janessa picked up one of her slippers to slide it on, however, she let out an exclamation of dismay. "Goodness! The soles of these are nearly worn through, and yet I have only had them these three months."

Recalling the way my aunt had chided Adalynn over the condition of her slippers, I couldn't keep myself from taking a closer look. Sure enough, the leather soles of Janessa's shoes were scuffed and scored, and wearing thin in several places. She certainly wasn't active enough to have caused so much damage in such a short amount of time, and yet I could not deny that her slippers were in a pitiful state.

"I will have to write to Papa and ask him to send me some more," she said mournfully as she tied her shoe ribbons around her ankles. "And he will chide me for being so careless with these ones. But I know I must do something, for they will not last the month in this state."

Janessa did not mind being frank with me, for she knew that my own immediate family was far from rich, and so she did not bother to hide that her own father possessed nothing near the wealth that my uncle did. Indeed, I rather thought it reassured her to have someone close by who would not hold her own lack of means against her.

Of course, I had a small secret of my own, one that I had not shared even with my aunt. My brother-in-law's magical gift involved working with precious metals and stones, and indeed conjuring them from the very air. He knew better than to send me finished pieces, for I would not be able to wear them without having to reveal from whence they had come, but with some of my sister's letters had also come small, undistinguished rocks—or at least, that was how they looked when they first arrived. I could not begin to guess at how Tobyn had managed the enchantment, but once I took those stones into my hand, they changed into a precious ruby, or a sapphire, or an emerald green as glass.

He sent me those stones because he knew how much my father had depleted my already meager dowry. The gems were small and easy to hide, and something that would be gratefully accepted by any suitor who otherwise might be put off by my very small dowry. I supposed at some point I would have to reveal that I had more means than I had let on, but some part of me was stubborn and hoped that if a man cared for me enough to ask me to be his wife, then he would not think of how much money I had to contribute to the arrangement.

But of course Janessa knew nothing of any of this, and so most likely thought her situation was equivalent to mine. I made sympathetic noises in response to her remark about her father being angry with her, and then said we had best be down for breakfast.

My cousins appeared just as bleary-eyed as Janessa; Carella couldn't seem to stop yawning. To look at them, one would have thought they'd been out all night, dancing with the local swains, and yet I knew they had all been safely in their beds.

Or....

Again that whisper of something forgotten tickled at my mind, although I couldn't quite grasp what it was. I told myself not to worry, that if it was truly important, sooner or later I would be able to remember what I could not currently recall.

"Goodness," Aunt Lyselle said as she gazed from one of her daughters to the other. Her brow puckered in a frown; I could tell that she, too, was puzzled by their weary aspect. "What has gotten into all of you this morning?"

"I don't know, Mama," Theranne replied. Her brown eyes looked enormous in her pale face. "I am just so very tired."

"You girls weren't up all night telling ghost stories, were you?" my uncle asked. He wore an amused half-smile, and clearly wasn't as concerned about their appearance as his wife seemed to be.

"I should think not," Adalynn said, her tone indignant. "That is, I cannot speak for Carella and Theranne, nor Janessa and Iselda, I suppose, but I know I went to sleep at a very respectable hour."

"It is no matter," my aunt said briskly. "You shall all have some tea, and that, along with your breakfast, should be enough to restore you."

None of the girls looked terribly reassured by her remark, although no one argued, either. The maids went around and poured a good measure of hot tea into the waiting mugs at everyone's place setting, and then it was time for the food itself—a great pie made of eggs and onions and cheese, and bacon on the side, and my favorite little rolls, the ones studded with currants. All in all, it was an excellent meal, and one which helped to make me feel restored, even though I still sensed an underlying weariness, one I could not fully explain.

I saw no sign of Lord Mayson, but that did not bother me overmuch, for he did not always break his fast with us. He tended to rise early and take only some bread and cheese with him as he went on his early morning walks, a practice that dismayed my aunt somewhat, although of course she did nothing to prevent him. Yes, he was her guest, but she would always allow him to go his own way.

Besides, it would have been difficult to face him this morning after what had passed between us the day before. I did not wish to avoid him, but I also preferred that our next encounter be something that didn't take place under the watchful eyes of my cousins, and my uncle and aunt.

All of the girls' feet were safely hidden under the table, or I would have attempted to see if my other two cousins' shoes were as damaged as Janessa's slippers, or Adalynn's. What precisely such a coincidence might mean, I didn't know, but it would seem to indicate that something very strange was occurring at my uncle's estate.

But because I could not slip from my chair and go about on my hands and knees, inspecting my cousins' footwear, I had to resign myself to waiting for another opportunity to present itself. Perhaps I could convince them to go wading in the stream, since the weather promised to be warm and sunny once again. If they left their shoes behind, then I would have my best chance at taking a closer look.

What that would prove, I had no idea. That the kingdom's shoemakers had all simultaneously become slipshod in their workmanship? Put that way, the situation did sound rather ridiculous, although I had to think something strange must be happening, even if I couldn't determine what it was.

The conversation at breakfast was mundane enough, consisting of remarks about the weather and the preparations my aunt was making in advance of Adalynn's upcoming nuptials, for guests would start arriving several days before the event itself. The castle was being scrubbed from top to bottom, and corners perhaps ignored for too long now returned to their original sparkling state. The gardeners were watching the flowers in the garden beds carefully, waiting to see which blooms would be at their peak when it came time to harvest them.

And we girls were not being ignored, either. True, much of the attention was on Adalynn, but each of the rest of us was to have a new gown, so we might not look shabby on the young bride's day. My dress was certainly the most beautiful I had ever owned, with its sweeping skirt of silver and sapphire-blue brocade, and the silver edgings on its slashed sleeves. The gown was a gift from my aunt, for certainly I would never have been able to afford something so fine on my own—well, unless I happened upon a way to sell one of the precious gems Tobyn had sent me. At any rate, even though the happy event was still several days away, the house had already begun to buzz with excitement.

The tea and the food did seem to revive my cousins somewhat, for their eyes grew less heavy and some of the bloom returned to their cheeks. My aunt watched them carefully, but said nothing as they rose from the table and went back upstairs—Carella and Theranne to prepare for the arrival of their tutor, Adalynn and Janessa to go back to their needlework. Janessa was very skilled, and although Delanis, Aunt Lyselle's personal maid, was overseeing the construction of Adalynn's wedding gown, Janessa had offered to embroider a matching silk purse.

Their departure put me rather at loose ends, and so I decided I would go for a walk. Not because I wished to have an "accidental" encounter with Lord Mayson, but rather because I thought some time outdoors might help to clear my head.

After absentmindedly nodding a "yes" to my aunt's admonishment that I put on my hat, I went out the side door that led to the gardens. Truly, summer was upon us with a vengeance; the hot sun overhead made me very glad of the hat, and the air was thick with the scent of roses and lilies and lilacs. Bees hummed away.

I took in a deep breath of the warm air. Despite the heat, it did feel good to be outdoors. I wore a gown of lightweight blue linen, and so did not feel too encumbered as I made my way down the path to the gate which opened on the rolling landscape beyond. Two guards stood there as well; they offered me a pair of quick but friendly bows as I went by, but I also noted how they paid attention to where I was headed. My uncle had all the appearances of an easy man, true. That did not mean he did not keep watch on the comings and goings of all the young women who lived under his roof.

Except last night....

The thought was so odd that I paused for a moment to consider it. Where in the world had that come from? As Adalynn had told her mother, we had all gone to bed early the night before, and slept more or less soundly. I had a vague recollection of hearing an owl hooting outside my window, sometime in the depths of the night, but there was nothing so very unusual about that.

Shaking my head—but not too firmly, for fear of dislodging my hat—I resumed my pace and strode down toward the stream. My hope of having my cousins accompany me had not come to fruition, but at least I could enjoy the shade of the trees there, and the delicious coolness of the water.

As I removed my slippers, I turned them over and inspected the soles for any signs of unusual wear. I saw nothing, however, except scuffs that I knew had been there for some time. And since the shoes had come from the same shoemaker in Bodenskell where my aunt bought all our shoes, I had no explanation as to why Janessa's slippers, and Adalynn's, should be so much more worn than mine.

I set the slippers down on a rock and unrolled my silk stockings, then hitched up my skirts so I might safely walk in the water. Perhaps such behavior was not entirely ladylike, but at the moment I thought of nothing more than getting some much-needed relief from the heat.

Cool water closed over my bare feet and rose to halfway up my calves as I went a little farther out into the stream. In the early spring, when the snow melt flowed down from the mountains, I would never attempt such a thing, for the water—besides being icy cold—would rush far more quickly than it was safe to stand in. Now, however, while I could feel the current as it flowed around my legs, I knew it was safe enough.

I waded upstream a few paces in the green-dappled shadows cast by the willows and sycamores that overhung the stream banks. A little ahead was a place where I liked to stop and sit down, a sandy stretch in between the otherwise rather rocky edges of the creek. When I drew close, though, I could only frown in puzzlement, for the usually smooth expanse of sand was now marred by a number of footprints. And not men's booted feet, either, indicating that perhaps my uncle's huntsmen had come this way. No, these prints were similar in size to my own, small and delicate.

Had my cousins come here without me? I supposed it was possible, although most of the time they preferred to stay downstream, at the natural fording spot with its stepping stones where I had left my slippers. Here, the bank was sandy but steep, and not that easy to reach. And yet it seemed that someone had been here.

I could feel myself frowning as I moved closer to the far bank of the stream. Because of the way it sloped so steeply, the easiest way to climb up was to grasp an exposed tree root and use that to haul myself from the water. As I did so, part of my hitched-up gown came loose and trailed in the creek. Damn. I tried to console myself that on such a warm day, the fine linen would dry in no time.

At any rate, I had more puzzling things to occupy my mind. For once I had carefully skirted the sandy area where the footprints were most prominent, I saw that they continued into the forest before they disappeared completely, obscured by fallen leaves and last year's carpet of pine needles. Perhaps a master woodsman would have been able to still locate their trail, but I certainly did not possess that particular ability.

So I stopped there, standing on a patch of thin grass in my bare feet, staring off into the woods and wondering. I knew my uncle's lands ended out there somewhere, and wild land began, owned by no particular lord, although I supposed it must then be the king's property. We had always been admonished to stay by the stream and not venture into the forest, for it was populated by bears and wolves and the gods knew what else.

Right then, with the sun shining brightly overhead through a canopy of fresh green leaves, the forest did not look terribly intimidating. But I was barefoot, and knew also that my aunt and uncle would be quite angry with me if I wandered off there by myself. The mystery of those vanishing footprints would have to be investigated at another time.

Repressing a sigh, I turned toward the stream and began to carefully descend toward the water. As I did so, however, I made a mental vow.

I would return, and see where those footprints led.

But not that day. When I returned to the castle—looking somewhat the worse for wear, I must admit—my aunt admonished me for disappearing for so long, and cast a jaundiced eye at my bedraggled skirts.

"For it seems that his lordship has seen fit to come visit his son, and now we are all in an uproar!" she announced.

"Lord Mayson's father is coming here?" I asked, wondering what on earth this sudden visit might mean.

"Yes," Aunt Lyselle replied, "and with very little warning. He will be here in only a few more hours, so go get changed, and have Tarly do something about your hair."

I put a hand to my head. When I had been roaming around near the stream, I had not paid much mind to how my hair might be behaving, but now I could tell that it had become something of a tangled mess. "Of course, Aunt Lyselle. I'll make sure I am completely presentable."

"See that you do."

There was nothing for it but to flee upstairs and ransack my wardrobe to see what would be appropriate for an earl's visit. I had several fine wool gowns, but of course they were far too warm to be suitable for a sunny day in early summer. The linen dresses seemed too plain, and the blue brocade must be reserved for Adalynn's wedding.

In the end, I settled on a pale green watered silk that was a hand-me-down from my cousin. It had suited Adalynn's coloring very well, but I'd never thought that particular shade did much for own pink-and-white complexion. But as I had little else that was at all suitable, I put it on. Really, I doubted it mattered much what I looked like anyway. The earl was coming here to see his son, not judge my charms...or lack thereof.

Tarly, the maid who attended Janessa and myself, appeared so she could comb the tangles from my hair, then wind the heavy curls around her fingers so they looked presentable. At least my hair did generally do as it was told, as long as it wasn't left to run wild, as Annora used to say.

Right then I missed her terribly, amidst all the hubbub. Yes, I had had six years to come to terms with her absence, to learn to become a part of this new family, but cousins were not sisters. And Annora had been far more forgiving of my whims and humors than any of my cousins ever were. If I had told her something odd was going on, and had described the footprints I'd seen going into the woods, she wouldn't have dismissed my suspicions, but would have talked to me seriously about them.

But she was gone, and had made a new life for herself in North Eredor. I could not blame her for the choices she had made, for I was sure I would have done the same thing, and yet...

...and yet I could not ignore the hole she had left in my world. Ever since our mother died, she and I were the only person the other one had. Our father was still very much alive, but that mattered little, considering how he had treated both of us.

Then I put those thoughts resolutely aside, for I could feel the sting of long-suppressed tears in my eyes, and it would certainly not do to appear before Lord Elwyn, Mayson's father, with a red nose and puffy eyelids.

"Thank you, Tarly," I said, once she was done with my hair. She bobbed a curtsey and headed out, no doubt to check on my cousins and make sure they also were fit to be seen by as exalted a personage as Lord Elwyn.

I studied myself in the mirror. Being out in the wind and the sun had added some color to my cheeks, and so the pale green silk of the dress did not wash me out quite as much as I had feared. Indeed, my eyes looked far greener than normal in contrast, and so I thought I should do well enough.

Besides, I told myself, *I am sure he can have no idea of what his son said to you about being his wife. The earl will only look at you as the niece of his friend. Then he will go, and you can spend your energies on trying to determine whose footprints those were—and where they were going.*

That sounded sensible enough. I could hear the chatter of voices out in the corridor, and so I knew my cousins must be ready to go downstairs. It seemed safest to fall in with them so I might descend the stairs as part of a group, and therefore escape any unwelcome attention.

Indeed, with Adalynn in fine rose-colored brocade, and Carella looking equally resplendent in bright sky-blue, I doubted that anyone's eyes would seek me out. Janessa and Theranne were somewhat less noteworthy, but still looked quite lovely.

As we came into the great hall, I saw that our visitor was already there, his son next to him. I had met Lord Elwyn several times before, and thought him to be a kindly enough man...but now I could feel my heart begin to race. In the past, I had only been one of the gaggle of girls who lived under my uncle's roof. Now I was the young woman his son had asked to marry him, although I still had no idea whether Mayson had divulged any-thing of our exchange to his father or not.

Like Mayson, Lord Elwyn was tall and dark-haired. His eyes, however, were deep blue, and his features had a more chiseled look to them. I guessed the slight roundness of his son's nose and chin must have come from his mother, although of course I had never met her, since she'd died years before I came to stay with my aunt and uncle.

His lordship smiled pleasantly as we girls came into the hall. Almost as one, we curtseyed, and my aunt looked on in approval, clearly glad that we did not have to be reminded to show the proper respect to our visitor.

"Ah," said Lord Elwyn, "I thought your gardens lovely here, but I see your most beautiful flowers bloom indoors."

Carella and Theranne and Janessa giggled, while Adalynn only inclined her head, as if she was far too used to those sorts of compliments. I could feel my cheeks flood with color, but as I stood rather behind the other girls, I felt I did not have to show any more response than that.

"We are truly blessed," my uncle said. "But now, if we might all go to the dining chamber?"

"Of course," Lord Elwyn said, with no apparent fading of his smile. He followed my aunt and uncle into the dining hall, a later addition to the building, with its windows of mullioned glass open to the gardens and a warm breeze blowing through. On that breeze wafted the scent of hundreds of roses, and their perfume made me relax slightly. I had detected no particular alteration in his lordship's expression as he looked at me, and so I felt buoyed by the notion that perhaps he did not have any idea of what had passed between his son and myself, and that this visit was only his idea of being neighborly, and possibly wishing to know how his son fared.

Mayson did not look at me as he fell in behind his father and also headed into the dining chamber. Whether his avoidance of my gaze was due to embarrassment over his words of the day before, or because he did not want his father to notice any particular regard paid to me, I could not say.

But I did breathe a little easier as we gathered around the long table of polished mahogany, and all took our respective seats. Whether by luck or by careful arrangement, I was seated at nearly the opposite end of the table from Lord Elwyn and his son, and so I thought I should be able to survive the meal without having to exchange a word with either one of them.

The servants came out first with a salad of field greens and dressing of honey and oil and fine red wine, perfect for the warm day. After that was cool strawberry soup, and then cold roast fowl and a compote of berries. Clearly, my aunt had made certain to put together a menu that would not have us all panting from the heat by the time we were finished, and I wondered how she had managed to ensure that everything was so perfectly done in such a short amount of time.

Conversation was light, and touched on the warm weather, and the news that Queen Lorelis was with child again. Ironic, when one considered that the old king had wanted his son to put her away for her barrenness. But almost as soon as King Elsdon was dead, it was announced that she was carrying Prince Harlin's child. That heir had been followed by two daughters, and now it seemed she would be adding yet another child to the family. Elsdon had been quite the frightening man, and I had to wonder if the queen's apparent "barrenness" had more to do with his oppressive presence than any physical cause.

But that was long ago, and certainly there did not seem to be many fears for the current succession. Peace was upon the land, and the weather favorable for good harvests, even though my country was known more for its mines than its expansive farmland. Still, we should all do well enough.

And so we made our way through supper without anything of much import being discussed. Again I found myself wondering what had brought Lord Elwyn here. Surely it had to be something more important than a mere desire for some light conversation.

As the meal came to its end, however, and the men were about to remove to my uncle's study for port and, perhaps, discussions not suited for young ladies' ears, his lordship looked over at me, then back at my aunt.

"I wonder, my lady, if I might have few words with your niece?"

"With Iselda?" she blurted out, obviously flustered.

"The very one," he said calmly. "If you do not mind, that is."

"No, of course not," my uncle put in, as if realizing that his wife was not quite up to the task of making a coherent response. "You may go into the library, if that suits you."

"It suits me very well." The earl rose from his seat, then added, "If you will, Iselda?"

I could not ignore that request, so I got up from my chair as well, attempting what I hoped was a polite smile. "Of course, my lord."

It seemed as if everyone's eyes were on me as I followed him from the room, then down the corridor to the library. Lord Elwyn seemed quite familiar with the layout of my uncle's castle, but then I realized he had visited here a number of times over the years.

Once we were in the library, he shut the door, although I noticed he left the windows overlooking the gardens open to the breeze. That was probably safe enough, for no one was about—and I was certain my aunt would make sure everyone remained in the dining hall until his lordship and I were done with our conversation.

Whatever its topic might turn out to be.

"Please, Iselda," he said, then pointed toward the divan in the center of the room. "If you would sit."

I did as he bade me. Certainly I did not have the courage to defy as exalted a personage as the Earl of Bellender Rise...even though every instinct was telling me to get up and bolt from the room.

He paused with his back to the window. Silhouetted like that, his features were cast into shadow, and I could not make out much of his expression. When he spoke again, his voice was calm, but I heard an edge to it that I did not like. "You know my son came here to see if he would find your cousin Carella to be a suitable wife."

"Yes, my lord," I said, even as I experienced a sinking sensation in my stomach. With an opening like that, I guessed that this conversation would not go in any direction I found pleasant.

"And yet when I write to my son and ask him how he fares, he replies by filling his letters with praise of you, and very little for your cousin."

I said nothing, only remained in my seat on the divan and stared at a particularly interesting spot in the intricate Keshiaari rug on the floor.

"You know why I wished my son to become engaged to your cousin?"

Faced with a direct question, I could not remain hidden behind my silence. "Because she is the daughter of a baron, my lord?"

"Precisely. And yet he will hear nothing of that, but will instead only sing your praises." Lord Elwyn stopped then, sending a piercing glance in my direction. "Your father is a merchant, is he not?"

I could not deny that all-too-obvious truth. "Yes, my lord."

"And one who is rather in disgrace."

Again, I could make no denials. "Yes, my lord."

He continued to regard me with those sharp dark blue of his as I did my best not to fidget or squirm or look away. After an uncomfortable moment or two, he said, "Well, I can understand something of his interest. You are quite a lovely young woman, Iselda."

Hot color flooded my cheeks. "I-I thank you, my lord."

Almost without pausing, he went on, "But he spoke far more of your kind heart, of how you have become friends. That is the true reason for his interest, and why I think I have little inclination to deny him."

For a few seconds, the meaning of those words did not quite sink in. But then I stammered, "M-my lord?"

"I told him I must come and see you again, for I will confess now that in the past you were not someone to whom I needed to pay any particular attention. But now I see that you are a sweet and well-mannered girl, and certainly lovely enough. So if it is Mayson's will to continue with this, I will not gainsay him."

Surely I had to be dreaming. I could not think of any other way that Lord Elwyn, Earl of Bellender Rise, could be standing there and telling me he thought I would suit his son well enough. So flustered was I that I exclaimed, "But this cannot be! I told him yesterday that I had no wish to be his wife."

Immediately, Lord Elwyn's dark brows drew together. Indeed, he looked so fearsome that I could not prevent myself from shrinking back against the divan's cushions. "You what?"

"I—" Telling myself I must remain calm, I pulled in a breath, then another. "My lord, I mean no disrespect. I do like and admire your son very much. But he told me that he had no wish to be married, but if he must, then better it be me, for at least some friendship had grown between us. Perhaps some young women would have been pleased by such a comment. However, I may be poor, and my family of little worth, but I still believe I should have a husband who loves me, not one who has taken me as his bride because he must."

How I had managed to summon the courage to make such a speech to someone like Lord Elwyn, I could not say. After I had delivered those words, I could feel my heart beating away, and yet I also experienced an odd feeling of relief, as if now I had spoken my piece, and I would let him say what he willed.

An uncomfortable silence fell. For another moment, his lordship continued to stare down at me, and I forced myself to remain quiet, with what I hoped was a neutral expression on my face, although something about his regard made an odd little shiver go through me. But then he let out a sigh and turned toward the window, the bright sunlight of late afternoon streaming over his features. He appeared calm enough, but beneath that calm I sensed a great weariness, one that I did not think had entirely to do with me.

"It is true," he said, voice heavy. "My son is not...." The words trailed off, and the earl shook his head. The light from the window picked out glints of dark umber and copper in his hair. Strange, since I knew he was of an age with my uncle, and yet showed no grey at all, unlike Uncle Danly, whose own hair was now as silver-grey as the tin his mines produced. "Mayson is not inclined toward marriage, true. There have been no young women to catch his fancy. Until you."

Once again I had the sense of missing a particular undercurrent to his words, although I could not begin to guess what it might be. "I do not think I have caught his fancy, my lord. I only believe he thinks that the two of us should get along better than he and Carella."

"And is that not enough?" His frown deepened, and he added, his voice growing rough, "Are your prospects so very grand that you will turn away from the opportunity to one day be the Countess of Bellender Rise?"

I flinched, but then I told myself that I should not let him cow me, no matter what his title or his wealth. Because I did not like the way he loomed over me as I sat, I rose from the divan and crossed my arms. "No, my lord. I have no prospects at all, if you must know the truth. But I am not yet so desperate that I will give myself over to a loveless marriage simply because I am afraid that nothing better will offer itself."

To my surprise, his frown smoothed itself somewhat, and a reluctant smile touched the corners of his mouth. In that moment, I could see how he must have been very handsome back in the day, perhaps handsomer than his son, and was still quite a fine-looking man. "'Loveless' is perhaps a bit harsh, my lady. I know that Mayson cares for you, even if he does not precisely love you in the way you seem to expect from the man who will be your husband. But," he went on, even as I opened my mouth to speak, "I can see that you do not believe me. You are young, and think that the world will come to you one day. Perhaps it will."

"My lord, I—"

"No, Iselda. I will not argue with you, for I can also see that your mind is made up. I will speak to my son, and tell him that it is not too late for him to set his sights on Carella. He will be disappointed, but perhaps that disappointment will be lessened by the joy such an outcome will arouse in the young lady herself, and your aunt and uncle." He stopped there, as if deciding whether to say anything else. Then he shrugged, and added, "Have a very good evening, my lady."

Before I could speak, he had offered me a slight bow and was gone from the room, leaving me to stand there and stare after him, my mind whirling. In that moment, I could not be sure whether I had just made the greatest mistake of my life... or whether I had saved myself from a comfortable yet suffocating prison.

Chapter Four

H is lordship left soon after that, saying he wished to take advantage of the lingering summer twilight for the journey home. It seemed likely that he and his guards would reach his estate before full dark fell; his lands could be reached in only a few hours, if one hastened the horses along and did not dawdle.

Everyone's eyes were full of questions for me—everyone's, that is, except Lord Mayson's. Perhaps he could read my expression, or the emotions on his father's face. But he exchanged only a few words with his lordship before nodding grimly and saying a brief good night. He would not look at me at all, and said that he was weary, and wished to retire early.

Of course no one gainsaid him. And although I could tell my cousins were overbrimming with curiosity, I ignored their pointed glances and also said I wished to go to bed. It was only after I had prepared myself for sleep and pulled the sheet up to my chin—for the chamber was still quite warm, and I had pushed the blankets aside—that Janessa exclaimed, "Oh,

Iselda, you must speak now! For I am quite eaten up by curiosity, and if you do not tell me what Lord Elwyn said to you, I fear I shall not be able to sleep a wink."

Letting out a sigh, I rolled over onto my side so I could face her. With only the faint moonlight to illumine her features, her face was a pale blur in the darkness, although I thought I could catch the gleam of her eyes. "It is of no import. Nothing has changed."

"No import! How can it be anything *but* important when a great lord like the Earl of Bellender Rise pulls you aside and asks for private conversation with you?"

Oh, gods. If I told Janessa the truth, then all of my cousins would know the facts of the matter as well, as soon as the sun came up and Janessa was able to go and speak with them. While I did not much care whether they knew that I had turned down Lord Mayson's suit, I certainly did not want Carella to realize she was a distant second choice, should Lord Elwyn have his way and somehow convince his son to transfer his "affections" to her.

"It was...a question about Lord Mayson's birthday," I lied quickly. "It is coming up next month, and Lord Elwyn wanted to know if there was anything in particular his son would like to have."

Even in the darkness, I could see Janessa frown. "He rode all this way, just to ask a silly question like that?"

"It is not silly," I returned. "Mayson is his only son, his only child. And he had not seen him for several weeks. No doubt his lordship thought to combine a visit with his son with an opportunity to ask me about his birthday."

A silence then, as Janessa seemed to mull over what I had just told her. It was a foolish lie, but the only one I could think of in the time that had been given me. And although none of the girls who shared the castle with me knew of Mayson's offhand proposal, they did know that he seemed to prefer my company. That would make me the logical person for his father to approach with a question about his son's birthday. I could only pray they would see nothing more in it than that.

"So what *does* he want for his birthday?"

I bit back a groan of frustration. Trust Janessa to keep asking questions; she was the naturally curious sort anyway, and I believed she tried to keep her mind as engaged as possible because then she would not be forced to dwell on her mother's death and the reason why she was staying here with us at all. Yes, she tended to be reserved around my cousins because of the perceived difference in their stations, but she had no such scruples around me. "He mentioned that he would like a new bow, as the pull on the one he has now is no longer sufficient."

Something that sounded like a sigh escaped Janessa's lips. "Oh, I can see that. His arms are very strong."

Yes, they were. Mayson enjoyed the outdoors, liked to hike and climb, fish in the stream, practice archery with the men in my father's guard. I'd noted that even in the time he had been staying with us, Mayson's arms seemed to have gained a good deal of muscle. I supposed they were worthy of a sigh, if one preferred that sort of thing.

A man's build did not concern me as much as his character, though. And I had always cared more about the symmetry of a man's countenance—and the purity of his heart—than the breadth of his shoulders.

But clearly Janessa's tastes lay elsewhere. In that moment, I could not argue overmuch, for at least it seemed I had given her an explanation she could accept, and, if all went well, she could fall asleep while contemplating the muscles in Lord Mayson's arms.

"Well, then," I said. "I am sure Lord Elwyn will bring his son a wonderful bow for his birthday. But we must keep it as our secret."

"Oh, of course," Janessa responded. "I wouldn't think of spoiling his surprise. Thank you for telling me."

"You're welcome. But now I do wish to sleep."

She murmured something that sounded like an apology, then rolled over on her side. I let out a breath and uttered a silent thank-you to the gods that she had not decided to press the matter further. Now I only wanted to sleep, and put this day behind me. That interview with Lord Elwyn had been more taxing than I'd thought.

Apparently my body judged it so as well, because I slipped away into slumber soon enough after that. Perhaps I dreamed, but if I did, nothing of what had passed through my mind lingered.

All I knew was that sometime later I awoke, eyes opening to the hazy moonlit chamber around me. Because a gibbous moon was visible through the window, I knew that not too much time could have passed—a few hours at most.

The night was still. This time I heard not even an owl, and the breeze which came through the open casement was so gentle that at first I could not be sure I had not imagined it. Something made me turn my head toward the bed where Janessa slept, and I went still.

She was gone. Again.

In that moment, it was as if the vague curtain obscuring my memories of the night before had been drawn back, and I recalled how I had awakened to find Janessa and my cousins all gone. True, wherever they had disappeared to, it could not have been terribly dangerous, for they were all back in their beds before sunrise, tired but certainly not harmed in any way.

But just because they were safe did not mean something very strange wasn't going on.

I pushed back the covers and rose from my bed, then went across the corridor to check the room that Theranne and Carella shared. It was empty, and so, too, was the large chamber Adalynn had as her own. This time, I saw that their dressing gowns still lay draped across the foot of all their beds, although I noticed their slippers were missing.

Those footprints in the forest....

Suddenly determined, I returned to my own room and hurriedly retrieved my plainest, oldest dress from the wardrobe, then drew off my nightgown. Fingers fumbling a little in the dark—for of course I could not light a candle and reveal that I was up and about—I got dressed and put on my sturdiest shoes.

I doubted that anyone would come to check on us, for we were all young women grown, and not small children who needed to be tended to in the middle of the night. Even so, I took the pillows from my bed and slipped them under the covers, so it looked as if someone slept there, then did the same thing with Janessa's bed. A few moments lost as I also created the same subterfuge in the other girls' bedrooms, but it was not so very long afterward that I slipped down the hallway and headed for the staircase.

The castle was dark and quiet. Once or twice when I had first come here, I had gotten up and roamed through its halls while everyone else slept, fascinated by the size of the place and wanting to experience something of it when the rest of the household was abed. However, after one of the maids caught me and gave me a good scolding, I stayed in my room like a good girl. Now I could only hope that no one would be up tonight, save the guards who always watched over the castle gates.

Those gates were not the only way out, however. While my uncle made sure his holdings were protected, it was not as if we had to watch for invaders from a neighboring land, or even bandits grown bold enough to attack such a formidable keep. So there was a door that opened from the kitchen into the kitchen garden, and another door through the wall that led to the fields beyond.

Going this way could be tricky, though, as there was always the risk of bumping into one of the household staff, who might be wakeful on a warm summer night. But somehow my cousins and Janessa had gotten out the night before and returned without anyone catching them, and so I had to hope I would have similar luck.

I crept along, keeping my back to the wall. At least that way no one could come up behind me, although I had to admit such a posture would look rather suspicious to any onlookers.

Not that there were any such watchers. The kitchens—and the servants' quarters which opened off that wing of the castle—were all silent and still. In the hearth, coals still glowed faintly red, banked down for the night, but their dull flicker was the only sign of life I was able to see. Hardly daring to breathe, I passed through the cavernous kitchen and to the door that opened on the gardens.

The latch lifted under my fingers, and in the next moment, I was outside, breathing in the cool night air. The scent of roses lingered, like a memory of the day's warmth, although by that hour the temperature had dropped enough that I was almost chilled.

An easy remedy existed for that mild discomfort, of course. If I walked briskly, I certainly would not notice how much colder it was now than it had been during the daylight hours.

The large moon, Taleron, had begun to dip toward the west. I could not see the smaller Calendir, and guessed it had not yet risen. There was still enough light for me to make my way through the gardens, and then through the door in the wall, which should have been barred but somehow, curiously, was not.

Beyond lay the open fields where barley and rye grew tall and golden. I found the path that traveled between two of those fields, and followed it as it descended toward the creek and its border of dark, secret trees.

. As I went, I had to wonder at myself, for I had no true evidence to tell me that my cousins and Janessa had passed this way. Yes, I had seen those footprints earlier, but the cottagers who worked the fields had daughters, and it could have been their footprints that marred the soft soil next to the creek. In truth, that seemed a far more rational reason for the prints I had seen.

But that explanation did not account for the inexplicable disappearance, and then reappearance, of the young women who dwelt in my uncle's castle.

A few moments later, I had reached the stream. This time I did not take off my shoes and wade in the water, but rather picked my way along the rocky banks until I came to the spot where I had seen those prints in the sand. Although I had not brought a lantern with me, for fear of being discovered, my eyes had adjusted to the gloom well enough that I could see even more footprints now, many of them blurred, as if the older marks had been overlaid by newer, fresher ones.

For a long moment, I stood there, staring down at them. It seemed obvious enough to me that whoever had passed this way earlier must have been headed into the depths of the forest.

Daleskeld Forest, to be precise. The great woods took their name from the province where they lay. They began here as a pretty border for the creek, but then expanded to the north and east to become a large forest of pine and fir, of oak and elm and beech and sycamore. The hunting was good here, and there were men in the province who made it their livelihoods to go and retrieve pelts so that young women like my cousins could have winter mantles trimmed with fox and beaver and ermine.

But there were also, I'd been told, bears and wolves and badgers, none of whom could precisely be called friendly. Surely it was madness for a young woman to venture there at night, unarmed and unaccompanied, with not even the small comfort of a lantern to guide her way. I could feel the fear begin to rise within me, and I paused for a long moment, wondering if I should go back inside before I truly got myself in trouble.

No, I would not turn back now. If I had intended to allow doubts and fears to prevent me from seeking the reason for my cousins' disappearance, I should have remained in my bed, eyes shut against the darkness, and sent prayers to the gods that those young women would come home safely.

Still I hesitated, staring into the gloomy woods, only faintly lit by the lowering gibbous moon. In a few more days, that moonlight would be much brighter, but I would have to make do for now. Here, the wind felt stronger, rustling in the trees. For the barest moment, it seemed almost as if I could hear whispered words in the sound of the leaves, words in an unknown language, sibilant and strangely beautiful.

A chill moved down my spine, but my resolve was unshaken. After taking in a breath to steady myself, I moved forward into the woods.

Chapter Five

Traversing the path was not as difficult as I had feared it might be. True, there was the occasional fallen branch or patch of weeds, but once I began walking, I found I followed a faint path that wound its way through the trees, taking me deeper and deeper into the forest. From time to time, I would hear a rustling off somewhere in the undergrowth and pause, certain that I was about to set upon by some fierce woodland animal. But nothing ever appeared, and I would make myself go on.

On several occasions an owl flew overhead, one time with the great night bird dipping so close to me that I could feel the rush of cool air as it went past, the great beating of its wings blowing stray strands of hair into my face. Each time I would stop, my heart hammering away in my chest, but of course the owls were not hunting me, but were intent on catching poor small creatures such as voles or mice or perhaps even rats.

And from time to time, the canopy of trees overhead would part just enough to allow more moonlight to flood down onto the path, and I would see those small footprints, leading me ever on into the heart of the forest.

Where in the world were they going? I'd been told that Daleskeld Forest had a number of clearings, and that nearly four miles from the borders of my uncle's lands, surrounded by pines and firs, was a beautiful lake, almost circular in shape, where one could catch all manner of fish. But I'd also been told that the way there was treacherous, and we girls had never been allowed to venture that far, even if accompanied by some of the household's guards.

Well, Adalynn and Carella and Theranne and Janessa certainly didn't have guards with them now.

The ground sloped upward slightly, becoming rockier at the same time. More than once I stumbled, but I did not fall, and that was enough to keep me moving forward. I did wish I had a walking stick—and perhaps a dagger—but I found if I took my time and chose where I stepped, I could manage to keep my footing.

I could not say how long it took to cover that particular patch of ground. It felt interminable, although I guessed it really had not been that great a span of time—perhaps half an hour at most. At last the path leveled out again and became smoother, and I let out a relieved breath, resolving that if I should come this way again, I would bring a walking stick, or at the very least find a fallen branch that would serve the same purpose.

But then all such mundane concerns fled my mind, for the forest opened up into a clearing, and in that clearing were the missing girls.

They stood hand in hand in a circle. As I watched, they moved slowly clockwise, making a complete circuit of that circle, then reversed, going widdershins so they went back to whence they came. There they stopped, then let go of one another's hands so each of them could spin in place, their nightgowns flowing ghost-like in the moonlight. After they each had spun around three times, they joined hands again and began moving once more in a circle.

All of this activity was accomplished in utter silence. There was something so odd, so eerie about their movements, that although I had intended to call out to them, some deep misgiving stopped me. Even at this distance, I could see the blank expression each of them wore. I had the uncomfortable sensation that even if their eyes should meet mine, I would see no recognition in their gaze.

"What are you doing here?"

An unfamiliar man's voice, hushed and angry. I whirled, and was confronted by an apparition the likes of which I had never seen before.

My first impression was that he must be elderly, because of the silver-white hair which fell around his face and brushed the high collar of his doublet. But as I stared at the stranger who confronted me, I realized he was probably only a few years older than I, features clear and chiseled and untouched by age. His eyes were as silver-bright as his hair, and seemed to bore into me with a mixture of anger and fear.

"Who are you?" I asked, my voice barely more than a whisper, just like his.

He glanced past me to the little group out in the clearing, still performing their strange dance. "That does not matter. What matters is that you should not be here."

"I do think I should be here," I responded, moved to protest despite the strangeness of the situation. "Those are my three cousins out there, and Janessa, who is my aunt and uncle's ward. I came here to see what had happened to them."

Those silvery eyes narrowed. "How did you come here?"

"By following their footprints on the path," I replied. "They are very accomplished young women, but they certainly do not possess sufficient woodcraft to cover their tracks."

This explanation did not appear to do much to ingratiate me with the strange young man. His mouth—which I noted was beautifully sculpted—compressed, and he said, still in the same harsh whisper, "You have put yourself in a great deal of danger by coming here."

"How? For I have seen no bears, nor wolves or foxes or badgers. The woods are quiet tonight."

"Of course they are. *He* made sure that nothing would molest your cousins as they came here."

"He who?" I asked, frankly curious.

Something like fear moved through the stranger's eyes, and he shook his head. "That does not matter. You must go."

"I will not," I said, planting my hands on my hips. "For they are my cousins, and so I have a right to know what you have done to them. They are under some kind of spell, are they not?"

He said quickly, "There is no such thing as spells, or magic."

But he would not quite look at me, and even though I had never met him before, nor ever seen anyone who shared his odd, fey appearance, I somehow could tell he was lying. I replied, "Oh, I must disagree with you on that, sir, for I have seen such things for myself, and know those who practice the forbidden arts. What else other than a spell would bring my cousins so far from their beds, and make it so they could not remember anything of such excursions the next day?"

For a long moment, the young man said nothing. He glanced toward the clearing, but my cousins and Janessa were still performing their strange, stilted dance. What was truly odd was that I could almost see the air swirling around them, as if it had taken on a strange luminescence only visible when the moonlight caught it the right way.

I shivered.

"It has not affected you," he said, apparently choosing to ignore my earlier remark. "We still don't know why. But if you linger, he will discover that you have come here, and then he will make sure to find out for himself."

Although his words sent another chill through my body, right then curiosity was still stronger than fear. "Who are you?" I asked again. "And *what* hasn't affected me? The spell that has caught my cousins?"

"You must go," he said, his tone taking on a fresh urgency. Once again he glanced toward the group of girls as they danced, but I could see nothing except their slender forms, graceful and haunting in the moonlight. Even so, another chill traced its way down my spine. "I promise that no harm will come to them, but I can make no such promise to you, if he should catch you here."

"Who—?" I began, but he caught me by the arm and propelled me toward the path.

"He is coming. Go, Iselda!"

There was such command in the stranger's tone that I had no choice but to hurry off whence I had come, as if he had placed his own spell on me, one that compelled my feet to propel me forward, down the path and back toward the safety of my uncle's lands. As I went, the branches overhead began to move in a fierce, unseen wind. Leaves tumbled all around me, and I started to run, ignoring the rocky ground, ignoring everything but the fear that had begun to rise in me.

Something was coming. Something dark and dangerous. I loved my cousins, but I knew I could do nothing to help them. Nothing except run, and run.

The stranger had said he would keep them safe. And they had returned home safely the night before, the only apparent damage they'd sustained to their slippers. I had to believe that he had told me the truth. As odd as the situation was, and though my mind was filled with unanswered questions, I knew I could not turn back.

My cousins might survive whatever lay ahead of them, but if I did not go, then I could not be certain of sharing such a pleasant fate.

As I ran, the rustling of the leaves overhead lessened, and the night air grew calmer. I let out a sob of relief when I heard the whispering sound of the stream as it moved over its stony bed. Yes, I had farther still to go, but for some reason that stretch of water, only a few yards wide, seemed like a barrier, or at least a boundary. Once I was across, I should be safe.

Heedless of my skirts, of my shoes, I sloshed through the water at a place where I knew it would be only ankle-high. And then I was on the other side of the creek, and I could glimpse the open fields of my uncle's lands stretching out before me.

My wet gown slapped against my legs, and my shoes squished uncomfortably, but I ignored them as I found the path that would bring me to the castle wall. And there was the door, which I had left unlocked but pulled to, so that none of the guards would notice anything amiss if they should pass this way.

Once I was inside, I closed the door and set the latch in place, then leaned against the wall and took in deep, heaving breaths. Surely I must be safe here.

But the spell reached all the way into the castle and summoned Adalynn and Carella and Theranne and Janessa from their beds, I thought, a new chill striking me.

Yes, that was true enough. But the silver-haired stranger had clearly believed I was unaffected by the spell, for whatever reason. Perhaps my forgetfulness on the subject of their disappearance was another spell, although I was not sure who had cast it—the same dark force that had summoned my cousins, or the young man who had clearly been trying to protect me.

And how had he known my name?

A puzzle I would have to work through later. For now, I knew I must go back inside and slip into bed, and pray that no one had taken notice of my nocturnal wanderings. And if the stranger was to be believed, when I awoke in the morning, I would find my cousins returned, no worse the wear except for a strange weariness—and some inexplicable damage to their shoes.

The castle still slept when I entered, returning the same way I had left, through the kitchens and on from there to the great staircase that led to the upper levels. Was this another spell, to cast everyone into a deep slumber so that my cousins' comings and goings might pass unnoticed? I did not think that so very strange, not when some unknown mage was capable of calling them forth from their very beds.

Nevertheless, I tiptoed up the stairs and hurried down the hallway to my room. Janessa's empty bed seemed to mock me with a host of unanswered questions. Who was this sorcerer, the one the strange young man had seemed so afraid of? And what on earth did he want with my cousins?

As I stripped out of my soiled gown and wet shoes, I thought again of the strange luminescence I had seen drifting around my cousins and Janessa as they danced. What it had been, I could not begin to guess, although now that I recalled the scene to my mind, it seemed almost as if that light had been emanating from them, rising from the tops of their heads to mingle in the air above.

Another spell, I assumed, although I could not think what its purpose might be. None of the girls seemed to notice that strange light as they danced. They had moved in perfect harmony, their steps as polished and precise as those of the most experienced dance troupe, and yet I did not think they knew what they were doing. Someone else had been controlling them.

I swallowed, and felt myself shiver, even though the room was far warmer than the night air outside, the stonework trapping the heat of the day. It seemed best to climb into bed and pull up the covers, although I had no intention of sleeping. No, I would stay awake to see Janessa when she returned—and to witness the manner of her return as well. Would the mage who controlled my cousins send them directly into their beds, or was such a thing quite beyond his powers? After all, he had made them come to him on foot. But perhaps that was merely another way he asserted his control, delighting in making them trudge over rocky ground to do his bidding.

That thought only made me colder. The stranger had said they would not be harmed, but I did not have any real reason to trust him. Only the look in his eyes and the pleading note in his voice, both of which had seemed genuine enough. Even so, although I had led a sheltered enough life, I was not completely naïve. There were many things that a man who had such powers at his command might do to a young woman...and dancing was certainly the most innocent of those things.

Gods. I pulled my knees up to my chest and hugged them, attempting to reassure myself that Adalynn and all the rest of them were all right, that they had only been summoned to perform the strange dance, even if I could not begin to guess at its purpose.

Should I have stayed? If anything terrible should happen to any of them, I knew I would never forgive myself. But they had survived the other night unscathed, and who was I to confront a mage with powers I could barely comprehend? I was only a young woman with no such gifts of my own.

And so it went, as I wrestled with my conscience, and tried to make some sense of my decision. All the while, the night wore on, and Janessa did not appear. And although I had vowed to stay awake as I awaited her return, at length my eyelids grew so heavy that I could no longer keep them up, and darkness washed over me, bringing with it an oblivion I could not escape.

"Oh, mistress, whatever happened to your gown?"

I opened one eye and saw Tarly, the maid who looked after Janessa and myself, holding up the dress I had worn the night before. Even in my bleary and unfocused state, I could clearly see the expression of dismay she wore.

With good cause, too, as I forced myself to look away from her face and at the gown she held. I had been in a hurry as I undressed, and had tossed the garment onto a chair. The linen was now badly wrinkled, but that was far from the worst of it. The edge of the skirt was splashed with mud and grime, and I could also see how part of the hem had been torn out. I had a vague recollection of getting it caught on a fallen tree branch, but I did not think I had done that much damage as I jerked it loose.

"I am sorry," I said, then risked a quick glance past her to Janessa's bed. It was now occupied, I realized, and relief flooded through me. Despite the commotion, she had not roused herself to see what was going on, which seemed to indicate that her exertions during her moonlit dance had wearied her even more than the other times she had been called out under the influence of that strange spell. "I was out looking for wildflowers and wandering along the stream. I suppose the skirt must have gotten caught on something."

Tarly did not appear terribly convinced by this explanation, and I could not blame her. I had gone picking wildflowers and walking by the stream many times before, but had managed not to ruin my clothes.

However, she also knew it was not her place to argue with a young lady of the house, so she let out a very small sigh and draped the gown over one arm. "I will take it to the laundry, my lady, and see what can be done. Luckily, it is not one of your better gowns."

Which was the reason why I had worn it in the first place, of course. Even so, my wardrobe was not so extensive that I could afford to damage many items in it. I would just have to hope that our laundress could work her usual miracles, and that the dress would be restored to some usefulness.

"Thank you, Tarly," I said.

Apparently I sounded meek enough—or perhaps truly grateful—because she only replied, "Think nothing of it, mistress. I will bring up your tea, and perhaps by then Mistress Janessa will also be awake and ready to have hers as well."

"I'm sure she will," I replied, although I had my doubts. She hadn't stirred once during this entire exchange.

Tarly nodded, then let herself out and closed the door behind her. Almost as soon as she was gone, I pushed back my covers and went to inspect the slippers sitting on the floor at the foot of Janessa's bed. Her footwear was not nearly as fancy as Adalynn's, but I could still see the scars in the soft, dark green kid, the soles scratched and scored, with a hole just beginning near the toe of the left shoe.

It was not the sort of damage one could sustain from walking sedately about the castle, or taking a turn in the gardens, but I'd climbed over that rocky ground on the way to the clearing where the girls were brought to dance. I knew exactly where and how that damage had been sustained.

The why still eluded me, however. What was the purpose in bringing them forth to perform that unearthly dance? I stole a glance at Janessa; although her dark hair was tumbled and tangled, she herself did not seem all the worse for wear, for her cheeks were pink and her breathing came regular and untroubled. Yes, one of those cheeks had a definite dirt smudge on it, but she could have suffered far more harm than that.

As I stood there, staring down at her, she stirred. Then her eyes opened, and she gazed up at me in some confusion. "Iselda? What on earth are you doing?"

She sounded normal enough, if rather irritated. I supposed I could not blame her for that, as I knew I, too, would be somewhat annoyed to wake up and find someone standing over my bed. "I—I thought I should wake you, for Tarly is on her way up with our morning tea."

A frown pulled at Janessa's brows, but then she nodded and pushed herself to an upright position. As she did so, she groaned faintly, as if her muscles pained her. "I cannot think what I did yesterday to make it feel as if I've pulled every muscle in my arms and legs," she complained. "I did not even go for a walk in the garden because the sun was too hot."

"Perhaps you slept in a strange position," I suggested, and although her frown did not disappear altogether, she did nod.

"Perhaps. It is so odd, for I feel as if I dreamt a great deal, and yet now I cannot remember any of it."

Were those "dreams" of hers actually memories of some of the things she'd done the night before, of making her way through a dark forest so she might dance in a woodland clearing under the humpback of a gibbous moon?

I dared not ask. Perhaps it was wrong of me to indulge such reticence, to not go immediately to my aunt and uncle and tell them what was happening under their very noses. And yet something stopped me, told me that to make such a revelation would do no good at all. My uncle might have been Lord Danly, Baron of Linsmere, but titles and lands were not of much use in a battle with someone possessing magical powers.

Indeed, even the king himself had not been able to withstand my brother-in-law's own particular gifts.

No, it seemed that more information was necessary before I did or said anything. If I had seen any actual signs of injury on Janessa—or on any of my cousins the day before—then I would have spoken. For the moment, though, they seemed well enough.

And I knew I would follow them again tonight, and perhaps encounter that strange young man....

"Goodness, Iselda," Janessa said then. "Whatever is the matter with you?"

"I beg your pardon?" I asked, coming back to the here and now with rather a start.

"You went all dreamy and vague, as if you were thinking of something very far away. Or perhaps someone," she added with a sly glint in her eyes. "Someone not so very far off after all?"

"No, of course not," I said at once. "I was only thinking of the weather, and if it would be so very hot again today."

She raise her eyebrows at this silly reply, although she forbore from saying anything else, as Tarly returned to our chamber in that moment, carrying a tray with our morning tea. She set it down on the table by the fireplace, although no fire flickered in the hearth now.

Janessa reached for her dressing gown and pulled it on over her shoulders before slipping out of bed. From the sudden pucker of the maid's brows, I could tell that Tarly had noted the smudge of dirt on Janessa's cheek. Would she say something?

I didn't quite hold my breath, but I couldn't help releasing a relieved sigh as the maid shook her head, then said briskly, "Here, my ladies. I've brought the honey, Mistress Janessa, just as you like, and the milk for you, Mistress Iselda."

Both Janessa and I thanked her, and she went out, saying that she would be back in a quarter-hour to help us with our hair and wardrobe. I thought it prudent to remain silent as I stirred milk into my tea, for none of the thoughts currently racing through my mind were ones I wished to share with my companion.

So we drank tea in blessed quiet. If Janessa was surprised by my taciturn behavior, she did not show it. I thought it quite possible that she was wearied enough from her activities of the evening before that she did not have the energy to expend on idle conversation. To tell the truth, I was more tired than I had thought I would be, and also enjoyed those moments of peace and quiet while we finished our tea. That peace could not possibly last, for I knew the frenzied cleaning of the castle in preparation for Adalynn's wedding was about to intensify, and after today we could expect to see the first guests arriving.

The prospect of having so many additional people sleeping under our roof made me wonder if the mage who summoned my cousins would be able to cast all our guests into a deep sleep so the girls' departure would still be kept secret, or whether perhaps he would abandon his game, at least until the celebrations were over and everyone had departed to their respective homes. Also, what would he do with Adalynn gone? Did it matter how many young women he called forth to do that strange moonlit dance? For of course Adalynn would leave here and become a great lady, the mistress of her own castle, with a title and husband, and a place at court, if her new husband was so inclined.

Far too many questions, and I feared I did not have answers to any of them. Although the day was fresh and new, I found myself wishing for the return of night, so I might venture forth again and attempt to learn more of the strange spell at work here.

And see more of that silver-eyed stranger, my mind jibed at me. I wanted to tell myself that was ridiculous, and yet....

Something about the strange young man had captured my imagination. I had never before seen anyone who looked anything like him—and I was not some provincial girl with no knowledge of the greater world. I had been born in Bodenskell, my homeland's capital, and lived there until I was thirteen years old. On the streets of that city I had seen dark-visaged men from Keshiaar, and fair-haired Southern Eredorians, and the handsome black-haired folk from the great empire of Sirlende…but I had never caught even a glimpse of someone with silver-pale hair and eyes to match.

His accents bespoke a man of Purth, a countryman of mine, although I supposed the accent was something he could have learned. Even so, he had to have come from someplace, but where?

Tarly reappeared then, and I was forced to put aside my musings as she helped us into our gowns and brushed our hair. Janessa looked on with envy as our maid took my gleaming strands of golden hair and twined them around her finger so they might fall in perfect spirals down my back.

"It truly is not fair that you should have hair like that," she said with a disparaging glance downward at her own mid-brown locks.

"I am not sure 'fair' has anything to do with it," I replied. "I was told my great-grandmother had hair like this, and so it came to me. But that was only luck, nothing else."

She heaved a sigh, and looked as if she intended to say more. But then Tarly finished working on my hair and said, "Mistress Janessa, your own hair is lovely—so thick and glossy. I am quite sure there is no reason for you to be jealous of Mistress Iselda's."

This unexpected compliment brought a flush of pink to Janessa's cheeks, and she sat quietly enough as Tarly brushed her long brown tresses until they gleamed, then twisted them into elegant coils and braids and held them in place with pins of silver and garnet. Once our maid was satisfied with her work, she went to retrieve Janessa's slippers—and made a shocked sound.

"What on earth has happened to your slippers, mistress?"

Janessa got up from where she sat at the dressing table and looked down at the pair of shoes Tarly held. In the bright daylight flooding in through the windows, the damage I had noted earlier was even more obvious.

"Oh, no!" she exclaimed. "What in the world could have happened to them?"

"I do not know," Tarly said. "For I am quite sure they were not in this sort of condition when you wore them last."

"No, they were not." Janessa did look truly dismayed; one hand went to her mouth, even as she shook her head. "And oh, those are the slippers my father sent as part of my birthday present. He will be so annoyed with me when he finds out what has happened to them."

Unfortunately, I thought he probably would be upset with her, even though the condition of those shoes was certainly not her fault. I had only met Janessa's father once, for after he had left her with my aunt and uncle, he showed no particular inclination to spend any more time with his daughter. The loss of his wife had hurt him, I believed, but he wanted to be alone with his hurt, rather than see his wife's features mirrored in his daughter's face. I knew that Janessa resembled her mother greatly, for she always wore a silver locket with a miniature of her mother's likeness contained within, and had shown it to me on more than one occasion. Even on that brief acquaintance, he seemed short-tempered and moody, and easily irritated. Moreover, their family was not overburdened with wealth. The cost of a pair of slippers did not mean that much to my aunt and uncle, but it was a far different matter for Master Marleton.

"Not if you explain that it was not your fault," I said gently. "Something is going on, that is for certain, because my cousins' slippers have also been damaged."

"That is true," Janessa said, looking a little more cheerful. "I wonder what could be ruining them in such a way."

"I am sure there must be a logical explanation," I told her, even as I thought, *Although I dare not give you the real reason. Even if I told you the truth, I do not think you would believe me.*

As I spoke, there was some commotion across the corridor. In the next instant, Adalynn stood in the doorway, another pair of tattered slippers in her hands and rage in her eyes. "What did I just hear? Janessa's shoes are ruined as well?"

"I would not say ruined, precisely," Janessa responded, although her voice was not completely steady. She would never admit such a thing out loud, but I knew that Adalynn intimidated her somewhat, and she would go out of her way to avoid a confrontation with the eldest daughter of the house. "But certainly they do not look new anymore."

Adalynn glared down at the shoes Tarly still held. "They look ruined to me," she said with a sniff. "I have been thinking on it, and it must be Daisy who is doing this."

Daisy was my aunt's little dog, a sweet creature who never even ventured upstairs, as far as I could tell. She spent most of her time sleeping on a soft down-filled bed in my aunt's chambers, and was her shadow when she did manage to venture out into the castle. At any rate, even if I had not known for certain that Daisy was innocent of any wrongdoing, I would have still argued that she could not possibly be responsible. Some dogs might enjoy chewing on slippers and the legs of chairs and anything else that came into their orbit, but Daisy was certainly not one of them.

"I don't think so," I said at once. "She is a good dog, and has never shown that kind of behavior before."

"Well, perhaps something has changed," Adalynn retorted. "Perhaps she does not like the heat, or perhaps she is upset by the preparations for the wedding. After all, she is a dog. One cannot apply logic to a creature like that."

I thought privately that Daisy showed more good sense than some people I had met, but I knew better than to say such a thing to Adalynn. The ruin of another pair of slippers had clearly incensed her, and I could also tell that the night's activities seemed to have worn more on her than Janessa, or Carella and Theranne, who had appeared a moment after their sister and were peering through the doorway, watching the goings-on. But Adalynn's eyes were shadowed, and there was a pallor to her face that I did not like. Had the spell fallen more heavily on her for some reason?

I did not know. I could not even make an educated guess, for I knew very little about magic and its effects. But I did make sure that I chose my next words carefully, as I had a feeling that Adalynn's temper, always somewhat short, was even more on edge this morning.

"Perhaps we should ask your mother," I said. "For Daisy sleeps in her chamber, and so she would know better than anyone else whether the dog had gotten out in the night."

If this suggestion did not precisely mollify her, it did make Adalynn at least nod and say, "Yes, I think that is a good idea. It is time to go down for breakfast anyway."

As it was. The group of us trooped down the stairs and on into the smaller chamber we used for less formal meals. I say "less formal," but the room was still much larger—and grander—than the dining room in the house where I had grown up. My aunt and uncle were already there, drinking their own morning tea. Larinda, one of the downstairs maids, had just set out platters of fresh fruit and several of my favorite, the breakfast pie made with cheese and eggs and bacon.

"Mama," Adalynn said without preamble as she entered the chamber, "Mama, another pair of my slippers has been ruined, and Janessa's as well. We think it must be Daisy, worrying at them in the middle of the night while we are asleep."

Looking rather startled, my aunt set down her teacup. "Another pair of slippers?"

"*All* our slippers," Theranne put in. "Only I had been wearing my older ones, and so I am not quite so put out as Adalynn. But still, Mama, I think it very bad of Daisy to treat them so."

"What on earth is this nonsense about Daisy?" my uncle demanded. "That dog was asleep in her bed when I closed my eyes last night, and she was still there when I awoke. The door to our suite was closed. So how, pray, do you think the dog got out at all, let alone went upstairs—where she never goes, because the staircase frightens her—and chewed on your slippers?"

My cousins all looked at one another, none of them apparently that eager to respond. Uncle Danly was a kindly man, but he did not appreciate a commotion at his breakfast table.

But then Adalynn said, "I do not know. I just cannot think of any other explanation for our shoes becoming so terribly damaged night after night."

For a few seconds, no one said anything. My aunt glanced over at me, then asked, "And what of you, Iselda?"

"I?" I responded, startled. I had been hanging back, watching but wanting to stay out of the conversation.

"Yes, you. I cannot help but notice that you do not claim to have suffered the same kind of losses as your cousins. What about your slippers? Have you found them in the same regrettable state?"

"No, Aunt Lyselle. They do not seem to have been harmed."

"Well, that's rather extraordinary, don't you think?"

I had to admit to myself that it was, although not for the reasons she might think. Perhaps very soon there would come a time when I was forced to admit everything to her, but at the moment I only wanted to steer the conversation away from me. How could I tell my aunt—and everyone else present—that I was more or less unscathed because the spell that had summoned the rest of the girls out to the nighttime forest had not touched me?

Either they would think I was mad, or, worse, they would summon one of the witch-finders from Bodenskell to investigate further. True, King Harlin had a far more relaxed stance about magic and mages than his crazed father, but even so, he had not abolished that investigative body, either. The last thing I wanted was for the witch-finders to track down the strange young man I had met in the woods the night before. He had sworn that my cousins would be fine, and they were—perhaps somewhat weary, but certainly healthy and whole.

I doubted very much that the witch-finders would take such a fact into their consideration.

All I could do was lift my shoulders. "Perhaps. But if it is Daisy who is doing these things, perhaps she does not like the odor of my feet."

Theranne and Carella both giggled, and even my uncle's mouth quirked.

"I do not think it is Daisy," Aunt Lyselle said. "It seems we have a mystery on our hands, but we will not solve it here. Do sit down, girls—having you stand there in the doorway like that is giving me a headache."

Everyone dutifully went to take their seats, and I sat as well. As my cousins occupied themselves with filling their plates, some of the tension went out of the room.

But I saw my aunt watching me closely, speculation in her eyes, and I knew I would have to be careful. She was right— there was a mystery, and so far she had not solved it.

I just feared she would do her best to unravel the puzzle before I had sufficient time to do so myself.

Chapter Six

Because of the hubbub in the castle—and because I thought it best if my path did not accidentally cross with that of Lord Mayson—I stayed in my room for most of the day, saying that I was rather tired and wished to read. This excuse for my isolation was met with a few raised eyebrows, but no one tried to stop me. By that point I had a well-earned reputation for being bookish, and so no one saw anything particularly odd in my wanting to spend the day with my nose in a tome of legends from days gone by, a gift Aunt Lyselle had gotten for me during her last visit to Bodenskell.

However, I did not use the whole time for reading. I sat by the window and let the warm breeze flow in, and gazed off to the north and east, to the dark blur of Daleskeld Forest. Immediately north, the land swelled into foothills and then real mountains, where my uncle's mining operations were located. But they were not what drew my interest. From this distance, and in the bright daylight, the forest did not appear all that intimidating. It did not look like a place which hid such mysteries as I had stumbled across the night before.

I had pulled down every book in my collection and leafed through it, thinking perhaps I would find some mention of a people who resembled the young man I had met, and yet I could find nothing. True, I had heard stories of those who were born with no coloring at all, but those stories had also stated that such unfortunates had reddish eyes. The stranger in the forest certainly did not possess red eyes. Even now I could recall the way the moonlight had glinted on his face, awakening shimmers of silver from between his thick lashes...which had been dark, startling against his pale skin.

Although it was not the sort of thing I wished to admit to myself, I realized then that he was quite the most beautiful man I had ever seen.

However, I could not allow myself to be distracted by such surface concerns. Far more important was how he seemed to know exactly what was happening with my cousins, even if he had been reluctant to tell me the truth. Based on what he had said, I knew he was not the one who had cast the spell...but did he work for, or even with, the mage responsible for that strange magic?

That was certainly the first thing I would ask, once I saw him again. I did not know why I was so certain such a thing would happen, when he had all but driven me from the woods the night before, but somehow I felt it in my bones that we would meet again.

And the second matter I would inquire of him would be why this strange spell, seemingly cast to capture all the young women dwelling in the castle, did not affect me at all. It could not be because of my blood, for I was related to the three sisters, and Janessa not at all, and yet she went out into the night and danced with them, where I, their own cousin, did not.

The stranger's warnings that I should stay away...well, I had decided to ignore them. Had I not survived my first journey into the woods completely unscathed? That is, except the damage done to my gown and my shoes, but those were minor things, and I would be more careful tonight, now that I knew what to expect.

At length it was time for dinner. Because the first of the wedding guests would not be arriving until the next day, our evening meal tonight would be a quiet enough affair, and I knew I would not need to change my gown. So I returned my books to their shelves and went downstairs, steeling myself to face Lord Mayson for the first time since his father had departed.

Luckily, my tidying up had made me late enough that I was the last to enter the dining hall. Everyone was already seated, Mayson in his usual place to my uncle's left, while Aunt Lyselle had the chair to the right.

Murmuring an apology for my tardiness, I hurried to my place, which was opposite Janessa and below Carella. When I had first come to stay at the castle, I had found myself somewhat angered by the designated spot where I must sit, since it seemed to signal to everyone my lowly position in the family, a cousin there by sufferance, a poor relation. I cannot say I was still completely reconciled to it, even though I understood the customs which dictated the placement. In that moment, however, I was merely glad my position at the bottom of the table meant I was safely separated from Lord Mayson.

As had been the case lately, the conversation centered mostly around Adalynn's upcoming nuptials, with more of the apparently ceaseless discussions of the placement of the flowers and whether another course should be added to the dinner, and what on earth they should do if dreadful Cousin Patrile should show up the way she had threatened. I listened with half an ear, my thoughts far more focused on what lay ahead for me that night after everyone had gone to bed.

Even so, I could not help but notice the way Mayson's gaze seemed fixed on me, so that every time I looked up from my plate, I saw his dark eyes glaring down the length of the table to the place where I sat. Although the food was quite excellent, I found my appetite wanting to desert me. Surely he was not going to pursue his suit, not after everything I had said both to him and to his father?

I couldn't know, and that was most definitely not the time to ask. The only positive note was that no one else seemed to perceive his unwanted attention, and so I thought I could still salvage the evening, if only I was able to slip away after dinner before he had a chance to speak to me.

My luck did not seem to hold, however. The servants came to clear away the plates, and everyone stood. This was the time when my uncle would go to his study, while we girls would head to Aunt Lyselle's sitting room for more conversation before it was time to retire upstairs for the night. But as I stood and began to inch my way toward the door, Lord Mayson said,

"Perhaps a turn outside, Iselda? For it is still quite warm."

Trapped, I could but nod. Everyone's eyes were on me, and I noted how my aunt's head tilted to one side, as if she was absorbing this new wrinkle and attempting to determine how it might alter what I had said to her previously on the subject of Mayson Bellender. Affecting an air of unconcern, I waited for him to come up to me. Then he offered his arm, and I had no choice but to take it so he might lead me out of the dining chamber and into the corridor, where a door opened up onto the gardens.

Despite my unease, I could not help noticing what a beautiful evening it was, the air still thick with the scent of roses, the first stars beginning to appear in the soft, lavender-tinted skies. A perfect evening for romance, some might think. Was that Mayson's intention—to bring me to a place where the conditions were perfect for convincing me to be his wife?

I swallowed, but said nothing as he closed the garden door and began to lead me down one of the graveled paths. When we were far enough away from any open windows that even the most avid ear could not have overheard our conversation, he stopped, dark eyes intent on my face.

"I think you have been avoiding me, Iselda."

Denials immediately bubbled to my lips. "No, my lord, of course not. It was only that it was quite warm today, and I did not much feel inclined toward activity. Up in my room, the breeze is very fine, and it is far more comfortable than in other parts of the castle."

That actually sounded quite plausible. I waited as he seemed to consider my words, and hoped he would believe them. Then he said, "I thought we were friends, Iselda."

My heart sank. Truly, I did not know what to say to him. Friends, yes, but he wished for more than that, or at least wished for me to be a friend while at the same time to become his wife. I did not think I could manage that.

Especially not after last night, I thought, even though I immediately pushed the ridiculous notion away. I did not know who the strange young man was, not even his name. Yes, I'd been struck by his beauty, but that was certainly no reason for me to expect anything else from him, other than an explanation as to why all the castle's young women were being summoned to perform their strange dance.

"We are friends, my lord," I said. "And I thought we had already discussed this."

"We did." He paused then, again searching my face. I thought of the contrast between his warm brown eyes and the stranger's glittering silver, and was vaguely ashamed of myself for making the comparison. I certainly had no reason to be doing so. "And my father told me what you said." Another hesitation, and he moved closer, then took my hands in his. "Do you really think a marriage between us would be loveless?"

How on earth should I respond to that? Even as I flailed about, attempting to come up with a reasonable answer, a spark of anger awoke inside me. Lord Elwyn should not have told his son that I had said such things.

"I—"

I could get no further than that, because in the next moment Mayson had pulled me toward him, was bending down...and oh, his mouth was touching mine, and he was kissing me, his fingers tight on mine, his lips sweet with wine.

I will not lie and say it was not pleasurable on some level. Indeed, I thought I could see why men and women desired to kiss one another, for the sensations flooding through me were both novel and at the same time curiously exciting. And yet…

…and yet I did not feel the world stop turning, nor did I feel as if my body was on fire, both descriptions I had read in books of how it was supposed to feel when a man kissed you. Perhaps those books had been exaggerating…or perhaps I was not sent into transports merely because it was Mayson kissing me, rather than the true match of my heart.

After a moment, he raised his mouth from mine and said, his voice somewhat hoarse, "You see? We will do very well together, Iselda. Do you deny it?"

I pulled in a breath, and then another. "Mayson, I—I am not sure what to say."

"What is there to say, except you will be my wife?"

Oh, gods. Very gently, I pulled my fingers from his. "Do you think one kiss is enough to change my mind?"

His eyes glinted in the semi-darkness. "I can give you another, if that is what you need to convince you."

This was a Mayson I did not quite recognize. Was he being more forceful because the kiss had awakened something inside him, something he had not wanted to acknowledge until this moment?

I did not know what to say. For I could not deny that I had enjoyed the kiss, even while I knew it was not everything it might have been. Or was I just being foolish, thinking that what the storybooks said had any bearing on the real world? Mayson was only a few years older than I, handsome and kind and titled. A girl such as myself could do far, far worse. Indeed, many would say that I now had no choice, that because I had allowed him to take such a liberty with me, I had compromised myself and must be his wife or face certain disgrace.

But no one had seen us. We were quite alone here. That was enough to convince me that I had no need to make that kind of sacrifice.

"I—I am not sure it would be wise for you to kiss me again," I managed at last. At once his expression fell, and I reached out to take his hands. "Oh, dear Mayson, you are making this so very difficult for me!"

Once again he tightened his fingers around mine, and once again he pulled me close to him. Truly, there was something rather heady about standing so close, of feeling as if I could almost hear his heart beating. He bent down, but this time his lips brushed my cheek rather than touching my mouth. In a voice barely louder than a whisper, he said, "I do not want to be difficult. And—and I am willing to wait for you to decide what it is you wish to do. But Iselda, please make sure that you are not making things too hard for yourself. We all have wishes and dreams...but dreams are chancy things. They can disappear very quickly. Do not ignore what is in front of you just because of a dream."

Then he let go of my hands and touched my cheek, so briefly I almost could have imagined the gentle caress. And at once he turned and walked away from me, hurrying off to a different door than the one we had used to let ourselves out into the garden.

For the longest moment, I could only stand there and watch where he had gone. My heart raced, and I warred with myself.

I did not think I would have any difficulty staying awake that night.

Nor did I. Oh, once again Janessa was avid, wishing to know everything that had passed between his lordship and myself, but I was in enough mental tumult that I snapped at her and said it would be a mercy if I got a moment's peace in this house. That remark was enough to send her flouncing to her bed in stony silence, and she turned her face to the wall so she would not have to look at me.

I sighed, and immediately regretted my hasty words, but there was no taking them back. Perhaps she would forgive me, perhaps not. In the morning I would apologize and tell her I was merely on edge because of all the upheaval in the house. It would not even be a lie, not really.

But how in the world could I confess to her that Lord Mayson had kissed me, and I had no idea what I should do next? For in our sheltered little world, a kiss such as that might as well be a betrothal. Men and women of our station were not meant to share such intimacies unless marriage was soon to follow.

At length her offended silence faded into sleep as she began to breathe deeply, not quite snoring, if the next thing to it. I sat wakeful, and watched the pale moonlight begin to pour in through the window. Everything was still, even the night breeze dwindling to nothing.

And then Janessa sat upright in her bed. Immediately, I looked over at her; her eyes met mine, but there was nothing in them, no recognition, not even a spark of her lively soul. It was like staring into a pair of black mirrors, depthless, almost inhuman.

Despite the stuffy heat in the chamber, ice seemed to trail down my spine, awakening gooseflesh on my arms. As I watched, hardly daring to breathe, she picked up the sheet and thin blanket that covered her, then carefully folded them back. Then she swung her feet over the side of the bed and stood.

Something about her movements seemed strangely jerky, as if she was a marionette being controlled by unseen strings. Was this part of the spell? Was the mage who had cast it forcing her through every step, every motion?

Next, she stepped into one of the slippers lying on the floor beside her bed, followed by its mate. Although a dressing gown lay draped across the foot of her bed, she ignored it. And I recalled how she and my cousins had danced in the moonlight in only their nightgowns. Not a one of them had bothered to cover herself.

Janessa went to the door and opened it. Almost at the same time, the door across the corridor opened as well, and Carella and Theranne emerged. The three of them moved to the center of the hallway and stood there, waiting. In the next moment, I saw why, for Adalynn approached them, and they all fell into line behind her as she headed down the hall and toward the stairwell.

That seemed to be my cue. I leapt out of bed and thrust my feet into the shoes I had hidden under the bed against just this purpose. There being no time for me to dress myself properly, I grabbed a shawl from the wardrobe before hurrying after them. The piece of thin wool was certainly not necessary on such a warm night. I had not taken it for warmth, however, but for modesty. If I should encounter the stranger again tonight, at least I would do so while being partially covered.

I followed my cousins and Janessa down the stairs and out through the kitchen. So it seemed they, too, understood this was the best way to slip from the castle without being noticed. At first I hung back, certain that if I made enough noise, they would realize someone tagged along behind them, but they only looked forward and seemed to take no real note of their surroundings.

This allowed me to move somewhat more freely as we left the shelter of the castle and headed out through the moonlit fields, the grasses rustling under our trailing skirts. As I had thought they might, the little group went unerringly toward the ford in the stream, then followed the bank along the other side and on up to the place where they might pass into the darkness of the forest.

At this point, I quailed slightly, wishing again that I had brought a lantern with me. Surely if they had not noticed someone following them this whole time, then there was a very good chance they would not notice a lantern, either. But I had not thought to bring one, and besides, since the moon was quite bright, only a few days from being full, I knew I should see well enough.

Besides, it was not as if I hadn't gone this way just the night before.

They led me deeper into the woods, their gowns ghostly blurs of white in the darkness. If any wild animals watched, they made no move to attack, although certainly all of the girls would have been easy prey in their current state. Perhaps the mage was keeping the beasts of the forest at bay with a different spell.

At length we reached the same clearing where I had first seen them dancing. Here, I hung back, for I knew I would be far too conspicuous if I followed them any further. Instead, I hid myself behind the thick trunk of an ancient oak, and settled myself in to watch.

The four of them took up the same positions as they had the previous night. At the time, I had been too flustered by the uncanny sight to attempt to see any rhyme or reason in what they were doing, but now I thought they had arranged themselves so they stood at the four points of the compass, with Adalynn taking north and Janessa south, and Carella and Theranne occupying west and east, respectively.

Once again, they reached out to join hands and began to move slowly in a circle, going clockwise, as before. The night wind rose, fluttering at the hems of their gowns and pressing the thin fabric against their bodies. Although their hair had been braided for the night, the breeze was brisk enough that it tugged strands loose so they blew into their eyes, but none of them blinked. Not even once.

A fierce whisper. "I told you not to come back here!"

Although I had hoped he would return, I could not help startling slightly at the sound of his voice. Then I gathered myself and turned back toward him, even as I tightened the shawl around my shoulders. Watching my cousins and Janessa dance had told me just how much our nightgowns could reveal.

His silver eyes were narrowed and fierce, and his hands were planted on his hips. The previous night I had been so preoccupied with his unusual looks that I had not paid much attention to what he wore. Now I saw that he had on a plain dark doublet and breeches and high boots. An unadorned belt with a dagger in an equally plain scabbard hung at his waist. The clothes were completely ordinary, and yet they somehow served to draw even more attention to his face, to the bright silver of his eyes and the smooth pallor of his skin. If he was able to grow any kind of a beard, I could see no sign of it in the dark-dappled moonlight.

"You did," I said calmly. "But you are not my lord and master, and since this forest belongs to the crown, I have just as much a right to be here as anyone else."

"Foolish, stubborn girl!" he shot back. "You have no idea what you are dealing with!"

I chose to ignore the insult. In an echo of his own posture, I set my hands on my hips and stared back at him, willing myself to forget that I stood before him wearing only a nightgown and a shawl. "No, I do not, for you refuse to tell me. But those are my cousins over there, and I deserve answers."

To my relief, his eyes remained fixed on my face. If he had taken note of my dishabille, he gave no sign of it. "You would return here, when I have already told you of the danger you bring upon yourself by ignoring my warnings?"

"Yes," I said. "You called me stubborn, and I suppose that is nothing more than I deserve. I would debate you on 'foolish,' though. Foolhardy...perhaps."

For just the barest instant, I thought I saw his mouth quirk, as if what I had said amused him, despite everything. But his voice was stern enough as he returned, "Did I not tell you that they would return unharmed? Did I lie?"

"No," I admitted. "They did return to the castle, and seemed well enough, if somewhat wearied by what they had experienced during the night, even though they recalled nothing of it. But I still know nothing of why they are here. Can you not tell me that at least?"

A certain tautness overtook his features then, and he glanced away from me, as if looking to see that we were still alone. I recalled the tumult in the sky the night before, how he had told me that something dark and dangerous was approaching. The woods around us still seemed calm enough, however, and so I guessed that the "he" the stranger had referenced the night before was not yet about to make an appearance.

"I cannot," he said. "It would change nothing, save to put you in even greater danger."

I did not like the sound of that. But, because I was stubborn, I said next, "Then can you at least tell me your name?"

He hesitated. A slight lift of his shoulders, as if he had debated with himself and decided he could allow me that trifle at least. "I am called Reynar."

"Reynar...what?" For everyone I had ever heard of or met had some sort of family name.

"Only Reynar. And now that you have that particular piece of information, will you go?"

"Why? Is *he* coming?"

A long pause. Reynar looked past me, to the clearing where the girls danced, graceful ghosts in the moonlight. My gaze followed his, and once again I thought I could see that strange luminescence, as if some sort of light or energy flowed from them and around them. If I looked too closely, however, it disappeared at once, as if it had never been.

"No," Reynar replied, somewhat begrudgingly, as if loath to tell the truth but also not wishing to tell a lie. "Not yet, at any rate. There is time for you to go in a more sedate manner than you did last night."

"Well, then," I said. "Last night you seemed puzzled that the spell did not affect me. Have you thought on that any more? For I must confess that I am curious as to why I am not out there dancing with the rest of them."

His gaze moved from the quartet in the clearing back to me, and for some reason I could feel hot color move into my cheeks. In that moment, I was glad of the gloom, glad that he probably would not be able to tell I had blushed.

"I did think on it," he said. "As did he. But neither of us could think of what the reason might be. As far as either of us are able to tell, you are an ordinary enough girl."

"Why, thank you," I said with some acid. "This is the first time I have found value in being *ordinary*."

He blinked, then shook his head. "That is not what I meant. I am sure many think you a most exceptional young woman."

This piece of backtracking did little to mollify me. I lifted my chin at him and said, "So which is it? Am I ordinary...or exceptional? I find it hard to believe that I can be both."

"Oh, for all the gods' sakes...." The words trailed off, and he seemed to set his jaw as he stared down at me. "You are exceptionally stubborn, and quite lovely, and so I suppose those qualities must make you more than ordinary. But at the same time, you are a young woman of quite normal birth, and no peculiar abilities. You are no user of magic, or anything of that ilk, are you?"

"No," I responded, even as a strange, warm little tingle went over me at the same time. He had said I was quite lovely. So despite his apparent focus on far more important matters, he had still noticed something about my appearance. "No, if that is your definition of 'ordinary,' then I suppose I am quite ordinary indeed. But still there must be something different about me, some reason why I am able to resist the spell, or you and I would not be standing here and talking like this."

For a second or two, he did not speak. I did not know him well enough to clearly read his expressions, and yet I would say he was feeling somewhat flummoxed. "My lady," he said formally. "It is a puzzle, true, and one I have not yet worked out. I suppose I will discover the answer at some point...or *he* will."

"Who is *he?*" I asked, for that was yet another question that had been preying on my mind. "For one would have thought we would have heard something, if such a very great mage was living somewhere near my uncle's lands."

Real fear flared in those silver eyes and was just as quickly gone. Indeed, that sudden flash of fright disappeared so swiftly,

I was not quite sure I had not imagined it. "It is forbidden to say his name. Pray you never hear it. As for the rest...." Again there came one of those furtive glances upward, as if Reynar was not quite sure that his master was not about to descend upon us. "How do you think all the mage-born have been able to survive into these latter days? Through stealth, through cunning, through being able to hide their true natures. You could have one living very near and yet have no idea that he possessed any of those gifts."

I shivered then. Perhaps the night wind had picked up... perhaps not. But as much as I wished to argue, I knew I could not. My own brother-in-law had lived for many years in the crowded capital of my land, and no one had known that he was a mage. They had all thought he was only Tobyn Slade, master goldsmith, a man who hid his face because of scarring from a terrible bout of smallpox he had suffered many years before. And if he could hide himself in plain sight, why not others who had been born with the forbidden magical abilities?

"Perhaps you are right," I said. "I will admit that I know very little about how such things might be accomplished. But still...how is it that you came to be his apprentice? For that is what you are, is it not?"

Reynar's fine features became clouded, and he would not meet my gaze. "That is a long story, and not one you have the leisure to hear right now. But yes, if it satisfies some of that misbegotten curiosity of yours, I am his apprentice. I am here to watch over them, to make sure they are safe until the spell has built to its height."

"And then...?" I asked, wondering deep within if I really wished to hear the answer.

"And then he will reap what he has sown, and they will go home, with no recollection of where they have been."

My voice dropped to a shaky whisper. "What is he sowing?"

"Nothing that hurts them. You have my promise on that."

I hesitated. For I had seen my cousins return, more or less unharmed. They were tired, true, but that was only to be expected from someone who had been out wandering around in the middle of the night. Their bodies knew they had expended that effort, even if their minds had forgotten.

And yet...I had heard that no magic could be worked, no spell cast, without some kind of cost. The strange dance that had my cousins and Janessa moving in that slow, stately circle was creating some kind of energy; I was almost sure of it. But to what purpose?

I could ask again, but I knew I would only be wasting my breath. Reynar had told me a good deal, true, but mysteries still existed that he had no desire to explain to me. If I pressed him, he would only become closed off and silent.

"And what happens when Adalynn goes away?" I asked then.

His silvery head tilted to one side. "What do you mean?"

"I mean that she is to be married the day after tomorrow. After the wedding, her new husband will take her away to dwell in his castle, on his lands. Will the spell work with only three women remaining?"

"It will work. Not as efficiently as it does now, perhaps. And he will also look for a new opportunity, another place where he might work the spell."

That reply relieved me somewhat. For not only would this unknown mage make no effort to prevent Adalynn from going, but he would actually move on to work his magic somewhere else. We would be left alone. No matter what Reynar had said about the magic not harming my cousins, I could not prevent myself from thinking that it had to hurt them in the long run, if only because of all the sleep they would lose.

He went on, his tone somewhat gentler, "I know you worry for them, but there is no need. However, you have tarried here long enough. Will you please go now, before you must hurry away and possibly harm yourself?"

I hesitated. But then I looked up into his face and saw true concern reflected there. He did not want me to flee in terror as I had the night before. A measured exit would remove me from the orbit of this strange, unknown mage, and would prevent me from tripping and falling.

"I will," I replied, noting the relief that passed over his features. "As long as you do not try to make me promise that I will not return."

"Oh, I know better than to ask that." He hesitated then before adding, "I must confess that it is pleasant to speak with someone other than my master."

Warmth went through me at those words. Just before, he had said he thought I was lovely, and now he was admitting that he enjoyed our conversations. That seemed like worthy progress, even if he still had a fearsome master to contend with.

"You see no one else? Only your master?"

Reynar spread his hands and sent a self-deprecating glance downward at himself. "As you might have noticed, I am certain to draw attention wherever I go. So I do not venture forth from his holdings very often, save for these nocturnal expeditions."

I did not bother to contradict him, for of course he was right—he would stand out dreadfully wherever he went. Even I tended to attract my own amount of attention, for golden hair such as I possessed was not very common in Purth. But still my heart was wrung as I thought of what must be a very solitary existence. We were certainly not acquainted enough for me to put a reassuring hand on his arm, or to twine my fingers with his, and so I only nodded and said, "Well, then, I am glad that we can speak here, even if this is the only place where we might do so freely." I stopped there and glanced over at my cousins and Janessa, all of whom still moved in their silent circle, dancing to music apparently only they could hear. They would do so until the spell was wrought, but then they would be sent home. I did not need to worry about them...even though I knew I would. "And I will go now. Thank you, Reynar—thank you for telling me as much as you have."

He smiled, and inclined his head, and after that I hurried off into the woods. This time, only a light breeze moved the leaves overhead, and I heard the ordinary sounds of the forest's creatures. Wherever the mage was, and whatever he might be doing, it seemed clear enough to me that he had decided to stay away a little longer tonight.

But as I crossed the stream and back into the open fields, I found I was not thinking so much of this fearsome mage—whoever he might be—but of his apprentice, of Reynar's quicksilver eyes and the fine bones of his face and the unexpected beauty of his smiles.

I thought if he had been the one to kiss me, rather than Mayson, I would not have demurred at that offer of a second kiss.

Chapter Seven

After I had sneaked back into my bed, I did not bother to try staying awake. Perhaps that was foolish of me, but I did truly believe that my cousins would be fine, that Reynar would watch over them until they returned to their father's lands and were once again inside his castle's walls. Had they not done so several times before? All I would do was weary myself, and I knew I needed to keep my wits about me. The next day our first guests would be arriving...and I would also have to decide what in the world to do about Mayson.

Even that particular worry did not keep me awake. It seemed that no time had passed at all before I opened my eyes once again and saw bright daylight slipping around the edges of the silk brocade curtains hung at the windows. A quick glance over at Janessa's bed told me that she still slept; her back was to me, but I could see her long brown braid falling over her shoulder, and I could hear her deep, regular breathing. Certainly she seemed no worse the wear for her activities of the night before, although I resolved to stay still and quiet in my own bed for as long as possible, so I might not wake her.

That quiet did not last for so very long, unfortunately. A few minutes later, the door to our bedroom opened, and Tarly bustled in with the morning tea on a tray. As soon as she was within a foot or so of the bed, Janessa rolled over with a groan and looked up at our maid with confused, sleep-blurred eyes.

"Is it morning already?"

"Yes, and then some. Her ladyship does not wish any of you to tarry too long this morning, for the Earl and Countess of Delmayne are due to arrive at midday, and there is still much to be done before they arrive."

This piece of information was met with another groan, but after that Janessa sat up and rubbed at her eyes. Tarly seemed to take this as an indication that she was ready for tea, and poured some from the pot into one of the waiting cups. Next, she came to me and offered me a cup, which I accepted gratefully. Even though I had slept well enough, I was feeling rather groggy myself this morning. All that nighttime chasing around, probably, and then there had been that encounter with Mayson in the garden. I still hadn't determined how best to behave around him. While I did not want to offer any encouragement, I also knew I couldn't be so off-putting as to draw attention.

Or maybe, a treacherous part of my mind thought then, *just maybe, you should let him kiss you again. That would give you a great deal more to work with.*

Oh, no, I could not do that. I thought of how Reynar had looked in the moonlight, all silver and steel, and contrasted his appearance with Mayson's friendly dark eyes and the handsome cleft in his chin. Perhaps that was not fair, but I knew where I was being drawn, and it was not to the heir of Bellender Rise.

I sipped my tea and tried to calm my tumultuous thoughts. For while it was true that it would be difficult to avoid Mayson completely, with the guests arriving and the castle being prepared for Adalynn's wedding, it would also be easier to keep myself apart from him than it might have been under different circumstances. I would make myself helpful to my aunt, and to my cousin, and, with any luck, they would keep me busy enough that Mayson would have to occupy himself elsewhere.

Those thoughts cheered me enough that I finished the rest of my tea with some alacrity, and then had a serious discussion with Tarly as to which gown would be most appropriate for the day's activities. Janessa drank her tea and seemed to be listening with only half an ear, her gaze fixed on the window. I could not guess at the source of her abstraction, although I thought that perhaps she was wondering if any eligible young men might be among the wedding guests. No one could have faulted her for those thoughts, for my aunt and uncle did not entertain as much as some of their peers did, and so Janessa was not often given the opportunity to meet with possible suitors.

For her sake, I hoped there would be someone promising. Someone who would recognize her worthy qualities and give her a home of her own, where she would not have to be dependent on the charity of my aunt and uncle, and could make a life for herself.

To tell the truth, that was an outcome I wished for myself as well. However, I did not know if I would be so lucky. Perhaps I flattered myself, but I had the impression that Reynar had begun to admire me...which would have made my heart leap, except for the small impediment of his being apprenticed to some fearsome, unknown mage and therefore certainly not free to give his heart to another.

A knock came at the door, even though it stood open. Outside in the hallway were two of the footmen with that morning's bath. Tarly ushered them in, had them deposit the copper tub in its designated space behind a screen in the corner of the room, and then shut the door. While she and Janessa debated Janessa's wardrobe for the day, I climbed into the bath. The water had already begun to cool, but I did not mind much, for the day promised to be warm, and an overly hot bath was not something I thought I required.

I lathered my hair and thought of Reynar, even though it seemed rather inappropriate to have him so present in my mind while I lay naked in a bath. Somehow, though, I could not help myself. Was it only that he was so very different, so strange and exotic? If I put the two men side by side, could I honestly say that Reynar was more handsome than Mayson?

In all truth, I did not know. All I did know was that I found something compelling about the silver-haired apprentice, whereas I liked Mayson but experienced no particular fire when in his presence, not even when he had kissed me.

It would have been much easier for me if my feelings were the opposite, but I already knew that feelings were not things which could be easily commanded.

Fighting back a sigh—for I certainly did not want Tarly and Janessa to overhear such a thing—I finished rinsing the soap out of my hair and then reached for one of the clean cloths that hung from the screen so I might rise from the bath and get myself dry. I had heard that some great ladies had their maids wash their hair and dry them off, but we were certainly not so grand here, and I was glad of it. Somehow it seemed very strange to let someone who was not your husband touch you in such an intimate fashion.

But of course that was probably the wrong thing to allow to cross my mind, for I thought of Reynar again, of the shape of his mouth and the strength in his hands, and of what it might feel like for those lips to touch mine, for those hands to move down my body—

I shivered, and thrust the thought away immediately. It was so very improper for even the barest hint of such things to enter a young lady's mind, and yet....

Concentrate on drying off the last of the bath's moisture and squeezing the damp from your hair. That was what I told myself, and through sheer effort of will, I somehow managed to do so. What had come over me right then, I could not say.

Except that perhaps Reynar had cast his own spell on me, one which had very little to do with actual magic.

A dressing robe also hung from the screen, and I took it and wrapped it around myself to cover my nakedness. When I emerged, I saw that Janessa and Tarly had apparently decided on her wine-colored silk, which did suit Janessa's glossy brown hair and warm hazel eyes very well. My other good dress besides the green watered silk I had already worn—and the splendid blue and silver gown that was being reserved for Adalynn's wedding day—was also pink, albeit a lighter shade than Janessa's dress. I went ahead and quickly slipped into my underthings and my chemise as Tarly went to help Janessa into the bath, for she was not quite as tall as I and sometimes had difficulty stepping over the sides of the tub.

Once she was settled, though, Tarly came back out to help me into my dress, to lace me tightly and begin twisting my damp hair so it would fall into the ringlets which were such a source of jealousy for Janessa. Throughout these ministrations, I was silent, my thoughts far away.

As far as the nighttime woods, and a clearing where four girls danced to music no one else could hear.

Again I wondered if now was the time to go to my aunt and uncle. But although they did not lack for wealth and influence, they would be of little use in this situation. They could set guards outside all our doors, I supposed...but what if the same spell that sent the house into such quiet made those men fall asleep? I recalled the strange lassitude that had overcome me the first night my cousins and Janessa had ventured forth. It certainly had not felt like ordinary weariness, even if it had not affected me on the nights that followed.

Besides, while my aunt and uncle were certainly some of the most amiable and open-minded people I had ever known, I could not help worrying what they might think if they found magic at work in their own household. Perhaps they would believe I had something to do with it, I with the mage for a brother-in-law.

And I also thought again of what might happen if the witch-finders should appear, and decided it was better to do nothing. In a few days, Adalynn would be safely married and gone, and the mage who had cast the spell would be looking for a new set of young women to influence with his spell.

Was that fair, though? Should my silence allow such a thing to continue? What if the next group the mage happened upon was not so lucky, and did encounter some kind of harm?

No, surely Reynar would not allow such a thing to occur. But while I trusted his intentions, I did not know if he had the strength to defy his master.

So I went, back and forth. If Tarly noted anything strange about my unusual taciturnity, she did not mention it, but continued to work on my hair, and then fastened the pretty rose quartz and pearl necklace that had been a Midwinter gift around my neck. When I gazed at myself in the mirror, I thought I looked well enough. Not that it mattered, for, unlike Janessa, I had no desire to seek out an eligible young man from among the wedding attendees. I already had two to contend with, one eminently eligible, the other not nearly so.

"Thank you, Tarly," I said as she stepped away from me, her work done. "It all looks lovely."

"Oh, that's because of the one who wears it, I think," she replied, then went over to help Janessa, who had already emerged from her bath and done much as I had, getting into her underthings while Tarly worked on my hair.

The unexpected compliment made me smile, for Tarly was usually not much of one for praise, preferring to leave that sort of thing for others. Perhaps she feared what might happen if she puffed up our vanity too much, although she would step in when we needed some cheering up, as she had with Janessa the day before.

At any rate, it is far too late in Adalynn's case, I thought then with an inward smile. Yes, my cousin was very lovely. Unfortunately, she was all too aware of that fact.

I told Janessa that I was going to head downstairs, and continued on my way alone, for I saw no sign of my cousins. Perhaps they were moving slowly this morning after their exertions of the night before. I could not exactly blame them, although I knew such tardiness would not sit well with my aunt.

It turned out I was correct in that assumption, for she frowned when I entered the small breakfast chamber alone, then said, "Are you the first to be ready, Iselda?"

"Yes, Aunt Lyselle," I replied as I took my seat. "I believe Janessa will not be too far behind, but I cannot speak for everyone else."

"Bother. I told them that the Earl and the Countess of Delmayne would be here at midday, and we do not have so much idle time that we can afford to be careless."

My uncle had been sitting at the table and drinking his morning tea, but at those irritated words, he stood and put a comforting hand on his wife's arm. "Beloved, it is not yet even nine o'clock in the morning. I assure you that all will be ready by the time the earl and the countess arrive, and their son with them."

For that exalted pair were the parents of Adalynn's betrothed, Coryn Landester, who would one day be the Earl of Delmayne in his own right. And my cousin would be a countess, and no doubt very grand.

And you could be a countess, too, if you would but accept Mayson's suit.

I did not want to think of that. Truthfully, I did not know what held me back. His kiss had been more than pleasant, so it was not as if I did not find some attractions about his person. Was I really going to let my strange fascination with Reynar, a man I had only laid eyes on twice in my life, keep me from having a secure future?

But no, I could not lay all my reticence at Reynar's feet. Even before I met him, I had told Mayson that I had no desire to be his wife. While some spiteful part of me thought it might be quite grand to be a countess as well, of equal rank with my haughty cousin, I would never do such a thing out of spite. Mayson deserved better than that. Even if I could not love him the way he wished for me to, he should have someone who would.

"I am not sure I have your confidence, Danly," my aunt said. Certainly she must be almost beside herself, for otherwise she would not have forgotten her manners and addressed her husband by his given name in front of me.

"Well, I have enough for both of us, I think," he replied in amiable tones. "So do sit down, dear wife, and have some more tea. All will be in readiness by the time our noble guests arrive."

She gave a dubious nod, but she did subside enough to take her seat, and sit quietly while Jax, one of the footmen, poured her some tea.

It seemed that my uncle's assessment was correct, for only a few moments later Janessa and my cousins appeared, all of them freshly scrubbed and in their second-best gowns, their hair gleaming. They uttered a chorus of "good mornings" before going to sit down and have their tea.

Aunt Lyselle relaxed visibly, her approving gaze moving from one of them to the next. Her eyes rested on Adalynn the longest, and I saw her mouth curve in a small smile. If I were her mother, I supposed I would have been proud of Adalynn as well, for she did look very beautiful in her gown of deep turquoise silk with its gold embroidery. Her hair hung in shining ringlets almost as intricate as mine, although I knew hers must have had some help from the long iron her maid utilized to create those perfect spirals of hair.

And I thought I glimpsed also the most subtle use of rouge on Adalynn's lips and cheeks, although I was not sure whether my aunt, who tended to be somewhat near-sighted, had even noticed. Perhaps my cousin had been looking rather wan after her latest foray into the nighttime woods, and so her maid had thought to remedy the situation. Certainly it would not do to be looking pale and lackluster upon greeting one's future husband and in-laws.

None of the other girls showed any signs of that kind of artifice being used, so perhaps they had fared better. I made a mental note to ask Reynar about that when I saw him again this evening. Was it possible that the spell somehow taxed my eldest cousin more heavily than the others?

This morning I paid more attention to the conversation about the wedding preparations than I might have the two preceding days, merely because I recalled my resolve to keep myself busy and therefore, I hoped, away from Lord Mayson as much as possible. When she mentioned that she was not sure the amount of roses that had been cut were quite sufficient,

I hastened to say, "Oh, I do not mind going out and cutting more for you, Aunt Lyselle."

She shot me a grateful glance, although at the same time she appeared rather troubled. "Are you quite sure, Iselda? It would not do for you to spend too much time in the sun, especially in one of your good gowns."

"It is no problem at all," I replied. "For I will wear my hat, and if I go out directly after breakfast, then the sun will not yet be too hot."

"Thank you, then. Because it seems all the maids are occupied, and your cousins—"

I wasn't sure what she intended to say then. Perhaps that it was more important for my cousins to remain looking neat and tidy, whereas I was more expendable? No, my aunt would never utter such a thing, even if it was only the truth. I saved her from her floundering by saying, "Everyone has a great number of matters to attend to this morning, and so I would not expect you to ask anyone else. I always enjoy going in the garden."

Those words seemed to convince her, for she smiled then and picked up her teacup. "Thank you so much, Iselda. For yes, there is still a great deal to do."

The meal was quiet after that exchange, as everyone ate quickly—presumably so they could get on with all their very important tasks. Once I was done with my bread and fruit and eggs, I excused myself from the table, then ran upstairs to my room so I might fetch my hat. As I did so, I cast a wary glance outside, trying to gauge whether I had overreached by saying that the sun should not be any trouble at all.

But some high, thin clouds had drifted in during the past hour, making me think that it would not be so very difficult to spend a half hour or so outdoors. If the clouds could only hold until I was done....

Tying the ribbons of my hat under my chin, I went back down the stairs, then out the nearest doorway that opened onto the gardens. Against the opposite wall, mostly obscured by a hedge, was a small shed that contained gardening implements; from there I fetched a pair of clippers and a basket. Then I went back out into the sun and began walking down one of the paths, eyes roving from side to side in search of the most likely specimens. Since Aunt Lyselle had not specified a certain type or color of rose, I was not all the discriminating, and only made sure that I snipped off flowers which were nearly at their peak.

Because the summer sun had been warm and the nights mild, I found an almost overwhelming number of worthy blooms. My basket began to fill up very quickly, and I thought I should be able to get indoors before I had even been out here a half hour.

"Iselda."

My heart sank, but I arranged a smile on my features and turned to face him. "Lord Mayson."

His gaze moved to the basket of flowers I held. "Let me take that for you."

"It's really not necessary—"

"I insist."

I subsided then, for I knew there was not much point in arguing. He would do the chivalrous thing, and despite our friendship—and the new intimacy of that shared kiss—I understood that it was not entirely wise to argue with the son of an earl.

So I surrendered the basket, saying, "I fear that poor Aunt Lyselle is rather in a state, what with so many guests about to descend upon the castle."

Mayson chuckled. "Yes, she is not her usual calm self. But I suppose it is not every day that one sees their eldest child married."

"True." I feared the topic of marriage was fraught with pitfalls, so I hastened to say, hoping I could steer the conversation elsewhere, "Do you think it will rain? For it seems that more and more clouds have begun to gather?"

One corner of his mouth went up in the lopsided smile that had become so familiar to me over the past few weeks. If his amusement stemmed from my obvious attempt to change the subject, he gave no sign of it. He replied, his voice grave, "Perhaps. But rain will cool things down for everyone, and your aunt does not have anything planned for out of doors, does she?"

"Not today," I said, relieved that he had decided to play along. "But tomorrow she intends to have an evening reception here in the rose garden, after more guests arrive."

Mayson tilted his head to look up at the sky. At that angle, the lines of his jaw and throat were thrown into sharp relief, and I had to force myself not to stare. He really was such a fine-looking man. Why, then, was I so reluctant?

I did not have the chance to puzzle out that particular conundrum, for in the next moment he turned back to me and said, "If we are to have any rain, I doubt it will stay with us long. Perhaps some brief showers this evening, but certainly not enough to inconvenience your aunt or her guests."

"That is good to hear." Whether he truly was one of those gifted at reading the signs that indicated whether rain would fall or move past without gracing us with a single drop, or whether he was merely trying to reassure me, I did not know. And perhaps it did not matter so very much. Even if we had a torrential summer storm move in, my aunt could always change her plans and have the reception moved to one of the great salons within the castle. It was not as if we lacked the space.

We had been moving slowly from spot to spot so I might stop here and there to clip off another rose, but Mayson stopped then and looked around, a small smile touching his lips.

"Do you know where we are, Iselda?"

Confused, I glanced from side to side, attempting to locate something that appeared out of the ordinary, but I could find nothing. "Other than in my aunt's rose garden, no, I fear not."

He shook his head at me, but when he replied, his tone was mild enough. "This is where I kissed you."

Oh, dear. Surely he was not going to attempt the same thing now, not when it was bright daylight and anyone might see us. True, it seemed the rest of the family—and the castle's servants—were occupied elsewhere, the entire reason why I was the one out in the rose garden with the basket and the clippers. Even so, I found myself praying that he would not forget himself in such a way. If he were to kiss me, and were anyone to witness it, then we would be as good as betrothed. No one would allow me to be compromised in such a way. My family might have had its own disgraces, but I was still a young woman of good birth, one whose virtue had never been questioned.

"Why, so it is," I said with a silly little giggle, one that sounded very unlike me. But I was so fearful of what he might do next that I was not quite in possession of all my senses.

"Have you thought of it since, Iselda?" he asked. His voice was soft, persuasive, but he made no move to come closer to me, which was something of a relief.

Of course I had. However, I could not admit such a thing to Mayson, for then he would believe that I recalled his kiss because I desired another one, and that was simply not the situation at all.

"I—"

He took one of the roses from the basket and held it to his nose so he might inhale its fragrance. "So very sweet," he said, "but not as sweet as the taste of your lips."

In that moment, I wished someone would come into the garden, for Mayson had not kissed me yet, and perhaps the presence of another person would help him to guard his emotions. But of course no one appeared. I was left to manage him myself.

"I do not think this is an appropriate topic of conversation," I said primly.

Those words only made him laugh outright. "Oh, do not take that tone with me, Iselda," he returned. "For I think I know you well enough now, and while you are many things, priggish is certainly not one of them."

No, I supposed not. Perhaps I had erred in being open and friendly with him, but I had not thought I would see such a shift in his demeanor, especially since only a few days earlier we had both resolved to be friends and nothing more. Could one kiss change a person so?

"Not priggish," I said, "but cautious. Forgive me, Mayson, but your sudden ardor takes me aback somewhat. At any rate, I do not think this is the time to be discussing such things. There is far too much happening to worry about whatever it is that you think you and I have shared. After the wedding is over—"

His eyes lit with sudden hope, and I realized I had said the wrong thing. "So once this is all done, we can go to your aunt and uncle and let them know this house will soon be blessed with another wedding?"

Even if I had truly wished to marry Mayson, I did not think Uncle Danly and Aunt Lyselle would be overjoyed to hear of such a match. They would be glad for me, of course, but their happiness would have to be tempered with disappointment, since they had wanted the heir to Bellender Rise to be their daughter's husband, not mine.

I did not look at him as I said, "That is not what I meant. I only meant to say that all is now in an uproar, and perhaps the very idea of marriage is preying more on your mind than it usually would. This is not the time to be making any decisions."

His hand tightened on the handle of the basket he held. The gold and ruby ring he wore on his little finger seemed to wink up at me like a baleful eye, and I selected a stem at random and snipped it, then deposited the yellow rose with its edging of deep coral along with the rest of the blooms already resting in the basket.

A silence fell, one too heavy and uncomfortable for such a mild summer day. A finch trilled away in a tree off to one side from where we stood, but the sound was certainly not enough to break up the pregnant pause.

At last Mayson said, "I cannot pretend to understand your reticence, but I will respect it. Only promise me one thing."

"What is that?" For I had read far too many stories to ever blindly promise anything, even if I was making that promise to Lord Mayson of Bellender Rise, and not some witch I had met at a crossroads.

He seemed to wince at my caution. When he spoke, his voice sounded almost too even, as if he was holding his anger in check. "It is a simple enough promise. All I ask is that, once the wedding is over and Adalynn has departed with her husband, you will meet with me here again in the moonlight. Let me kiss you once more, Iselda, and see if that will not change your mind."

Did he really think I was so easily swayed that a single kiss could make me alter my opinion of him? But his expression was so pleading that I relented, and said, "Yes, Mayson. I will make you that promise—if you will promise me in return that if my mind is not changed, then you will abandon this subject forever."

"I will make that promise," he said. "For I do not fear its outcome."

Perhaps he did not...but I thought I rather did.

Chapter Eight

The Earl and Countess of Delmayne arrived just before noon, bringing with them a sizable retinue, as well as their son Coryn. I had met him previously and thought him to be amiable enough, although not particularly handsome, with his long nose and rather close-set eyes. However, his smile did a great deal to improve his countenance, and it was clear from the way he looked at Adalynn that he thought himself very lucky to have been betrothed to her, even though his family outranked hers by a good deal.

Settling in these august visitors and their attendants took a good deal of time, and so we did not all sit down for luncheon until well after one in the afternoon. No thought of using the smaller, less formal dining chamber for such a function; we all gathered in the great hall we used for grand events, even though the table there could easily have accommodated more than twice our number.

As usual, I was relegated nearly to the foot of the table, and so, since our group had swelled to nearly double its normal count, I was even farther away from where Mayson sat. As Coryn's equal, he had been placed across from the other one-day Earl, with Adalynn at Coryn's side.

The separation relieved me, for it gave me time to gather my thoughts and sit quietly as I ate the delicious food that had been set in front of me, the cold pheasant and the melon salad with its dressing of mustard and honey, and all manner of other dishes that had been selected for both their flavor and their ability to prevent any of us from becoming over-warm in the heat of the day. All around, the roses I had brought in bloomed from a number of vases, filling the air with their sweet scent.

Indeed, they seemed to have impressed the countess, for she said to my aunt, "You do have very fine gardens here, do you not?"

I was too far away to see if Aunt Lyselle blushed, but she did give an airy wave of one hand and replied, "Oh, well, they have been here for many years, having been laid out by the late baroness. I only had to make sure that they continued to flourish."

"It seems that all things flourish here," said the countess, her clear blue eyes taking in the complement of young women sitting at the table. She was one who could be called more elegant than beautiful, with a long nose nearly identical to her son's, and the same thin, proud bones to her face. But her gaze was kindly enough. If anything, there was something almost pitying in it, as if she wondered how in the world my aunt and uncle would manage to marry off all those girls to anyone even remotely suitable.

Well, I knew they themselves had wondered the same thing on more than one occasion. And here I was, stealing away Lord

Mayson and dashing their hopes for Carella. No, I would not take that burden on myself. I had done nothing to encourage him.

Except kiss him, but he had initiated that contact as well. I was sure if my cousin had been put in that same situation, she would have kissed him back soundly—and probably would have also made sure there were witnesses to the act, so he had no chance of making an escape.

My aunt smiled, but I thought I could detect a bit of strain in her expression. However, she deftly maneuvered the conversation to the countess' journey here with her family and servitors, and said how lovely it was that they had arrived before there was any rain.

The discussion was mainly commonplaces after that, and so I only listened with half an ear as I ate my luncheon. From time to time I would look up from my plate and catch a smoldering stare sent by Lord Mayson in my direction, but of course he was sitting too far away to even attempt to engage me in conversation, so I was allowed to eat more or less in peace.

Afterward, my aunt took the earl and the countess, my uncle, and Adalynn and her betrothed away so they could inspect the site of the wedding ceremony, as well as the ball to be held afterward. I took advantage of the measured chaos to head back up to my room, since it seemed to be the only place where I was safe from being accosted by Mayson. He had glanced in my direction as I left, but I was too quick for him, and was already out the door while he was still excusing himself from the table.

Once in my room, I let out a relieved breath and prayed that Janessa would not come and make her escape here. But I thought not, for by doing so she might miss out on something interesting, and so she would most likely stay downstairs with the rest of the girls.

For myself, I was glad enough to retrieve one of my books and settle down on the bed with it. Rereading one of my favorite tales would pass the time until supper. I was also glad that dinner promised to be another quiet meal, much like the one which had just ended. It was tomorrow that the rest of the guests would arrive, and the peace of the castle shattered until two days hence, when Adalynn would ride forth with her new husband and we would all be able to settle back down into our regular routines.

At least, I prayed that was what would happen...just as I very much hoped that Mayson would forget the promise I had made him earlier that afternoon.

As I had thought, dinner passed without incident. The addition of the earl and countess and their son seemed to have a sobering effect on Lord Mayson, for he was very proper and correct, and spent far more time conversing with Carella and Janessa and Theranne than he did speaking to me. This attention was enough to make Carella's cheeks flush and her eyes twinkle as she stood next to him.

I should have been relieved, except I was fairly certain that he did so only to avoid attracting any particular notice. He and Coryn, Adalynn's betrothed, also seemed acquainted, and they spoke of getting together a hunting party in the autumn, once the season was upon us again.

All in all, it was quite an unexceptional evening, albeit one that did not pass swiftly enough for my taste. But at last it was time to go upstairs, although Janessa kept chattering away, saying what a gentleman she thought Lord Coryn was, and how she was certain Adalynn would be very happy. I supposed she would, if she would allow herself to be; while her betrothed was not the handsomest man in the room—that honor must go by default to Lord Mayson—still he seemed all amiability, and very much besotted with her. In general, I thought it must be easier to be in love with a man when he was already in love with you.

Except, of course, for my conundrum with Mayson. But I sensed something strange about the intensity of his regard, as if it had grown from some cause I could not quite identify. If he really was madly in love with me, why had that emotion blossomed into being only during the last few days? Surely there must be something more to his attraction than that, for we had been living under the same roof for nearly a month now.

Unfortunately, I could not deduce whence had come this sudden ardor, and so I had to push the problem away for now, and arrange a placid expression on my features, lest Janessa ask me what the matter was. It was hard enough to say good night to her in ordinary tones, and pretend to fall asleep without actually doing so.

By that evening, I was almost used to the ritual. Some time later, she sat up in bed, eyes blank and unfocused. And then she climbed out from under the covers, pulled on her slippers, and headed into the hallway.

I had prepared myself this time. As soon as I had determined she was asleep, I slipped out from under the covers, then went to the wardrobe and got out my oldest frock, the one the laundress had saved from my previous depredations, even though there were still some faint stains along the hem. I pulled the dress over my nightgown, as it only differed from my daytime chemises in the thickness of the fabric. Finally came my shoes, which I had stowed under the bed so they might be immediately to hand.

The other girls had already begun to descend the staircase by the time I emerged in the hallway, but no matter, since I knew exactly where they were going. Once more I trailed after them, and once more emerged into the cool night air and headed out toward the forest.

Even though I had managed to slip out without being noticed several times before, on this night I was more tense than usual, probably because we had so many new people sleeping under the castle's roof. What if the spell used to keep them all slumbering and unawares lost its effect when it had to be cast on that many?

But no one stopped us. The castle slept under the nearly full moon, indifferent to the comings and goings of the young women who lived there.

The air was warmer tonight, the night breeze almost a caress against my cheek. As I followed Janessa and my cousins across the stream and then deeper into the forest, I listened carefully, but heard nothing, not the hooting of an owl, nor even the faint rustlings in the undergrowth that I'd come to associate with the movements of mice or chipmunks or other small denizens of the woodlands.

The clearing gleamed under the moon's white orb. No sooner had the girls formed themselves into the usual circle than I caught a glint of silver, and Reynar stepped out from between the trees. His features reflected resignation, along with a certain weary amusement.

"My lady, if we keep meeting like this, I am sure people will begin to talk."

I flashed a grin at him. "I would agree with you, sir, except that we have no observers to our conversations, unless you can count my cousins. But since they cannot recall the next morning what they have been up to, let alone what I have done, I cannot say that they would make the most reliable of witnesses."

"I suppose you are right." He pointed at a fallen log, over which he'd draped a light blanket of fine wool. "Would you care to sit?"

Well, this was an unexpected wrinkle. During our previous encounters, he had not shown much inclination to be hospitable. But perhaps he had determined that he was not going to succeed in keeping me away—or preventing me from asking questions—and so had decided he might as well be comfortable while we conversed.

So I sat down on the log, and he followed suit. Although he took care not to position himself too close to me, he was still near enough that I could see the glint of moonlight on his heavy pale hair, could tell that his doublet was made of linen. An intriguing fragrance clung to his clothing, one that reminded me of pine needles and warm moss.

Indeed, to sit this close was to send a little thrill through my body, although I told myself that he clearly had no intentions toward me, other than talking as we had the night before. But that would be enough...at least for now.

"Adalynn will be married the day after tomorrow," I said.

"I know," Reynar returned. "And my master has already planned for that contingency. He does not seem overly troubled."

"Are you going to tell me now what this spell is for?"

"No," he said, but his tone was so mild that I could hardly take offense. "That is my master's business, and none of yours, Lady Iselda."

"I'm not Lady Iselda," I pointed out then. "I'm no one much of anything, actually."

His brows—which were as dark as his lashes, startling against the pale hair and eyes—pulled together. "I would beg to differ. Perhaps you were not born of titled parents as your cousins were, but that does not diminish you in any way."

A flush rose in my cheeks, and I took in a breath. I could not let him see how that simple compliment had affected me. "Perhaps," I allowed. "But still, please just call me Iselda. Surely we are friends now, after sharing confidences these past few nights?"

"If you wish...Iselda." He seemed to linger on my name, and again I could feel a little thrill pass through me.

"I do wish," I said. "And since you will not speak to me of your master, perhaps you will tell me something of yourself?"

A flash of surprise in his silvery eyes, as if he had not thought such a subject much worthy of note. "Myself?"

"Yes, you," I replied. "Did you always know you were a mage? How did your master find you? Are your family like you—that is, with the same extraordinary hair and eyes?"

If the sudden darkening of his cheeks was any indication, I was not the only one who had been made to flush. Even so, he held up a hand, as if to prevent me from asking any more questions. "No, I did not always know I had mage blood. I began to notice strange things, like whispers and voices in my mind, when I was not quite ten years old. At first I thought I was going mad, but then not long afterward, my master found me, and explained that the voices were only my powers awakening."

"How did he find you?" I asked, intrigued beyond all measure. These were the sorts of questions I would have liked to pose to Tobyn, my brother-in-law, but the secrecy required in my correspondence with my sister quite prevented me from making such queries.

"Mage-born can sense other mage-born," Reynar said. "Or at least, if the blood is strong enough, then a user of magic can usually tell when he encounters another of his kind. There are many, my master says, who have some of the old blood running in their veins, but it is not strong enough that they are able to actually practice magic. All they can do is pass the talent on to their children, and perhaps one day those children will be true mage-born."

His answer awakened so many questions in my mind that I was not quite sure where to start. But, as my sister had been wont to point out, when you are feeling muddled, it is always best to begin at the beginning. "The old blood? What is that?"

For a few seconds, he didn't answer, but looked away from me so he might cast a watchful glance in the direction of the dancing women in the glade. But they moved in the same graceful formation, with only the night wind to ruffle their hair, and so he seemed satisfied as to their safety. "Once there was a race of beings known as the Althuri. No one knows precisely where they came from, only that they were not like us."

"'Not like us'?" I echoed, puzzled. "What on earth do you mean?"

"In form they were like men, only they also had great white wings. And their hair and eyes were like mine."

"So you have this old blood?"

"Yes." Reynar reached up to scratch at his left shoulder. "No wings, of course, but I fear I am quite conspicuous enough as I am."

I did not bother to contradict him, for he spoke only the truth. That silvery hair would attract attention wherever he went. "Is the rest of your family like you? That is, do they share the same coloring?"

"As to that, I do not know. I was raised in the orphanage in Heathskell, for someone left me on the doorstep there when I was only a few days old. It was there that my master found me, and from there he took me. I supposed they were kind enough, or tried to be, but I believe the matrons there were frightened of me. More than once I caught them making the sign of the evil eye behind their backs when they thought I wasn't looking."

"I am sorry," I murmured.

A casual lift of the shoulders, one that did not really fool me. "It is all right. But I'm sure you will believe me when I say that I had no regrets about leaving the orphanage and going with my master to be trained. It is no small thing, to be given a purpose."

No, I supposed it wasn't. Perhaps my own underlying discontent had everything to do with not really knowing what my place in the world was supposed to be. I had been given a home, but I did not know what direction my life should take.

Well, Lord Mayson thought he knew, but I was not quite ready to set my feet down that particular path. Especially not now, when I sat next to Reynar and listened to his low, musical voice and watched the moonlight glitter in the matching silver of his eyes.

Because I could see a shadow of pain in his face, and knew that he did not wish to speak of his own childhood, no matter how detached he might sound, I deemed it best to guide the conversation back to a topic that was not quite as fraught with pain. "What happened to the Althuri?"

"No one knows. Clearly, they intermingled with our own kind, but how that came to pass, and why they disappeared, no one seems to know. My master told me that there existed no gift of magic among ordinary people until their blood was blended with that of the Althuri, but that is all he knows. They are gone, lost forever in the past."

Even though I had only heard of these Althuri for the first time tonight, I could not help but feel a sudden twinge of sorrow at their loss. Whoever they were, they had changed mankind forever. Some might say the magic that came with

At last he appeared to relent. "Very well, Iselda. I cannot say I am pleased, but I understand your reasoning."

"Thank you, Mayson."

He sipped at his wine, then said, "But do not think I have forgotten your promise to me. I will see you here the day after the wedding."

I nodded, said, "Of course," and then fled into the castle. My heart pounded as if I had just run all the way from Daleskeld Forest, and I knew the reason why.

Mayson's last words had not been a promise.

They had been a threat.

Janessa came up to bed very late. I was already under the covers, pretending to be asleep, although sleep was the furthest thing from my mind right then. All I wanted was for Janessa to let slumber overtake her, so that the spell might summon her and I might go to the forest to see Reynar.

She bustled about getting ready for bed, making far more noise than was required. I rather thought that she wanted to wake me so she could discuss her evening, but I knew better than to oblige her. I kept my eyes tightly shut, and after a time she heaved a rather exasperated sigh and then climbed into bed.

Thank the gods.

A few minutes later, her regular breathing seemed to signal that she had fallen asleep. I turned over onto my side and cautiously opened my eyes, just in case she was in fact still awake and waiting to pounce.

But no, she most definitely seemed to be deep in slumber. I watched her, and waited for the spell to take hold and draw her forth from her bed.

And waited. And waited.

Lying there, I felt my heart sink. Had the mage not cast the spell tonight, for whatever reason? Would all the girls stay in their beds this evening?

I fervently hoped that was not the case. I wanted—no, I *needed*—to go see Reynar.

But it seemed my wishes were of little worth, for the minutes passed, and still Janessa did not stir. I lay in bed, warring with myself. Of course the wise thing to do would be to stay where I was. If the spell to summon the girls to dance in the forest had not been cast, then very likely the accompanying spell, the one that made sure all the castle's residents slept soundly while my cousins and Janessa crept outside, had not been used as well. I would be risking a great deal by attempting to leave on my own.

For several minutes I warred with myself, but in the end, the compulsion to go see Reynar was simply too strong. But I dared not put on one of my gowns, for if I were caught, that would result in even more questions. At least if I was seen slipping down the corridors in my nightgown with a shawl flung about me, I could make excuses, could say that I was hungry and was headed to the kitchen to find something to eat.

And if I happened to be caught outside, well, there was always the excuse of sleepwalking, although I had never done such a thing in my life...and in general, sleepwalkers did not pause to put on their shoes first.

So I sat up cautiously, then slid out from under the covers with equal care. Luckily, my slippers sat underneath the bed, for with all the commotion in the household today, Tarly had not bothered with anything except the most cursory of tidyings-up. The shawl I sought had been hung up inside the wardrobe; I opened the door as slowly as I could, but it still squeaked. I paused, heart pounding away in my breast, but Janessa did not stir.

At least the shawl hung from a hook on the inside of the wardrobe door, so I did not have to rummage for it. I pulled it off and wrapped it around my shoulders, then closed the wardrobe and began to inch my way to the door, my eyes on Janessa the entire time.

Still she did not move, and I was able to slip out into the hallway without her noticing. I closed the door with the barest whisper of the latch, and began to tiptoe down the corridor, acutely aware of how every room behind every door had its occupant, and how any of them could appear at any time. For all I knew, some of the servants were still down in the court-yard, cleaning up now that the last of the revelers had gone to bed.

That notion set my heart pounding all over again, so I hurried over to one of the windows that overlooked the rose garden and peered out. I was still far too tense to allow myself a sigh of relief, but I did relax slightly, for the courtyard was dark and still, all the torches snuffed out, and with no sign of activity. So it appeared Janessa had lingered long enough that even the servants had retired for the night.

Thus encouraged, I hurried to the staircase and then began to descend it, with each step becoming a little braver. Not bolder, though; I hugged the wall and made sure my slippers were as quiet as possible as I took each step. A few candles burned here and there in sconces, but otherwise the place was dark and still, with not a hint of anyone stirring.

Perhaps they had all overindulged, and were now fast asleep, an abundance of wine making them sleep more soundly than they normally would. I could not question my good luck, but only hurried from room to room until I reached the kitchens, and at last came upon the door to the outside world.

There I finally let out a breath. Was it luck or a spell that had guided me thus far? And if it was only luck, how long would it hold? Could I be sure of reaching Reynar safely?

I supposed there was only one way to know for sure. I put my hand on the latch, and let myself out into the night.

Chapter Ten

Even as I hurried out the door and into the kitchen garden, I kept expecting to hear a voice halting me and calling me back—Linsey, the cook, or perhaps the dignified Alister, my uncle's steward, who kept a tight rein on the household and who never seemed to overlook much of anything.

But apparently he missed me, or there truly had been another spell cast to keep everyone asleep, for I was able to disappear into the fields without anyone apparently noticing my departure. Overhead, the moon floated bright and nearly round, lighting my way. If anyone had been watching from the castle, they could not have helped seeing me, but all remained still as I hastened down the between the waves of barley and rye, their stalks rustling with the night wind.

At last I came to the stream, and took off my slippers so I might wade across in my favorite spot to ford the waters. No sooner had I paused on the forest side than I heard Reynar's voice, sounding somewhat resigned.

"I thought you would come tonight." He emerged from behind a tree, the moonlight making a halo of his silvery hair.

"Did I not tell you I would?"

"Yes, but when the girls were not summoned to dance...." Stopping there, he reached out a hand to help me up a rocky part of the path.

Grateful, I took his fingers, let him steady me as I clambered up to stand next to him. Here was also a fallen log, on which was spread the same thin wool blanket he had used the night before. I cast a questioning glance at it and thought on what he had just said. "So there truly was no spell cast tonight?"

"No." He went over to the log but then waited, clearly not planning to sit down until I did.

I didn't bother to argue, but took my place on the log and sat, even as I pulled the shawl I wore more closely about myself. "So why did the mage not summon my cousins and Janessa to dance?"

"It is your cousin Adalynn's wedding day tomorrow. He did not think it fair to bring her out and have her be weary for such a special event. I suppose you can consider that his wedding present to her."

"That is—" I broke off then, for I was about to say that it was very kind of him, but truly a kinder thing would have been not to cast the spell in the first place. However, as I did not think that a most politic statement, and because I was not sure how Reynar would react to such a remark, I thought it best to avoid the subject. Instead, I ventured, "But it seemed so easy for me to leave the castle tonight, even with so many guests staying there—"

enough to attract a man with a title, not because she was born with one. So I think we are far more equal than you have made out."

Reynar was silent for a moment, clearly thinking over what I had just said. When he spoke again, his voice was measured, slow, as if he forced himself to consider each word before he uttered it. "That may be true, Iselda, but I am an orphan from nowhere, in possession of powers that would have me arrested... or worse...if they were to be discovered. Even if I were free to leave my master—"

"About that," I said, for I hoped now he would clarify some of the concerns that had consumed my thoughts ever since our last encounter. "What are the terms of your service with him? Surely he does not expect you to be his servant for the rest of your days? You have already spent more than a decade with him, so what else does he want?"

My voice had hardened somewhat as I asked that last question, and I saw how Reynar's lips thinned in response. When he replied, however, his tone was a good deal more gentle than mine.

"Like all masters, he wants to make sure that I have sufficient control of my gifts so that I no longer require his guidance. This is not like being apprentice to a woodworker, or an ironsmith. It is not merely a matter of serving my seven years and then going forth to make my own way in the world."

"You certainly seem in control of your powers," I protested. "I cannot see what else he thinks he has to teach you."

Reynar's lips brushed the top of my head, and, despite my current worry, I could not help sighing somewhat at the thrill his touch evoked. "I can go to him and ask to be released. But doing so will be at his discretion. And I must abide by his decision."

Even though I tried to tell myself that I should be calm, that I did not want to cause an argument, I could not help saying, "I cannot understand why you would give him so much control over you."

At those words, Reynar let go of me and stepped back a pace. "Am I not supposed to show gratitude toward the man who took me from the orphanage and gave me a home?"

"That's not what I meant at all." I took in a breath and resisted the urge to lay a hand on his arm. He looked stiff and angry, and even though we had kissed, I did not know him well enough to judge how he would interpret such a gesture. Voice softening, I went on, "Have you not shown your gratitude by doing his bidding for more than ten years? Have you ever *not* done as he asked?"

These questions did not seem to move Reynar overmuch. When he spoke, he only gave me a grudging, "No."

"Well, then," I said, telling myself not to be too discouraged. "If he is as wise and learned as you have hinted, then surely he must understand that there would come a time when you would wish to be free to pursue your own destiny."

At first Reynar did not reply. He watched me closely, though, and I could almost see the emotions flickering behind his eyes—need, and worry, and an all-too-fragile hope. In barely a whisper, he asked, "And this destiny? Does it include you?"

I went to him and put my arms around his waist, and laid my head against his chest. "Oh, yes, Reynar. I want it to. All the gods only know how much I want that."

He held me tight, and kissed the top of my head. "Then I will do whatever I must."

And so, as simply as that, we sealed our fates together.

No matter what happened.

I would have liked to stay out all night with him, but he told me I should go back to the castle and sleep as best I could. "For it is your cousin's wedding day tomorrow, and I doubt she would be happy to have a bridesmaid who was tired, or cross, or had great dark circles under her eyes."

"I do not get circles," I told him. "I never have."

"Ah. Well, that is good to know. But I still think it best that you go back. I will hold the sleep-spell for the next hour. I think that will be a good incentive to make sure you get back before it fades."

Since I knew he was only right, and because secretly I did not want to appear haggard or weary in front of all those exalted wedding guests, I did not argue, but kissed him again before I headed back toward the castle and my comfortable bed. It was something of a relief to know that I could enter the sleeping building and not have to worry about anyone catching me sneaking about. However, I did not dally, and was still careful after I had slipped through the kitchen door and was making my way back up the stairs. Only after I'd entered the room did I allow myself a quick breath of relief, right before I hung my shawl up in the wardrobe and then slid under the covers.

A hasty glance at Janessa told me that she still slept soundly. I murmured a silent thank-you to Reynar and this particularly handy spell of his, and closed my eyes and told myself I must sleep. Already it was long past midnight, and I knew Adalynn would have us up at dawn so that no possible detail would be overlooked in the hours before the ceremony, which was set for noon.

I did not know if it was my own will exerting itself on my body, or whether Reynar sent a small tendril of his spell to twine itself around me. I only knew that within the minute I was asleep, falling into a slumber that I hoped would be haunted with memories of his arms around me, and his lips on mine.

Chapter Eleven

"**G**et up, Iselda! I cannot believe you would lie abed, today of all days!"

I opened one eye and saw Janessa hovering over my bed, practically dancing in impatience. As I knew she would not go away until I responded, I pushed back the covers and managed to maneuver myself into a sitting position. "Pray, tell me why you are so excited," I said. "For I was certain this was Adalynn's wedding day, not yours."

"Well, yes, it is, but you left so early that you did not see how Lord Gwyllim flirted with me all last evening, and that he asked me to dance the opening promenade at the ball with him tonight."

"Oh, well," I responded. "That is definitely a good reason to want to get out of bed. Anyway, see? I am awake, and the sky outside is just barely turning light."

So it was. The first flush of dawn had begun to spread over the countryside, turning everything pink and gold. A few clouds dotted the sky, but they were certainly not enough to evoke any kind of worry about rain.

All in all, it seemed that Adalynn would have a perfect day...which she probably thought was no more than her due. But no, that was an uncharitable notion. She could be high-handed and occasionally downright thoughtless, but she was not a cruel person, exactly, more that she had always gotten her way because she was the eldest and so very beautiful. I might as well put the blame on my aunt and uncle for spoiling her the way they had.

Her betrothed seemed like a very kind, generous man, and so I had no reason to think that Adalynn would not improve once she was his wife and constantly in his company. Some of that graciousness would have to wear off on her.

Or so I hoped.

I did not have much opportunity for further ruminations, because Tarly arrived shortly after that, looking far more harried than usual. Today she had brought up our tea and a tray as well, for we girls were to be sequestered until the time of the ceremony, when the guests would finally be able to see us in all our glory.

That arrangement suited me very well, for it meant that I would not have to see Mayson until afterward, by which time I hoped I would have more or less composed myself. Some part of me worried that he would be able to tell I had kissed another, although I tried to tell myself that was ridiculous. He certainly was no mage, to be able to look into the minds of others.

So Janessa and I ate a hurried breakfast, and then the footmen arrived with the bath. I told Janessa she could go first, and sat and stared out the window while she washed her hair and Tarly bustled about, laying out our new gowns and all the items that went along with them—chemises of linen so fine you could nearly see through it, and silk stockings and slippers of delicate kid, and jewelry to match our gowns, rose quartz and pearls for Janessa's pink gown, a few shades lighter than Adalynn's glory of deep rose, and moonstones and tiny blue river pearls for my gown of silver and blue brocade.

Not that I cared for any of that right then. I gazed out at Daleskeld Forest, and thought of Reynar, and the feel of his strong hands, the gentle caress of his mouth. A curious warmth spread through me as I awakened those memories, and I wished more than ever that he was free to come and go like any other young man, that he could come to the ball tonight and lead me in the promenade, just as Lord Gwyllim had promised Janessa.

That dream, I knew, would never come to pass, for by necessity Reynar must hide himself away. True, he had the ability to mask his appearance, to make himself look quite unexceptionable, but I wondered how long he could maintain such a spell. For hours and hours?

Possibly, since he could certainly make the sleep-spell last for goodly length of time. How much of a strain was it to maintain such a thing, though?

So many questions, and all of them were merely a thought exercise, for it would not be enough for Reynar to merely assume a different appearance. He would also have to come up with a way to get into the wedding itself, since my aunt personally knew everyone who had been invited and would be sure to question any interlopers, or at least would summon the steward to investigate further. Perhaps that was no very great matter for one with Reynar's powers. I still did not have a very clear idea of what he could or could not do. It seemed very likely to me that he would not take the risk of attending a wedding when he had not been invited.

No, I would not be able to dance with him. Far more likely that I would be Mayson's partner, whether I liked it or not.

Usually a bath soothed me, but as I settled myself into the water and began to wash my hair, I only wished for all the preparations to be over, for the wedding to be done, the guests gone home, and those of us who remained to return to our ordinary lives. But I could not expect that to happen, could I? For I had promised Mayson that we would discuss matters further after the wedding.

Damn.

I rinsed my hair, then took a towel from the chair next to the tub and climbed out. Once I was dry, I put on the robe Tarly had left hanging for me and emerged into the main part of the bedroom, to find our maid lacing Janessa into her gown. I gathered up my chemise and other undergarments, and hung the towel once more on the hook on the screen.

"Sit in the sun, lady, and let your hair dry," Tarly instructed me, so I did as I was told, taking up my previous position at the window. Then I retrieved the wide-toothed wooden comb she had left on the windowsill and began to carefully work through the knots in my hair. This took some effort, for even though I had braided it the night before, my sojourn in the woods had helped to tangle it more than it should have.

Or perhaps those snarls had only come from Reynar running his hands over it.

I willed the image of his face from my mind. If I was too preoccupied today, someone was bound to comment on my abstraction. Also, if I allowed my mind to wander, there was a far greater chance that I might do or say something to arouse suspicion. I did not dare let anyone know of how I had slipped away from the castle, and even less did I care to have anyone find out about my assignations with Reynar. His was the far greater risk, since he had taken such care to keep himself hidden, but I would be ruined, all chance of making any kind of a respectable match gone forever, if word should get out that I had indulged in such wanton behavior. After all, I had very little to recommend me, other than my virtue.

At length Tarly was done with Janessa, who looked resplendent, her cheeks glowing with color, her dark hair glossy and gleaming. I thought that glow had come not only from the fine gown and the extra care our maid had spent on her hair, but also from the prospect of seeing Lord Gwyllim again, of realizing that she, too was worthy of attention and admiration, even if she was not a daughter of this household.

I went to sit in the chair she had just vacated, and resigned myself to spending the better part of an hour there as Tarly laboriously twisted my hair into long spiral curls. Most days she would take less time with this task, but of course everything had to be perfect for Adalynn's wedding. Midway through this procedure, my aunt knocked on the door and poked her head in, wishing to check on our progress. She seemed glad that Janessa was ready, less pleased that my hair was taking so long.

"We must all be down in the great hall no later than eleven-thirty," she admonished me.

I did not answer as tartly as I might have under other circumstances, for I knew she must be feeling ragged already, and had a very long day ahead of her. "That is two hours from now," I said gently, "and Tarly has already finished half my head. It will not take me so very long to get dressed. Really, Aunt Lyselle, you have nothing to fear. Janessa and I will be down there with plenty of time to spare."

My aunt flashed me a relieved smile. "Of course you will. It is only that Lord Alstron broke out in hives after something he ate did not agree with him, and Lady Penelly complained that her bath was too cold, and—"

"I am sorry about all that. Do what you must, but you need not worry about the two of us."

"No, of course not," Janessa chimed in, all good humor because she had an assignation to look forward to. "And of course I would be happy to help you with anything you might need, Lady Lyselle."

That offer was met with an emphatic shake of the head—although not so emphatic as to shake the diadem she wore loose from her elaborate coiffure of braids and curls. I hated to think how early my aunt must have been up to have achieved such a hairstyle at such an hour. "I thank you for the offer, Janessa, but you know that none of you girls can be seen until the ceremony. I am sure that between us, Alister and I will be able to manage. I shall see you downstairs in a few hours."

With that, she shut the door, and Tarly went back to toiling away on my hair. If I had been in Janessa's position, I would have taken advantage of the idle time to pick up a book and read, allowing myself some peace and quiet before the certain hubbub of the wedding descended, but Janessa was not at all bookish. Instead, she sat on her bed and watched as our maid created one perfect spiral curl after another in my waist-length locks.

"How many are riding in today, do you think?" Janessa asked, even though she knew the answer to that question as well as I did.

"Some thirty, I believe," I said, since to not reply at all would be churlish. "Of course Lord Elwyn, and Sir Locksen, and the Dalensons of Vandar's Well."

"Lord Elwyn is quite handsome, don't you think? You can see where Lord Mayson inherited his looks."

Although I was rather surprised that Janessa would have taken note of Lord Elwyn's appearance, since he was so much older than we, I could only nod. To say that his lordship was unattractive would have been a complete falsehood. "Yes, he is quite a fine figure of a man," I said cautiously.

"One must wonder why he did not remarry after Lord Mayson's mother passed away. I should think there must have been many ladies who would have been glad to take her place."

Perhaps. Lady Danelle Bellender had died when Mayson was only ten, and therefore a number of years before I had come to live with my aunt and uncle. No one seemed to speak of her much, and I had never asked Mayson about her, mostly because the subject never seemed to come up in the natural course of conversation, and I certainly didn't wish to pry.

"It is possible that he loved her so much that he didn't want to have another wife," I suggested, holding back a wince as Tarly accidentally pulled at my hair. She murmured an apology and kept working.

"I suppose so." Janessa went silent then, perhaps pondering her own father, who was still desolate over the loss of his wife, three years later.

Or possibly that was the narrative he wished her to believe, rather than admit that he didn't want to manage the rearing of a young woman on his own. I had to wonder how Janessa felt about being fobbed off on us when her father had had no trouble keeping his son close to home. She rarely talked about either of her parents, and again, I didn't press her. I knew what it was like to be asked for information you had no desire to give.

"But it does seem odd, especially when a title is involved," she went on. "For if anything should happen to Lord Mayson, then what will Lord Elwyn do?"

"I doubt there is much to fear on that score," I said. "Lord Mayson is young and healthy, and there is no reason to think he will not live a very long and happy life."

"I should think he would be very happy...if you would agree to be his wife," she said slyly.

At that comment, Tarly shook her head. "Lady Janessa, that is not the sort of thing to be discussed in light conversation. Surely if his lordship had offered for Lady Iselda, she would have told the family by now."

I feared that Tarly's trust in me was woefully misplaced. For of course I had said nothing to anyone of what had passed between Mayson and myself, just as I had kept silent on the subject of Reynar and the strange spell that had drawn my cousins from the castle each night.

So I only nodded, since I did not quite trust myself to speak. Janessa sent me a sideways glance from under her lashes, but appeared to subside for the moment. Instead, she went to the mirror that hung on the wall next to the wardrobe, and turned from side to side as she inspected her gown. I had no doubt that she was imagining the effect her appearance might have on Lord Gwyllim, and I could not blame her. My aunt and uncle had given Janessa as loving a home as they could, but she must be pining for a place she could call her own. And if that place should include a title and a handsome young husband, all the better.

"There," Tarly said, moving away from me slightly so she might better inspect her handiwork. "All done, so now let me help you into your gown."

This task was accomplished with a great deal of care, for of course my maid would not wish to jar any of my curls loose as she slid the gown up over my shoulders and then began to lace it up the back. I did not think she needed to be quite so cautious, as, once it was set, my hair tended to stay in those curls, unlike my poor cousin Theranne, whose own unruly locks always fell back into their natural waves no matter what her maid did. Would they risk fate today and attempt to curl her hair, or be practical and adopt a style that embraced those loose waves?

Knowing Adalynn and how she wanted everything just so, I guessed that she would make her younger sister suffer the hair-curling process, no matter what. I could only hope that the bride would be so occupied with other matters that she would not be paying much attention to her sister's hairstyle, should it begin to suffer the effects of gravity partway through the day.

Tarly fastened the necklace of moonstones and pearls around my neck, then handed me the earrings to match. I slipped them into the holes in my earlobes and went over to the mirror to inspect my appearance. My motivation for doing so was very different from Janessa's, for all I cared about was that there should be nothing in my appearance for Adalynn to find fault with. I certainly did not care about attracting the attention of any young men, since the only man I was concerned with would not be here to see me.

That thought elicited a small sigh, and I quickly looked over at Janessa to make sure she had not noted anything out of the ordinary about my demeanor. Luckily, she was still fussing with her necklace, making sure that all the little rose quartz drops lay flat against her skin, and so I doubted she had seen anything at all.

"You are both very beautiful, my ladies," Tarly said as she replaced the brushes and combs in the dressing table's drawers. "And a credit to this household, I am sure."

Janessa blushed, and I smiled at our maid. "And a credit to your hard work, Tarly. Thank you for taking so much time with us."

She bowed her head, but her words were deprecating enough. "Well, I would have heard about it from Lady Adalynn, and from her ladyship, if I had not done my very best. But there is still some time before you can go downstairs, so I believe you should sit down and be comfortable—only not too comfortable, as I don't want to see those dresses wrinkled."

"We shall be careful," both Janessa and I said in unison, and Tarly gave a satisfied nod.

"Very well. I will go down and see how things are faring, and then I will be back up to fetch you when the time comes."

We both agreed to this plan—not that we had much choice in the matter—and the maid departed. I had left a book on the table by the window, and so I retrieved it and sat down, preparing to read. Janessa did not appear overly happy about my choice of diversions, but since she had little choice, she too, went and fetched something to occupy herself—an embroidery hoop with a half-finished handkerchief held within.

So we sat in silence for the space of an hour, although it felt much longer, and then Tarly returned to fetch us downstairs. As we descended the staircase, we met up with Carella and Theranne, although there was no sign of Adalynn. She would come last, after the rest of us had taken our places in the great hall. Both her sisters were also resplendent, Carella in a blue gown trimmed in gold, and Theranne lovely in a dress of a soft, coppery-blush shade. They smiled at us, and Theranne looked as if she wanted to gush about everyone's gowns, although a warning glance from Tarly was enough to make her subside into a respectful silence.

The castle itself was quiet, all the guests already seated in their designated places. Everywhere, though, were flowers, and a warm summer breeze flowed through the open windows and doorways. I thought again of what a lovely day it had turned out to be, and how lucky Adalynn was to be married on such a day. I could only hope that I would have similar luck in my own wedding.

If that were ever to happen at all. Yes, Reynar and I had pledged that our destinies should be as one, but what did that mean? He had not asked me to marry him. He had not even said he loved me. I thought he did, but I had only feelings to go upon, and not much else. And of course there were probably many who would say we could not possibly have true feelings for one another, not after such a short acquaintance. I supposed it did seem mad, but I could not deny the effect Reynar had on me, the way he occupied my thoughts in a way no other man ever had. Surely that must be love, mad and impetuous as it might seem.

However, I knew I had to push those thoughts aside. It would not do for me to be distracted by such matters on my cousin's wedding day. Let me survive all this, and then the next time I saw Reynar, we could put together a real plan. Would we have to elope? Possibly, for I saw how his master held him under his sway, and I did not know if he possessed the strength to confront the man who had been both father and teacher to him.

An elopement would hurt my aunt and uncle terribly, I knew. They would think me ungrateful, and I could not even blame them for that. And where on earth would Reynar and I go? We could not stay here in Purth, a land where use of magic was outlawed.

North Eredor, I thought then. *Of course. For not only are my sister and her husband there, but in that land there is no prejudice against those who work magic. We could live openly, and not have to fear what might happen if someone were to guess that Reynar was a mage.*

"What on earth are you thinking about?" came Janessa's rather irritated voice. "You almost stepped on the train of my gown!"

"I'm so sorry," I replied at once. "I supposed I was woolgathering."

"Thinking about Lord Mayson?" she asked in arch tones.

Theranne giggled, and Carella sent Janessa a very pained look. I opened my mouth to protest the insinuation, but Tarly intervened, saying, "My ladies, we are almost to the hall. Please show some decorum."

Our maid had very little power to control or punish us—but she could make a less than favorable report to Aunt Lyselle, who no doubt would take us to task for our behavior, should word of it get back to her. The girls all subsided, although Carella kept shooting daggers with her eyes at Janessa, who affected not to notice.

And then we were at the doors to the hall, and the footmen were opening it for us.

Truly, if I had not known it was the same space where my aunt and uncle held all their large gatherings, I should not have recognized it. The long tables placed up against the walls were gone, and instead the enormous chamber had been filled with row after row of wooden benches—all of which had been made by the craftsmen who lived on the estate. Those benches were now crowded with lords and ladies in their best finery, so my eyes could barely take in the array of colors, the gleam of metal embroidery, the glint of jewels at throats and wrists. Along the walls were tall vases filled with roses and lilies and ferns, their perfumes at war with those worn by the guests.

At the end of the hall was a dais, and on that dais were more flowers, and the priest of Inyanna who would oversee the ceremony. We four girls were charged with walking down the aisle between the rows of benches and scattering rose petals as we went. Once we were done with that all-important task, we were to take our positions, two of us to either side of the priest, so we might stand there as guardians of her virtue until the priest had completed the ceremony and Coryn and Adalynn were officially bound as husband and wife.

More footmen stood inside the door. They handed us our baskets of rose petals—I knew several of the maids had been up early preparing them—and we all headed down the aisle. I was first, because I was the eldest, followed by Janessa, then Carella and Theranne. A murmur of approval went through the crowd as the four of us passed, and I could feel my cheeks flush with embarrassment. I was not used to having so many eyes upon me.

Even worse was catching a glimpse of Mayson, who sat in the second row on the right. His dark eyes shone as he looked at me, admiration clear on his features. Oh, dear. If he was already this starry-eyed....

But I did not have time to think of him further, because it was time to climb the two low steps to ascend the dais, and to take my position to the left of the priest. Janessa stood next to me, while Carella and Theranne headed to the right, so they might stand in locations that mirrored Janessa's and mine. I had been so overwhelmed by the crowd that I hadn't even realized music was being played; the musicians sat to one side of the dais, the harp and the flute and the fiddle playing a pretty country melody. Then the tune shifted, became more solemn, and another murmur moved through the crowd as Adalynn appeared in the doorway to the hall, the light streaming in from the corridor behind her and outlining her in a golden glow.

Yes, she and I had had our differences over the years. But in that moment, I could feel my breath catch at how beautiful she was, how queenly her posture as she glided down the aisle, the silken skirts of her train rustling as she went. My gaze flicked to the front row, where my aunt and uncle sat. Aunt Lyselle was dabbing at her eyes with a handkerchief, while Uncle Danly practically glowed with pride at the sight of his eldest daughter.

Coryn, too, seated on the opposite bench with his own parents, looked as if he couldn't quite believe that this glorious creature was about to become his wife. She paused next to the bench where he sat and held out a hand, and he nearly stumbled over his own feet in his haste to get up and take her fingers in his. Perhaps one corner of her mouth twitched, but otherwise she did not react.

Then the two of them came to stand on the dais, and the priest began to speak the words of the ceremony. This was where I would allow my thoughts to drift, for I had attended enough weddings to know that this part of the proceedings was quite dry, and contained a number of words on the subject of obedience and duty and a whole host of admirable qualities that managed to make marriage sound quite dull.

I did not think it would be dull. Not if I could have Reynar as my husband.

My gaze shifted, and I caught sight of Mayson staring up at me. He, too, did not appear as if he was terribly interested in the words of the ceremony. No, he seemed far more occupied with watching me, as if he had never seen me before and wanted to commit every detail of my appearance to memory.

Oh, dear. There would be no escaping him during the festivities that would follow the ceremony itself, and it seemed clear enough to me that he had no desire to spend those hours with anyone else. In that moment, I wished I were mage-born like Reynar, so I might cast a spell to take me far, far away from here.

But I could not let my worries show in my expression. No, I had to stand there and fix a small half-smile on my lips, and pretend to be interested in the proceedings. It did not help matters that I could also see Lord Elwyn sitting next to his son. His lordship glanced from Mayson to me and back again, and his mouth pursed slightly, as if he was considering something that had not entered his thoughts before.

To my relief, the priest said the words that invited Coryn to kiss his new bride, and the newly made husband and wife shared a very chaste kiss. From the intent look Coryn gave Adalynn, I guessed that the kiss was only chaste because it was so very public, and that things might be very different when they were alone together.

The hall erupted in cheers as everyone stood to congratulate the couple, and they strode in triumph from the dais, out through the doors, and into the corridor, where they would stand with their parents on either side and personally greet all the wedding guests. Luckily, we attendants were not required to stand there as well, although we were certainly not allowed to do as we pleased. No, we must join the long line of well-wishers, taking our place at the very end so as not to make anyone wait longer than they must.

To my relief, Mayson did not attempt to join us, but stood with his father near the head of the line. I saw him bend toward the happy couple and say something, but of course it was too noisy in the hallway to hear anything of what passed between them. Next was Lord Elwyn, who also smiled as he offered his congratulations. The line slowly lurched forward, and I found myself wishing I could curse my new slippers, for they were not fully broken in and pinched my feet. The other girls were in the same position, for Aunt Lyselle had had to hurriedly order new shoes for them all to replace the ones that had been ruined during their moonlit dances.

At last, though, our little group reached Coryn and Adalynn. I smiled and said I wished them every happiness, and Janessa and Carella and Theranne offered similar sentiments. Adalynn gave us what looked like a genuine smile in return, and told us how lovely we all looked, to which Coryn chimed in as well and said that he thought himself a very lucky man, to have the most beautiful bride in all of Purth. To their right, Coryn's parents thanked us as well, and Aunt Lyselle beamed at us and said, "You have done beautifully, girls. Now you may go and enjoy yourselves."

Freed from our duties, we hurried out into the courtyard, where a great pavilion had been erected on the green lawn at one end, and where the other guests had already gathered to drink wine and eat the delicacies that our servants had prepared. Some others wandered along the paths that wound through the rose garden, chatting and sipping wine.

Altogether, it was a very festive sight. Janessa and Carella and Theranne made a beeline for the pavilion, dragging me in their wake. Theranne especially was excited, for Aunt Lyselle had said she might have wine today, whereas under ordinary circumstances she had been forbidden anything stronger than cider until she was past eighteen.

I made a mental note to keep an eye on my cousin and make sure that she did not do anything to call attention to herself. Perhaps that should have also been the task of the other two girls, but I could see the way Janessa's eyes roved the crowd, clearly looking for Lord Gwyllim. And Carella wore a rather defiant expression, one that told me she thought she had done quite enough for everybody else and was now going to enjoy herself.

Very well. I had only resolved to survive the afternoon and the evening that would follow. I could not expect more than that, not when I knew I would have to deal with Lord Mayson at some point. If I were very, very lucky, perhaps his father would keep him in check, but I could not plan on that.

But as I had not seen him yet, I followed the other girls into the pavilion, which was quite crowded, enough so that I worried whether the skirt of my gown would survive the day, or whether a misplaced foot would tear out the hem. Out of deference to us as attendants of the bride, however, most people moved out of the way so we might go to the table where the enormous bowls of wine punch had been set out, and where the footmen were pouring cups for all who approached.

I noticed that Branwell, the elder of the two footmen pouring out the wine, was careful about the serving he gave Theranne, and that her cup was only a little past half full. Her lips formed into a pout, and I feared she was going to protest, so I said, "Go on, Theranne. For there are others waiting for their drinks as well, so it is best not to linger here."

She heaved a sigh but did not bother to argue, and went off to be lost in the throng—no doubt hoping she would meet up some of the girls she knew but did not see that often, for their parents' estates were not within easy riding distance of her own. I did not think I needed to fear her flirting with the young men among the guests, since she had never shown that much interest in that sort of thing—unlike her sisters, or Janessa. But still, I thought I should keep something of an eye on her to make sure she did not have too much wine. Her mother would be preoccupied, as would Adalynn, and Janessa would be occupied with Lord Gwyllim. Carella had no such distractions to prevent her from watching over her little sister, but I feared she would not be of much use.

Branwell poured wine punch into my cup, and I headed into the crowd. I knew I was expected to be social, and merry, and yet, now that I had performed my required duties, I wanted only to flee to my room and hide there. Such a retreat would be even more enticing if I knew that another assignation with Reynar lay at the end of it, but I knew such a wish was but a vain hope. He would not expect me to come to him after such an exhausting day. No, he would wait until the guests had departed and things had returned to normal, or at least as normal as they could be with Adalynn gone off to her new home with her new husband. We would have to find a different rhythm in our lives without her.

That seemed rather a melancholy thought—even though Adalynn was certainly not my favorite person in the world—and I brought my cup to my lips and drank, even as I attempted to find an inconspicuous corner of the pavilion where I might hide myself. For a few moments, my stratagem seemed to be working, but then I heard Lord Mayson's voice.

"Ah, Iselda. I wondered where you had gotten to."

Automatically, I summoned a smile, even though I was not all that happy to see him. My happiness decreased that much more when I noted a certain bleariness to his gaze. Barely past two in the afternoon, and yet he must have already consumed several cups of wine punch, judging by his appearance.

I knew I would have to tread carefully.

"Lord Mayson," I replied. "I thought it best to stay out of the sun, and this seemed the best place to stand, as here I do not have to worry so much about being bumped into, or spilled on."

He glanced around, seemed to take note of the corner where we stood, and nodded. "Yes, that does seem rather wise. This pavilion can barely accommodate half the guests."

Was that a hint of disapproval in his tone? "Well," I said, my tone perhaps crisper than it should have been, "this lawn is not so large that we could possibly erect a pavilion here big enough to contain everyone. But no one else seems to mind strolling through the rose gardens, or going inside if the sun should become too strong for them."

Mayson was not so far into his cups that he could not see his mistake, for he said swiftly, "No, everyone seems to be enjoying themselves. I have been to many weddings, but I think this has been one of the most lovely. Your aunt has outdone herself."

These words should have mollified me, but didn't. For I knew he had only said those things to ingratiate himself, and not because he truly believed them. But since I would not pick a quarrel with him here, I made myself smile and say, "She would be very glad to hear that. I know she has been running ragged these past few weeks. But Adalynn has had her day, and a very lovely one it is."

"True." Mayson fell silent for a moment, clearly turning something over in his mind. I did not like his quiet, for I could guess all too well what he might be thinking. "But what of you, Iselda? Do you not wish to have a day like this for yourself?"

I sipped from my cup of wine punch and desperately wished myself elsewhere. Unfortunately, since I did not possess any magical powers, I remained standing right where I was. "Of course I do. Sometime in the future," I added quickly as I saw a certain light begin to kindle in his eyes, "after I have had a chance to recover from this one."

Those words did not seem to have the quelling effect I had intended, for he said, "Oh, not too far in the future, I hope?"

This time I could not prevent myself from letting out an exasperated breath. "My lord, we already said we would discuss this later. This is simply not the time, nor the place. I have been up since dawn, and I can barely think straight!"

As soon as the words had left my mouth, I regretted them, since I could not be sure how he might react to such an outburst. However, he did not appear angry. In fact, he gave a sympathetic nod and said, "You are right, of course. You have your duties to manage today, and I should leave you to them. But you will dance with me tonight?"

"I already said I would." And oh, how I regretted that promise, even though I knew there was no way I could possibly avoid him during the rest of the festivities.

If he noted the churlishness of my tone, he gave no sign. Instead, he made a very slight but graceful bow, and said, "Then I will see you later this evening, my lady. Until that time."

And he was off, weaving through the crowds before he disappeared from view. I could not allow myself a sigh of relief, for I knew that I had only been granted a brief reprieve.

I would still have to face him that night.

Chapter Twelve

As was the custom at these sorts of events, the reception lasted until the heat of the afternoon was too much for everyone, and then we all retreated to the comfort of our rooms within the castle, which, with its thick stone walls, provided a more than adequate buffer against the summer sun. Some took the opportunity to nap and sleep off some of what they had drunk earlier that afternoon, while others only sat and perhaps loosened the lacings on their gowns, so that they might be comfortable for a time before being required to make a some-what more fashionable appearance at the evening's events. The servants, of course, were not granted such leisure, for during this time they must go to the great hall and remove the benches where everyone had sat for the ceremony, and redecorate the space so it would be ready for the ball later that night. Dinner would be served in both the dining chambers, and there would also be tables set up in the pavilion outside for those who wished to dine by the light of the setting sun.

During this lull, I gratefully escaped to the room I shared with Janessa...but she never appeared. I suspected that she had taken advantage of the respite to retreat to a forgotten corner with Gwyllim, and I certainly would not begrudge her that stolen time. If only I had been able to do the same with Reynar! But of course I had no idea where he even made his home, and, desperate as I was to see him, I was not so desperate that I would attempt to slip away from the crowded castle and make my way to the forest. No matter how careful I might be, I couldn't know for certain that I would not be spotted. Besides, I had made no arrangements to see Reynar, and so I had no reason to believe he would even be waiting there for me.

No, all I could do was retrieve the book I had been reading, kick off my too-tight slippers, and allow myself to enjoy a few hours of peace and quiet before I must put on my public face again and endure the rest of these celebrations. I had no real duties at dinner or at the ball which would follow, save to be gracious and charming, and make sure that I did not favor one young man over another during the dancing. Right then, I could only thank all the gods that my aunt had requested such behavior of me, since that stricture would make it far easier for me to beg off from dancing too much with Lord Mayson.

I read, and drank some cool water from time to time, and began to feel restored. Not more than a quarter-hour before we were due to go downstairs, Janessa reappeared, her careful coiffure somewhat disarranged, and a few telltale reddish marks showing on the fair skin of her throat.

"I am glad to see you are still with us," I remarked dryly as she went to the mirror and began repairing the damage to her hair as best she could.

"Oh, well, I was talking with Lord Gwyllim," she replied in somewhat breathless tones, "and I completely lost track of the time."

"'Talking'?" I repeated as I lifted an eyebrow.

Her hand went to her throat. "Yes, *talking*. I cannot think how I got these marks! There must be some kind of biting insects in the garden."

No doubt something had been biting her, although I rather doubted it was insects. But since she was clearly inclined to protest her innocence no matter what, I only said, "Best you should put some powder on those marks. To take out the sting," I added with a smile I could not quite suppress.

She opened the cabinet that contained our hairbrushes and combs, and the chamomile mixture we used for our hair. Hidden there was also the small pot of rice powder, along with the lip and cheek stain Tarly had mixed up for us and had made us promise that we would never, ever tell Aunt Lyselle where it had come from, as young ladies of good birth were not supposed to resort to such artifices.

Janessa pulled out the powder and the hare's-foot brush we used to apply it, and dabbed at the red marks on her neck. They did seem to subside somewhat, although they did not completely disappear.

"Do you think your aunt will notice?" she asked anxiously as she peered into the mirror and turned this way and that, no doubt trying to see how well her artifice held up under the shifting light.

I set down my book and rose from the bed, then went over to the mirror so I could get a closer glance at Janessa's throat. When looking at them up close, I thought there would be little doubt as to what had left those marks. "On any other day, she would take note of them right away. But as distracted as she is—and no doubt will be, until the last of our guests goes safely home—I do not think you have too much to worry about it." Then I hesitated, unsure as to whether I should leave matters there. Janessa was not my sister, nor my cousin, and so I really had very little say as to what she did or did not do. Still.... I cleared my throat before I continued, "I must say, though, that I am rather surprised you would take such a risk. Do you care so little for your reputation?"

Color flooded her cheeks, color which had very little to do with any sort of cosmetics. "Of course I care. But Lord Gwyllim has said that he has never met anyone like me, and that he knows it might be importunate, but he wishes to speak to my father as soon as he returns from Bodenskell."

For yes, Janessa's father had not come to attend Adalynn's wedding, stating that he had urgent business in the capital which he could not put off. Although no one had asked for my opinion, I rather thought this "business" of his had far more to do with wishing to avoid seeing his daughter rather than anything that required his immediate attention.

But if Lord Gwyllim truly wished to ask for Janessa's hand, then her father would not have to worry about avoiding her any longer. She would have made a far more advantageous match than he had probably dreamed of, and she could go and make a life of her own without having to concern herself with her father's neglect and the reasons behind it.

"Well, that is wonderful news," I told her, "and I am very glad to hear it. They say that love is in the air at events like these, and makes people want to confirm their own happiness when confronted by the happiness in others."

She nodded, even as she continued to cast a critical eye at her reflection in the mirror. "Perhaps that is it. I am still not sure how it all came about, but it will be quite a wonderful thing to be the Lord Gwyllim's wife, and the Baroness of Linsmere."

Of that I had little doubt. For Janessa would escape her life as a ward in this household, and would have a title of her own. I thought that Carella would be quite green with envy, and knew that she would be impossible to live with for some time before she became resigned to the situation. Not that she'd had any particular designs on his lordship, but rather that she would find it quite insufferable that quiet, simple Janessa could land a titled husband when she herself was quite unattached.

If only Lord Mayson...but no, I would not allow my thoughts to go there. He seemed quite fixed on me, for better or worse. Perhaps I would be able to persuade him to look elsewhere, but even if I happened to be successful in such an endeavor, I could not hope that he would transfer his affections to my cousin.

A deep bell tolled from the courtyard, and Janessa let out a sigh. "That is the signal to go downstairs. Are you quite sure I shall pass muster?"

"You will be fine," I assured her. "Only let me fix that one pin on the back of your head."

I went to her and inserted the offending hairpin at a more elegant angle, then shifted another that had begun to slip as well. "Good as new, and if you need any further assistance, please come and find me."

"Thank you, Iselda." Impulsively, she hugged me. "You have been like the sister I never had. I cannot say the same for the others."

Tears pricked at my eyes, for I had never heard her say such a thing before—and also because I guessed those words were her way of starting to say goodbye. Once Lord Gwyllim had spoken to her father, everything would begin to change for her.

I thought then with some spite that I would tell whoever asked for me—if and when such a thing might happen—to speak to my uncle, and not my father. For his treatment of my sister Annora, and because of his complete neglect after I had come to live with my aunt, he did not deserve to be given that honor.

But perhaps I was getting ahead of myself. Certainly Reynar had not spoken of such things, and although Mayson had, I definitely did not intend to accept his suit.

"I thank you for that," I said softly, "and I am so very happy for you. But we must go down now, and play our roles."

Janessa made a face as she seemed to think of the hours that lay ahead. "It will be torture to dance with anyone except Gwyllim. But I do not want to attract too much attention, and so I will do what I must."

"I suppose that is all any of us can do."

We went out then and shut the door behind us. I did not see any of my cousins, and so I guessed they must have already gone downstairs. Adalynn certainly, for she and Coryn must take the place of honor in the main dining hall, and be sitting there as the guests arrived. Under normal circumstances, I would have been banished to one of the lesser tables, but since I was one of my cousin's attendants, I, too would sit at the head table, along with my aunt and uncle, and Janessa and Carella and Theranne. This was something of a relief, for although I did not much care to be put in display in such a way, at least I would be able to avoid Mayson during dinner, even if doing so at the ball which followed would be nigh impossible.

It seemed that Janessa and I were somewhat tardy, for everyone else was already seated when we entered the hall. My aunt sent us a disapproving look but said nothing; she would never reprimand us in front of the guests, although we might hear something from her later about our conduct. We both murmured apologies that no one else could hear as we took our seats. Whether she accepted them or not, I could not tell, for she only gave a very faint nod before gesturing toward Alister, to let him know all the guests were present and that the servants could begin bringing out the first course.

All of the maids and the footmen had been drafted to serve, even those who normally would never be seen outside the kitchens. On this special day, they all wore new ensembles of blue and silver, and looked very fine. But I could tell my aunt was worried, from the way she watched all of them with an eagle eye, clearly concerned that all it would require was one dropped cup, one spilled salad, to demonstrate to everyone that our household was not quite as equipped to handle such crowds as she wanted everyone to think.

I scanned the hall, but could not catch a glimpse of Mayson. He would have been sitting with his father, and they would have had a place of some importance because of Lord Elwyn's rank, but I supposed that my position at the end of the head table meant I was not sitting in a spot where I would be able to see them. Just as well; I was not sure how well I would have fared if I had had to worry about Mayson's eyes being on me all through dinner.

Alister himself waited on us, so of course no one at the head table needed to worry about any mishaps. The food was excellent, and I wondered whether all the kitchen staff would be in a state of utter collapse after this wedding was over. Certainly my aunt would not expect us to entertain again for some time.

Good, I thought then, *for once we are all back to normal, it will be much easier for me to slip out and see Reynar. Will those midnight dances resume with Adalynn gone, or will the spell still be effective with only three girls dancing?*

Hard for me to say, since I still had no idea what purpose the strange spell even served. That was one piece of information I could not seem to pry out of Reynar.

At least the meal went smoothly enough, course after course being brought in and taken out, until I began to wonder whether I would be able to last through dessert. My gown was not even laced that tightly, and so I could not imagine how some of the more corseted ladies must have been feeling.

Eventually, though, we were done, and Adalynn and Coryn rose from their seats so they could lead all the guests from the dining chambers down to the main hall, which had been transformed into a fairylike ballroom, with chains of roses swagged from the vast wrought-iron chandeliers, and hanging from the sconces along the walls. The air was thick with their scent, combined with the spicier, more exotic fragrance of the lilies that spilled from tall vases where the musicians sat.

The quintet played as we entered, a pretty, quaint tune older than the hills—not really suitable for dancing, but a charming way to come into the hall and prepare ourselves for what was to come next. As the new husband and wife, Coryn and Adalynn took their places near the musicians, and a set began to form beneath them, two long lines that stretched the entire length of the hall.

I began to wander toward the refreshment table at the far end of the chamber. I had had wine with dinner, but I was thirsty, and thought some cool water or punch would help. But I had not gone more than a couple of paces before I heard Mayson say, "Lady Iselda."

With some reluctance, I turned. At the same time, though, I did my best to fix a pleasant smile on my lips. After all, I had managed to avoid him for a goodly number of hours. I could not hope to do so all through the evening. "Lord Mayson."

"Will you stand up with me for the promenade? I think there is still some room at the bottom of the set."

"Of course," I replied demurely. "That would be lovely."

He beamed at me and led me to what would turn out to be the very end of the set, for we could not add more dancers without running the risk of having them bump into those who were attempting to get something to drink or nibble at the refreshments table. True, a second set could be formed, but it was not fashionable to do so, for there was always a good deal of jockeying for position involved.

We faced one another across the set. Inwardly, I could not help but be relieved that he had asked me to dance the promenade with him, for we would have no more intimate contact than holding one another's hands. If it had been a *verdralle,* he would have had to put his arm around my waist, and I would have had to hold his free hand with mine, and put my other hand on his shoulder. No, this was much better.

The music began, and he bowed as I curtseyed. Then we turned toward the head of the line and joined inner hands, and began to walk in time to the slow and stately music.

One drawback to this sort of dance, compared to the more lively ones, was that it did not provide much impediment to conversation. As we strolled toward the top of the hall, Lord Mayson said, "Everything seems to be going very well so far."

That seemed like a safe enough topic. But then, we did have Lord and Lady Pellyn directly ahead of us, and so perhaps Mayson did not wish to say anything that could not be overheard in polite company. "Yes," I replied as we split off to follow the column of people moving to the right of the hall. When we reached the bottom again, Mayson would take hands with the lady of the couple who walked parallel with us, and so we would move four abreast and go back to the head of the chamber once again. "All is as it should be. I believe my Aunt Lyselle is very relieved that there have been no mishaps."

"And will be even more relieved when all of her guests have gone home, no doubt," Mayson responded with a glint in his dark eyes.

I cast a quick glance at the couple who walked with us, but they seemed to be engrossed in their own conversation and did not appear to be paying us much mind. "As to that, my aunt is a very hospitable woman, but I do believe that she will be glad enough when things are not quite so hectic."

"Well, I doubt anyone could blame her for that."

We both fell silent after that, for the dance required a bit more concentration going forward. Our little group of four joined up with another group of four, and we walked eight abreast up the length of the hall, where the gentleman leading our group joined hands with a lady at the tail end of her particular octet, and the entire group of dancers shifted into one long line that made its way around the room, twisting and turning as we moved into a tighter and tighter spiral.

By the end, I was laughing along with everyone else, for a good deal of concentration was required not to step on anyone's toes, and Mayson laughed with me, a deep, throaty chuckle that seemed to indicate he truly was amused. Afterward, he guided me to the refreshments table so I might have some punch, but he did not linger, saying he had promised the next dance to Theranne.

I could not be jealous of that—far from it—and so I smiled as he went off in search of his partner. Anyway, I did not lack for partners myself, for almost as soon as he had left my side, I had several young men approach and importune me for a dance.

If I could not be with Reynar, then this was not a poor substitute. None of my partners appeared interested in anything except sharing a dance and enjoying themselves, and so I was able to spend the first hour or so of the ball quite happily entertained. And after a little while longer, I would have done my duty and shown my face for quite long enough, and then I would be able to slip away to my room. On the morrow, the guests would begin to depart, and our lives would settle back into their regular patterns.

After a quite breathless *verdralle* with a knight's son who possessed far more enthusiasm than skill, I went to fetch myself a cup of water. As I paused by the refreshments table, I gazed across the room and saw Mayson and his father, apparently deep in conversation. At this distance and because of the clamor of conversations around us, I could not hear anything of what they said, but apparently they reached some sort of agreement, for Mayson nodded and turned away before disappearing into the crowd.

What all that had been about, I couldn't begin to say. Perhaps Lord Elwyn had decided he had had enough of revelry, and was making plans to return home. If he left now, he could still reach his estate before midnight.

Although all the doors and windows to the hall had been opened to let in the cooler night air, the chamber was still far too warm. I could feel my hair sticking damply to the back of my neck, and a rivulet of perspiration trickled down my spine. It would probably be best if I went out into the gardens for a few moments so I might allow myself to cool down somewhat.

So I murmured an apology to the young man who had just begun to approach and ask for another dance, and threaded my way through the crowd and on into the rose garden. Overhead, the moon was very full and bright, its blue-white radiance quite overpowering the warmer light from the torches that ringed the courtyard.

I paused on a quiet little path, one where no one was currently walking. Although it was quite unladylike to do so, and Tarly would have scolded me for disarranging the curls she had spent so much time forming, if she had been there to see me, I took the mass of hair at the back of my neck and lifted it with one hand while I fanned away at the exposed skin with the other. In my rush to come downstairs, I had quite forgotten to bring my feather fan with me, and I certainly regretted that oversight now.

"Iselda?"

Oh, damn. I let my hair fall back down on my neck, and assumed what I hoped was a pleasant smile. How Lord Mayson had found me here, when I'd thought this was quite the isolated spot, I had no idea. Or had he been watching to see where I went? No, that was a most unsettling notion. The whole evening he had been quite offhand, friendly but certainly not pressing his suit in any way.

"Lord Mayson," I replied, sounding far too formal. But what else could I do? I certainly was not that happy to see him here, and yet I dare not let my dissatisfaction show. "It seems you also had a need for some night air."

He came to stand next to me, and glanced up at the full moon overhead before replying, "Yes, it is rather stifling in the hall. I suppose I should be glad not everyone had the same idea that we did, or this courtyard would be far too crowded."

"Yes, it would be quite unbearable, whereas now it is most pleasant."

"I am glad you think so."

Oh, dear. That was not what I had meant at all. And yet I could not say anything that might insult him. I began to cast about for excuses that would allow me to go back inside, but my mind betrayed me. Had I not just said that I required the cool night air? To return to the hall so precipitously would surely signal him that I had no desire to share his company.

But before I could reply, he went on, "I know you said we would speak after the wedding was done, but we are so near to that now—and have this wonderful quiet spot to converse— that I see no reason why we could not have our talk here."

Never had I wanted to simply run away as I did right then. Perhaps that was cowardly of me, but the day had been long and tiring enough as it was. I did not want to speak to Mayson about anything important, let alone this insane notion he had taken into his head to make me his wife.

"Oh, I do not think it is quite as private as you think," I said hastily, hoping the possibility of being interrupted would be enough to dissuade him from pursuing the topic. "People are coming and going all the time. Far better that we wait until tomorrow, or even the day after, when I know all the guests will be gone."

He took a step closer, and I had to force myself to remain where I was, to not let him see how much he had discomfited me. "But what if I do not wish to wait?"

"Mayson, I—"

I got no further than those few words, for in the next instant he had taken me by the arms and pulled me to him. And immediately after that he was lowering his head to mine, his mouth forcing my lips open. He tasted of wine, and I wondered in despair how much he had drunk this night. Surely he must be somewhat intoxicated to take such advantage of me in such a public place.

And though I struggled, he would not let go of me, kept forcing that kiss upon me...until I heard a startled exclamation, and my aunt's voice saying, "Iselda! What on earth do you think you're doing?"

At last Mayson released me, even as he took a guilty step backward. I stared past him in shock to see Aunt Lyselle standing there on the path, Lord Elwyn and my uncle right behind her. Worse, I could see they were not alone, either, that they had been accompanied by quite the group of noble lords and ladies, all of whom had probably decided to venture outside to get their own chance at some fresh air.

My cheeks burned, and I quite wished that a hole would appear in the ground and swallow me up. I was certainly disgraced beyond all measure now. The only remote comfort I could take in all this was that Reynar would not care about my reputation. We would run away as soon as we were able, and then I would not have to worry about Mayson Bellender ever again.

Even so, I could not quite bury my rage at Mayson, that he would so knowingly imperil me. What on earth had he been thinking?

My uncle turned toward the group of watching nobles, and murmured a few words I could not hear. Apparently they thought it best not to ignore the wishes of their host, and so they went off immediately afterward, heading back toward the hall. I did not want to think of the gossip they would spread once they were inside, but at least they were gone.

Lord Elwyn moved forward so he stood next to my aunt. His clear blue eyes flicked from his son to me and back again. When he spoke, his words were a knell in my heart.

"There is only one thing you can do now, my son. You must marry her, and marry her quickly. If everyone believes you were already secretly engaged, then the gossip will die down soon enough."

"That is all I wanted," Mayson said, his dark eyes gleaming. With triumph? For it seemed he must have planned this all along.

And in that moment, even as I seethed with frustrated fury, I realized there was very little I could do to escape.

❦ Chapter Thirteen ❦

"Oh, it's so very exciting!" Janessa exclaimed as I packed my meager belongings. "To think that you and Lord Mayson have been engaged for this past week! However did you manage to hide such a thing from all of us?"

Because there was nothing to hide, I thought sourly. *That is, I did have a great many things to hide, but this sham of an engagement to Mayson Bellender was not one of them.*

Of course I could not say such a thing to Janessa. I had to pretend that I was happy, that I wanted nothing more than to be the Countess of Bellender Rise.

For truly, I could see no way to escape my doom. As soon as word of the "engagement" spread, Lord Elwyn seemed to take over, telling my aunt and uncle that he and Mayson would bring me back with them to their estate, and there I would stay until the day of the wedding, which he announced would take place a week from now. Precious little time to plan such an elaborate event, but perhaps his lordship only wanted to make sure his son and I were married as quickly as possible, before we could elicit even a whiff of any more scandal.

This was all rather unconventional but not completely unheard-of; it used to be the custom that a bride-to-be would go to stay with her betrothed's family if she had none of her own. No one could claim that I was all alone in the world, but an aunt and an uncle were not the same as a mother and father, especially since my own father was still alive, if absent. It seemed that Lord Elwyn was determined to take advantage of the opportunity my uncertain status represented, and since he outranked my uncle, there was little Uncle Danly could do to protest. Neither he nor my aunt would do anything to stop this marriage, not when I had been caught in such a public embrace with Mayson. They were probably thanking the gods that Lord Elwyn was so eager to have me marry his son at all, for there were some noble fathers who would have made sure their sons remained free to marry someone of elevated birth, and then left me to suffer my disgrace on my own.

And so I was packing my meager collection of gowns and other trifles into a pair of leather satchels that Aunt Lyselle had lent me. Perhaps I should have left the task to Tarly, but I needed something to occupy myself. My thoughts chased each other this way and that as I concocted ever wilder schemes to extricate myself from the situation, and yet I knew in the end there was very little I could do. Everyone seemed to be watching my every movement. I had no way to escape.

If only Reynar had known anything of what was happening to me. But there had been no more spells, not on the night of Adalynn's wedding, nor the evening that had followed. He had already hinted that his master would not cast any more enchantments during the festivities, and had told me to be circumspect until all the guests were gone.

Well, now they had departed, except for Lord Elwyn, who had sent one of his men back to his estate to fetch some of his belongings, so he might stay with us for a few days after all. He took an empty room the first night, then moved into one of the suites which had just been vacated that morning. I knew he would not leave again until he accompanied his son and me back to what would be my new home.

Adalynn was gone, too, safely away with her new husband. If she had been startled by the announcement of my sudden engagement, she showed no sign of it. But then, she had her own changes and beginnings to keep her occupied. She was not going to concern herself with my fate, except perhaps to be somewhat annoyed that we would soon be of equal rank.

I had seen very little of Carella, for she had greeted the news with an eruption of hysterics, and promptly disappeared into her room. The outburst surprised me somewhat, because I truly had thought she wasn't interested in Mayson at all. Unfortunately, all she had done was hide her feelings until they exploded like a summer thunderstorm.

Ah, well. If I had had my choice, I would gladly have allowed her to take him off my hands.

I closed the satchel and locked it, then went to fetch the little wooden box I kept underneath my bed. In there were my few pieces of jewelry, and, hidden in a small leather pouch, the stones my sister and Tobyn had sent me. They had hoped to give me something of a dowry, but it seemed I had no need of such a thing now. Even so, I was glad of the jewels, for at least I could still take them out and hold them, and think of my sister and the happiness she had found with her husband.

It seemed such happiness would be denied me.

Now you are just being dramatic, I told myself. *For if you were to look at any of this logically, you would understand that you had no real understanding with Reynar. A few stolen kisses, and that is all. Mayson cares for you, and is young and handsome besides. You should do your very best to make him a good wife.*

Sound advice, I supposed, the sort that a mother might have given me, if mine had still been alive to deliver it. But I found I could not quite believe those sensible words. I had no experience with broken hearts, but I rather thought mine was breaking now.

I would not weep, though. Somehow I would find the strength to go downstairs and meet my future husband and his father, would keep my chin up as I rode away from the place that had been my home for the past six years.

Would Reynar even know what had happened to me?

Impossible to say, for I still understood very little of the doings of the mage-born. They each had their own powers and abilities, and yet they were far from all-knowing. They were not gods. So it was entirely possible that Reynar would think himself utterly abandoned, jilted for a man with a title, without ever knowing the real reason why.

I pushed that thought aside, for I knew if I allowed it to dwell in my mind, I would begin to weep and never stop.

Janessa was watching me curiously, as if trying to interpret my prolonged silence. I needed to be careful, for too much woolgathering would certainly signal to her that something was wrong.

"We did not want to speak until after Adalynn's wedding," I said, for I knew I must tell some falsehoods, even though the thought of doing so made me want to grind my teeth. However, since I had been thrust into this role, I could do nothing but play the part I had been given. "But we were overcome by the moonlight, and quite forgot ourselves."

"Oh, I can understand that," Janessa returned with a smile. "For I cannot say that Gwyllim and I were being perfectly proper that night, either. Only we were fortunate enough not to be caught. Even so, he said before he left that seeing your happiness has inspired him, and he will be going to speak to my father very soon. So yours will not be the only wedding we should be celebrating in the near future."

I left off my packing and gave her a quick, fierce hug, then said, "I am so very glad to hear that. Lord Gwyllim is a very worthy man."

"Well, I certainly think so. And I am sure my father will think so, too, if only because that way I will be well off his hands, and to someone with a title, no less."

"Janessa!"

She shrugged, watching as I closed the flap of the satchel I had just finished packing and fastened the clasp. "Why should I lie, or try to make it sound better than it is? My father has very little use for me, so I must make my own future elsewhere. Just as you are, Iselda."

I supposed I could not argue with that. Lord Elwyn had said very little about the plans for my marriage to his son, only that his steward would manage the wedding preparations, and that I need not worry about any of it. Whether those preparations would include an invitation for my father, I could not begin to guess. He and I had been estranged for so long, and a whiff of scandal still clung to him, and so I could see why his lordship might wish to exclude my father from the celebrations.

To my shame, I could not really bring myself to care.

A knock came at the door, and Janessa went to answer it. Outside in the corridor were Tarly and one of the footmen, so he might carry my two meager bags downstairs. At least Tarly was to come with me, and so I was not quite as afraid as I might have been, for I would have one familiar face in my new home.

If she detected any of my trepidation, she gave no sign of it. And if she minded being sent from the household where she had served for so many years, she gave no indication of that, either. All smiles, she said, "They are waiting for you downstairs, my lady. Steffan will take your bags."

He came into the room and gathered up the two satchels as if they weighed nothing at all, and I followed him out into the corridor. Tarly gave a quick look around the chamber after I had exited it, as if to reassure herself that I had not forgotten anything. If I had, I did not think it would be that much of a problem, since Lord Elwyn's estate was less than a day's ride from here.

Then we all went downstairs, Janessa at my side as if to lend her support, Tarly and Steffan behind us. Waiting down in the foyer were my aunt and uncle, Carella and Theranne, and Lord Elwyn and Mayson. Carella still appeared red-eyed, and she would not meet my gaze. Ah, well. I certainly had not intended to take anything away from her, but I knew nothing I might say would convince her otherwise.

Of course Aunt Lyselle and Uncle Danly looked very pleased, although I assumed they would have been even more pleased if it had been their own daughter who was leaving the castle as Lord Mayson's betrothed. However, if they felt any disappointment on Carella's behalf, they gave no sign of it.

Lord Elwyn stepped forward. "Thank you, my lord, my lady, for your excellent hospitality. While we are saddened to leave, know that we depart to take Lady Iselda to a new home and a new life."

My aunt smiled, and Uncle Danly said, "And thank you, Lord Elwyn, for providing such a welcome for her." He turned to me, then grasped my hands and gave them a comforting squeeze. "Take care, Iselda. We will be there to stand with you on your wedding day in less than a week, and so do not be too sad now."

I nodded, and if perhaps my own smile wavered a bit, I did not think anyone would blame me overmuch for that. "I look forward to seeing all of you again very soon."

He let go of my hands then, so I might embrace my aunt, and then Carella and Theranne as well, although I thought Carella would have been glad enough to dispense with that particular display of affection. After that, there was nothing to do but allow Mayson to take my hand in his so we might follow his father down the corridor and out the main entrance to the castle, which stood open, letting in the bright sunlight and a warm summer breeze. Outside waited their two mounts, and horses for myself and Tarly as well.

Steffan the footman went ahead and fastened the satchels he carried to the saddle of Tarly's horse, and then assisted both of us up onto our mounts. She did not appear very pleased at being so high off the ground, and I doubted I looked very happy, either; while I had been taught to ride, I would not say I possessed a great deal of skill. But we did not have far to go, and it was a cheerful, sunny day, and so I supposed matters could have been worse.

Well, except for being dragged off to marry a man I did not love.

Lord Elwyn and Mayson mounted their horses with far more skill. As they did so, a group of five men came from the stables to join us—his lordship's escort, although one could argue he hardly had need of such a thing in these times of peace. But still, no man of his rank would ride about the countryside unescorted, and so we all waited while the guards fell in around us.

Then it was time to ride.

Even though I almost lost my precarious seat, I had to turn in the saddle so I could get one last glimpse of my family disappearing behind me. They all stood on the steps of the castle, the building itself a great grey pile rising up behind them, the bright clothing they wore a startling contrast to the drab stone. Their hands were raised to wave me goodbye—well, all except Carella, whose arms were crossed and whose lips seemed to form a pout I could see from yards away.

A lump grew in my throat, and I forced myself to look straight ahead, at the tall, proud forms of father and son on their fine horses, at the guards with their livery of green and

gold. Surely this would not be so terrible. Mayson loved me—
or at least he wanted me—and certainly Lord Elwyn was very
agreeable. In time I would come to accept my new life, and I
would forget all about the silver-eyed man I had met in the
depths of the forest, would forget about the feel of his lips on
mine and the way he had awakened both fire and ice within my
veins.

No, I thought then, *I will never forget him. I will not allow
myself to. And all is not completely hopeless, for I am not yet Lord
Mayson's wife, and perhaps I can still find a way to escape this
forced marriage.*

Perhaps those were foolish words, and vain hopes. But I
could not allow myself to give up hope, for without it I was
surely lost.

Chapter Fourteen

Bellender Rise was far grander than Mirfeld Hall, an edifice made of the same grey granite but more massive in scale, with large wings extending from the central rectangular structure and many towers and turrets of various sizes. From the spires on top of those turrets fluttered banners in the green and gold of the Bellender family colors. I supposed they soon would be my colors as well, unless I could think of some way to stop this farce.

A veritable throng of servants came out to greet us, and I was spirited away to a sumptuous suite like something I might have imagined a princess would live in, with a sitting area and a separate bedroom, and an enormous tiled bath chamber with a tub large enough to fit two or three people. That thought brought a flush to my cheeks, and I thrust it away. I certainly did not want to imagine sharing a bath with Mayson, although I did not know for sure precisely what intimacies were involved when it came to marriage. I could only hope he was not quite as unschooled as I.

Tarly unpacked my things, hanging them up in the enormous wardrobe, and then she bustled about as she disposed of the rest of my belongings, the brushes and combs and shoes and all the little oddments of one's existence. When she lifted the little box containing my jewelry from the satchel, however, I moved forward and took it from her, saying, "I will put that away, Tarly. Thank you."

One of her sandy eyebrows might have lifted slightly, but otherwise she showed no response, and only said, "Of course, my lady. Whatever you wish."

Usually she was not so formal, but it seemed our new surroundings had cowed her somewhat as well. I took the box and placed it on the shelf in the wardrobe, and reminded myself to remove it someplace safer when she was not looking. I did trust Tarly, but that box contained the few things of actual value that I owned, and I wanted to make sure I could give them a secure resting place. Besides, the last thing I wanted was to attempt to explain whence had come all those precious stones....

While we were busy with these tasks, one of the maids came and paused at the door, and said that Lord Elwyn and his son wished to see me once I was done settling in.

"Of course," I replied, although my heart began to beat more quickly than I would have liked. Mayson and I had not exchanged above ten words that day. Perhaps he felt he had very little to say to me, now that his goal had been accomplished. Or perhaps he simply did not feel comfortable speaking confidences to me in the presence of his father. Either way, I could not help but be a bit trepidatious at the thought of going to see both of them. But I knew I could not demur, so I added, "I am done now, actually. If you could show me the way?"

The maid dropped a quick curtsey and inclined her head. "Yes, my lady. If you will follow me, please."

I was certainly not used to that sort of deference, although I supposed I should get used to it, now that I was to marry the heir of the estate, and one day would be the Countess of Bellender Rise. No, that seemed impossible. I could not marry Mayson. My heart was given to another.

And yet here I was.

After nodding at Tarly in farewell, I followed the other maid—a young woman only a few years older than myself—out of my suite and down several flights of stairs, and then across a large landing to a pair of double doors. Here she paused and knocked, then said, "My lord? The Lady Iselda is here to see you."

A pause of only a moment, and Mayson was there, opening the door and smiling down at me. "Of course. Thank you for bringing her here, Elyth."

The girl curtseyed and hurried off. There was nothing I could do save enter the suite, and follow Mayson as he led me down a short corridor to a large sitting area where his father waited next to the fireplace. It was an impressive structure, carved of stone and with basilisks serving as caryatids at either end. No doubt in the winter, when it held a roaring fire within, it would be even more impressive. Now, however, with the hearth cold and unused, there was something bleak and rather sad about it, as if it knew it had a good while to wait before its days of usefulness returned.

Or perhaps I was merely placing my own feelings of worry and isolation on something that had no feelings at all, was only an object to be used when it was necessary, and otherwise ignored. Then again, that notion hit a little too close to home as well.

"You are well settled in?" Lord Elwyn asked. For the first time, I noticed that a small table stood next to him, and on that table were three silver goblets. Now he lifted one and extended it to me, even as Mayson stepped forward so he might claim his own drinking vessel as well.

"Oh, yes," I replied as I took the goblet from Lord Elwyn. "The suite you have provided is lovely. I had not expected anything so beautiful."

"The least I could do, for my son's affianced wife," his lordship said. "You have made us both very happy, Iselda. So let us drink to your upcoming wedding, and your joining with the Bellender family."

I knew there was no way to refuse, and so I did not even try. Instead, I lifted my goblet and clinked it against Mayson's, and then against Lord Elwyn's. For the briefest instant, I thought I saw a cloud of confusion in Mayson's eyes, as if he was not quite sure what we were toasting. Then his expression cleared, and he smiled at me, and I thought I must have imagined that flash of uncertainty.

"Yes, we should all drink to that," he said. "For this is an auspicious day, with even greater ones to follow."

The best I could do was maintain my own somewhat wavery smile before I sipped at the wine. It was a pale gold, almost as pale as the silver goblet which contained it, and was quite cool. Lord Elwyn must have been keeping it in one of his deepest cellars.

"Now, my dear," his lordship said, "I fear we must broach a rather unpleasant subject."

"Erm...yes?" I managed before swallowing more wine. I could not imagine what he might be hinting at. Had he somehow looked past my watery smile and tentative enthusiasms, and seen that I was not quite as enamored of the prospect of becoming his son's wife as everyone wanted to believe?

In a way, I hoped that was exactly what he intended to discuss. For then I could tell him that this had all been an awful mistake, and that I should be sent back to my aunt and uncle forthwith. A pleasant fantasy, even if I doubted it was one that would come true.

But of course that was not what he had meant at all.

"I refer to your father," Lord Elwyn went on. "While some eyebrows might be raised at the prospect of excluding him from the festivities, because of his current disgrace, I cannot in good conscience recommend that he attend. But my son and I wanted to speak to you about this in private, so we might know your mind. If your heart is set on having him present, then of course we will accede to your wishes."

A little bubble of laughter rose to my lips, but I somehow managed to choke it back. "Oh, no," I said at once, in tones of such utter sincerity that I knew father and son would have no choice but to believe me. "I have no desire at all to have him attend. Why, we have not spoken in years. I believe my last letter from him came two years ago. I cannot even recall whether it was on my birthday or—no, it was at Midwinter, I think. So you see, there is no connection I wish to maintain."

At my words, Mayson's expression softened, and he came closer so he might take my hand in his. I did not even bother to attempt to pull it away, for I knew better than to make such a display in front of Lord Elwyn. "You see, Father?" Mayson said. "It is just as I told you. Her aunt and uncle gave her a worthy home, but she is still quite alone in the world."

His lordship gave his son a fond glance. "Yes, it seems you were right. I should have trusted your judgment, for of course you have spent the last month in Lady Iselda's company, and so know her very well." He looked over at me before continuing, "I will respect your wishes, my lady, and do my best to ensure that you and my son have the perfect day you both deserve."

I began to stammer my thanks—false though they might be—and he raised a hand.

"It is the least I can do, as your new father. We will continue with the preparations, and if there is anything you should wish for the ceremony, please be reassured that we will do everything to make matters proceed just as they should."

Everything except releasing me from this regrettable obligation, that is, I thought, but I only smiled. Lord Elwyn had no way of knowing that my feelings for his son were not quite as deep as they should be, and that I in fact loved another.

I only said, "You are all kindness, my lord," and he smiled at me.

"It is easy to be kind, when I look forward to having such a lovely and worthy daughter-in-law. But now, Mayson, she is probably wearied from the ride here, and would wish to rest until dinner. Help her back to her room, for I doubt she remembers the way."

"Of course, Father."

Mayson put his hand on my elbow and guided me from the chamber. While I would have preferred a less intimate touch, at least Lord Elwyn's instructions seemed to indicate that I would have some time to myself, a small space to try to regroup and come to terms with my new life.

During the climb up to my suite, neither Mayson nor I spoke. It was only when we stopped in front of my door that he said, "You are very quiet, Iselda."

"Oh, well," I replied. "It is only as your father said. I am not used to such long rides, and I am feeling rather tired. I am sure I will be quite myself by the time dinnertime arrives."

Whether he accepted this explanation or not, I was not sure, but he did not contradict me. Instead, he took my right hand and pressed a kiss on my palm. "You will be very happy here, my love. I will make sure of that."

Then he bowed and turned away, and I let myself into my room. It was only a moment later that I paused, heart pounding much harder than it should, and tried to tell myself that an echo of a threat hadn't underlain his parting words.

Dinner went smoothly enough, however, with Lord Elwyn explaining more of his plans for the wedding, and how he intended to make it a great event, even with so little time to prepare. How precisely he intended to accomplish such a thing, when my cousin Adalynn's wedding had required several months of planning, I was not sure. But then, he was an earl, and so had far more resources at his command than an ordinary man, or even an ordinary baron, such as my uncle.

So I smiled and nodded at the appropriate times, and did my best to seem enamored of his son, even while I inwardly had begun to catalogue what I had seen in the castle so far—how many doors, how many guards, how many opportunities for escape.

Deep down, though, I knew such plans were all for naught. I would not be able to get away. The household at Bellender Rise was far larger than what I was accustomed to at my aunt and uncle's home, and the chances of escaping detection frighteningly small. Beyond all that, though, I could not find it within me to bring such disgrace upon Aunt Lyselle and Uncle Danly. Even if I did somehow manage to get away and return to them, the scandal would be well-nigh insurmountable. I did not care much if my own name was to be dragged through the mud, but how could I do such a thing to those kindly souls, who had stepped in and given me a home so I might not be outcast forever?

And so my thoughts twisted this way and that, even as I laid myself down in my new bed later that night. The bed was even more luxurious than the one I had slept in at my aunt's home, with a new feather mattress and a coverlet of silk, and yet I knew sleep would not be my friend. I would have to fight it, wrestle it into submission, for I could not get my roiling mind to settle down enough that I might get the rest I so desperately required.

In the darkness, just as the edges of the silvery moon began to touch the arched window opening a few yards from where I lay, I heard a voice I thought I had lost forever.

"Iselda?"

Although I could not be sure that I was not dreaming, still I sat upright in bed, the silken covers clutched to my breast. "Reynar?"

He stepped out of the shadows, moonlight glinting silver in his hair. As I stared at him in shock, he came over to my bedside and dropped to his knees there, just as he took one of my hands in his. "Yes, it is I. But you—you are quite unharmed?"

"Why, yes," I replied, puzzled. "That is, I have been greeted with the utmost hospitality here, even though I would much rather that I was at home."

His fingers, which had wrapped themselves around mine, tightened their grasp. Indeed, his grip was almost painful, but I was so glad to see him that I cared little for a bit of discomfort. "So...you do not love Lord Mayson?"

"Of course not!" I replied with some indignation. "How could I love him, when you know my heart has been given to you already?"

For a few seconds, he said nothing, but only continued to hold my hand. His eyes caught mine and held. When he spoke, there was a certain roughness to his tone which seemed to belie an emotion held barely in check. "I had hoped...but then I heard the dreadful news...."

Although I knew how terrible it must be to anyone who did not understand how I felt about Reynar, I could not help leaning over and pulling him toward me so our mouths might meet. I did not care that I was in my bed, and clad only in a nightgown. I had kissed him thus once before, albeit out of doors, and not in the questionable surroundings of a bedchamber. Right then, however, it seemed more important to me than anything else that he know I loved him and only him, no matter what the world might think.

And oh, the sweetness of his mouth, the despairing intensity with which he deepened the kiss so we might taste one another, could remind ourselves of how we could only be with the person we now held, and no one else. Again shivers and heat flooded my body, and I had the stray thought that it would be so easy to pull him to me so we might press against one another, limb to limb. I had only a very hazy idea of what might happen after that, but I was willing to take the risk. Surely Reynar would know what to do.

But then he pulled away, shaking his head. "You make this very difficult for me, Iselda."

"What is difficult about it?" I asked. "I kissed you then because I wanted you to know that my heart is yours...only yours. Lord Mayson trapped me into this horrible engagement. I had thought we were friends, and that he would at least respect my wishes not to discuss any future plans until after Adalynn's wedding. But then he kissed me, and made sure to do it in a place and time where we were certain to be seen. After that, I had no choice but to accept his suit, or at least pretend to. Do not think that I have not been planning my escape ever since, although I must confess that it has seemed rather impossible."

Despite the direness of my circumstances, Reynar's mouth lifted into a smile. "Yes, I believe you would have rather a difficult time scaling down the walls of this tower."

"Oh, do not tease me," I said, not amused at all. "You are here now, and so you must have a plan to take me away."

"I am trying to come up with one," he replied, the smile disappearing as if it had never been. "It is not all that simple, you know."

"But you are a mage," I told him. "How did you even get in here? Surely if you were able to sneak in, you should be able to spirit me away."

His shoulders lifted. "As I've shown you before, I have the ability to change my appearance. Anyone who looked on me as I walked down the corridors would have thought me merely another of the earl's guards. In the same vein, I have cast a spell to make any who might pass by decide they have urgent business elsewhere, and another so that even if someone should draw near, they would not be able to hear us. So I do not fear getting caught."

"But...."

"But I cannot do the same for you, Iselda. I cannot change your appearance, hide you in any way so I might walk you out right in front of the guards with no one noticing."

In that moment, I rather wished that mages were more like the fearsome creatures I'd read about in my storybooks, powerful men who could cast any spell they liked and who commanded powers that leveled mountains. The reality was somewhat disappointing. But I did not want to be disappointed by Reynar. He had come here, after all, and that meant a great deal. Together, we should be able to devise some sort of plan for getting me away. "A sleep spell, such as the one you cast back at Mirfeld Hall, so my cousins might slip out of the castle without anyone noticing."

He shook his head. "That would not work here, I am afraid. And I fear the situation is even more perilous than you might imagine."

A small tendril of cold began to unfurl its way down my spine, but I tried to sound calm as I said, "And how can that be, Reynar? For I am engaged to a man I do not love, and surrounded by his family's servants and guards. And even if I do escape, I will disgrace both myself and my family. So forgive me if I am having a difficult time understanding how things can be any worse than they appear to be."

"Oh, they are." He hesitated then, eyes shadowed with worry. "You know how I never told you who my master was, how he carefully guarded his name so no one could guess his true identity?"

I nodded, wondering what that had to do with my current predicament. Yes, I was sure Reynar had taken a risk to slip away and come here to see me, but....

Another pause. Then he said, "My master is Lord Elwyn."

Chapter Fifteen

I could not speak. I could not do anything except stare at Reynar in horror, for my mind did not want to accept what he had just told me. It was not possible. How could such a thing be possible?

His mouth curved in a grim smile. "You are surprised."

Somehow I found my voice. "No, 'surprised' is what you might be when the cook promised venison for dinner and you are given chicken instead. This...this...." I floundered for a moment, then asked, "How is such a thing even possible?"

"Do you think the old blood appears only in the veins of commoners? True, Lord Elwyn appears to be an ordinary man...unlike myself...but he was born with the same gifts. Or rather," Reynar added, "his own particular gifts. And he was trained, just as he trained me, although his education was undertaken in secret, under the very nose of the former earl, from what I have been able to gather."

My mind did not want to accept this new and strange reality. Mages by their very nature must keep in the shadows, must do everything they could to escape notice. And yet Lord Elwyn was by all accounts a very sociable man, one who did not turn up his nose at an invitation to come to dinner, or to step out on the dance floor, should the occasion warrant. He clearly doted on his son. But....

"What are his powers?" I demanded, although my voice dropped to a near-whisper. Yes, Reynar had reassured me that we could not be overheard, and yet I could not help but think Lord Elwyn would certainly discover us, would....

In truth, I did not know what he would do. I could only think that he would not be happy to learn that his apprentice and his future daughter-in-law had formed an alliance without his knowledge.

"He is powerful in many ways. The more so because many of his powers are subtle ones, gifts he can bring to bear to hold others under his sway, to make them do his bidding. As he has done with Lord Mayson."

"What about Lord Mayson?" I asked then, my voice sharpening despite my best efforts to keep it low. "What has he forced him to do?"

"Why, to compromise you so the two of you must be married," Reynar replied simply.

I slumped back against the pillows and stared at him in shock. At once he took my hands, holding them tightly before continuing.

"I cannot speak of Lord Mayson's feelings for you, because I have never had any kind of speech with him. His father made sure that we never met, that he did not even know I existed. I did gather, however, that Lord Mayson was not terribly eager to be married. This reluctance annoyed his father to no end, as you might imagine."

"Lord Mayson does not possess his father's powers?"

"Oh, no. He is an ordinary enough man. But still, he is Lord Elwyn's heir, and I know my master hoped the old blood would appear in any children Mayson might father, even if he himself does not possess any magical gifts."

"But...." I clenched my cold fingers around Reynar's, needing their warmth to drive away the chill that had entered my body, even though the night was quite warm. "Why me? If Lord Elwyn only wanted to make sure that he had grandchildren who could carry on the magical blood, he would have done far better to have Mayson pursue my cousin Carella, who was more than eager, and who also is the daughter of a baron, rather than a commoner like myself."

"That much, I do not know," Reynar replied. He did not relax his grip, but seemed to understand that I needed to hang on to him like a drowning swimmer might cling to a rope. "I am sure he has his reasons, for my master does nothing without a plan, but I cannot begin to see what his motivations are here, and he has not explained them to me. I am sure he believes it is none of my affair, since this involves the continuation of the Bellender name."

My heart sank. For if Reynar, who had known Lord Elwyn for years and years, could not begin to guess at his intentions in having Mayson claim me rather than some other young woman, then I certainly had no idea, either. Some called me beautiful, but Carella was beautiful as well. I had no wealth, no title. And I was not precisely alone in the world, and therefore easy to take advantage of, because I could always go to my aunt and uncle for help if I must.

No, the whole situation had me completely flummoxed.

"So...why the dances under the moon?" I asked then. "Did that have something to do with the spells he was casting on his son?"

"No," Reynar replied. "At least, only partially. It is a ritual he performs once a year, to gather the power of the young and vital, and bring it into himself. Have you not wondered why he has the air of a man some ten years or even more younger than he is?"

Well, I had, but I had not thought on the subject too much. After all, there were always those who seemed blessed in that manner, who appeared more youthful than their peers. "I suppose it crossed my mind once or twice," I replied slowly, then added, guilt overcoming me that I had remained silent and had said nothing to my aunt or uncle, "Did it...did it hurt them?" For while I already quite hated Lord Elwyn, I certainly did not want to think that Reynar had been complicit in any sort of activity which might have caused harm to my cousins or Janessa.

"No," he said at once. "I have already told you that. It is something he has done every year for the past decade. At first, he was able to perform the spell on young women who lived near the estate—daughters of farmers and cottagers, that sort of thing. There must always be at least three. Four is better, and five the most desired, but harder to come by. He could not use the same girls year after year, for they must be between fifteen and twenty, and as you know, young women grow up and get married, and move away." Reynar's fingers tightened on mine, as if he wished to give me more reassurance. "The light you saw dancing around them—that was the energy he was drawing forth and collecting so he might bring it into himself. But your cousins, or any of the girls he had taken it from, would not notice it gone, any more than you might miss the few strands that remain in your hairbrush each morning."

That explanation did reassure me somewhat. I had not noted any ill effects of the spell, save that Janessa and my cousins seemed rather tired the morning after one of their outings. And who could blame them, when they had lost several hours of sleep? But if that was the only harm they suffered....

"Very well," I said. "It is done, and my cousins and Janessa are safe now. But what should *we* do?" I asked, hating how hopeless I sounded, but unable to do much of anything about it.

Reynar bent and kissed me on the forehead, very gently, and then let go of my hands. "I am not sure yet. But we have time—your wedding will not take place until three days from now, and within that span, I am sure an opportunity will arise for me to get you away from here. Now, however, I fear I must go. My spells must be doubly strong when cast here in my master's stronghold, and I cannot maintain them indefinitely."

"No, please—" For I thought I should go mad to be left here alone, knowing what I knew now.

"My dear, I must." He kissed me again, this time on the mouth, the taste of him sweet and warm. I reached up and seized his hands, and attempted to pull him toward me.

But he was too strong. He remained standing where he was, his face a pale mask, one taut with worry and fear.

"Do not tempt me, Iselda. You have no idea—" He broke off his words there, his jaw clenching. "If I am caught, I can do nothing to help you. Do you understand?"

Of course I did. I released his arms, and slumped once more against the pillows. "I understand, Reynar. I do not wish to jeopardize you in any way. But perhaps—" I sat up a little straighter as a sudden thought occurred to me. "What if I speak to Lord Mayson? His father cannot hold sway over him at all times. I have seen it, I think—when Lord Elwyn's control begins to slip, and Mayson appears confused, or not sure precisely what is happening. If I could wait for one of those moments—"

"It is far too dangerous," Reynar cut in. "For when my master has control of his son's mind, he can see everything he sees, hear everything he hears. He would guess at once that you know far more than you should. Do you understand why you must say nothing?"

Damn. Even though these latter-day mages were not as powerful as their counterparts of long ago, clearly they were still a force to be reckoned with. Things would have been so much easier if I could have enlisted Mayson's help during one of his lucid moments.

But it seemed that was not possible, and so I murmured, "Yes, Reynar. I understand."

His mouth twisted, and then he bent and kissed me again, but so swiftly that I did not have time to respond. And as he stood up straight, his appearance shifted to that of a man some ten years older, bigger and broader, with heavy dark hair and a nose that appeared to have been broken several times. He wore the green and gold uniform of one of the household guards, a short sword at his belt. A quick smile, one that showed off crooked white teeth, and then he was hurrying out the door. It shut behind him, and I was alone.

Alone, and afraid, for I did not share Reynar's confidence.

I very much feared we would not be able to devise a plan in the limited time we had left.

Sleep eventually did come to me, although I tossed and turned for nearly an hour after Reynar had departed. Tarly cast a critical eye at me when she appeared with my morning tea but said nothing. Perhaps she thought it normal enough for me to have had a restless night, since it was my first time in this new place.

Instead, she bustled about, telling me what a lovely welcome she had had from the other servants, and how the kitchen staff had been so helpful in making up my tea that morning. I listened to her chatter, and smiled and nodded at what I hoped were the appropriate intervals. Part of me wished very much that everything was as normal as she made it sound, but I knew better. I did wonder how the prosaic Tarly would react if I told her the lord of this castle was no mere nobleman, but a mage who wielded strange and fearsome powers.

Knowing my maidservant, I rather thought she would probably laugh outright and then tell me I needed to make sure I got my rest, as lack of sleep was clearly giving me strange notions.

So I said nothing, and listened with some relief as she informed me that Lord Elwyn and Lord Mayson intended to ride the estate this morning before it got too warm, and so my breakfast would be brought up to me. That reprieve gave me some much-needed breathing space, although I knew I could not avoid father and son forever. I was sure they would expect me to sit down with them this evening. Could I hide my newly acquired knowledge from them? I supposed I would have to, or else all would certainly be lost.

Tarly left me for a time so she might fetch up my breakfast, and I went to the window and looked out. The morning appeared quite fine from my vantage point up here in the tower; the sun shone down, clear and golden, illuminating the gardens that surrounded the castle, and the fields which lay beyond. Past all of the cultivated land was the dark blur of Daleskeld Forest, which followed the path of the stream and created the northeast border of Lord Elwyn's lands. Here, the woods were much closer than they had been to my uncle's property. Perhaps it was somewhere within those dark stands of pine and fir and oak that the place where Reynar dwelt was hidden. He had never said exactly where he lived, only that it most certainly was not here with Lord Elwyn and his son. The forest made sense to me, for Reynar could travel within it and not be easily seen, and I thought it would probably be easy enough to conceal some kind of dwelling there as well.

I saw a pair of riders moving down a lane which separated two of the fields, and realized those riders must be Lord Elwyn and his son. Did Mayson have any idea of the sway his father exerted over him? Were those brief moments when he was in control of himself the times that felt like a dream?

A shiver went over me as I recalled what Reynar had told me the night before, that when Mayson was in the grip of one of his father's spells, then Lord Elwyn could see and hear everything his son saw and heard. Which meant he must have seen his son kissing me.

Had he felt that as well?

My stomach lurched, and I hurried back over to the table where Tarly had set down my tea, so I might take a few sips and, I hoped, calm the nausea that had begun to rise in me. As repulsive as the thought might be, I could not let the knowledge that Lord Elwyn might have seen all of my dealings with Mayson upset me too much, for then I ran the risk of not thinking clearly when the time came.

Tarly returned a few moments later, carrying a tray with fresh bread and butter and raspberry preserves, and a slice of the egg and cheese pie I loved so much. Had Mayson requested that I have such a meal for my first morning here because it was comforting and familiar...or had Lord Elwyn known already?

I grabbed my teacup and drained it, then filled it again. My maid sent me an inquiring glance.

"Are you quite well, my lady? You are looking very pale."

"I'm fine," I responded quickly. "I suppose I am only still rather weary."

"Well, breakfast should mend that, I suppose. And if you wish, I can have word sent to their lordships that you are tired from the journey, and would prefer to be quiet in your chamber today."

Oh, bless Tarly! And Aunt Lyselle, for having the fore-thought to understand that I would need my maid's steadying presence in a new place. "That would be wonderful, Tarly," I said. "I do think I would fare better if I were to have some quiet time to myself."

"I'll see what I can do. I know that the seamstress was com-ing up to see you later this morning, but I can try to put her off—"

"No, that's fine," I cut in. While Lord Elwyn and his son might not press me too hard about wanting to remain in my room today, I knew if I did anything that made it seem as if I were attempting to postpone the wedding, they might inter-cede. Better to appear that I was eager to marry Mayson, although now that I knew the real reason behind his ardor, I felt as if I wanted to be sick again. "I am quite well enough to manage the seamstress."

"If you wish, my lady," Tarly replied. Her voice was neutral enough, but I thought I detected a note of relief in her tone. It seemed that was one battle she had no particular wish to fight, either.

So I ate my breakfast, forcing down every bite, since my appetite had quite deserted me. As I ate, Tarly laid out my clothes for the day, and when I was done, she helped me out of my nightgown and into the dress she had selected for me, the green silk that I did not much care for, but was certainly fine enough for my role as Lord Mayson's affianced bride.

After that she took the breakfast dishes away, and I was left to my own devices for a time. I had brought several of my books with me, and I had thought to read to pass some of the time, but I could not seem to concentrate, my thoughts jumping this way and that. In the end, I laid down the book and again took up my post by the window. No sign of either father or son, unfortunately; I wondered what they were doing in that moment. Did Lord Elwyn have to keep Mayson close by, in order to maintain control?

No, that didn't sound right, for clearly Mayson had been under that dark spell's sway even when his father was miles away from my uncle's estate. I had a notion, however, that the spell had to be refreshed from time to time, which would explain why Lord Elwyn had unexpectedly come to dinner that one night not so long ago.

Which again led to the central conundrum of the whole affair. Why on earth had Lord Elwyn determined that I should be the one to become his son's wife? I could not flatter myself that there was anything particularly outstanding about my person. A pretty face, perhaps, but there were many more of those to be had, and plenty among the nobility as well. Possibly fewer who were not already betrothed, but....

My musings were interrupted by a knock at the door, followed by Tarly's voice. "My lady? The seamstress is here, and her assistant."

"Come in," I said, and turned away from the window. I would find no answers in the view outside, and I knew I must pretend to be engaged in the activities of the next hour or so, unless someone might begin to guess that I had no wish to be Lord Mayson's wife.

The seamstress was a tall, commanding woman of late middle age, with grey-streaked dark hair and an expression that did not invite commentary. Her assistant was perhaps a few years younger, but quiet and cowed. She curtseyed to me and seemed to do little of her own volition after that, for her mistress made sure she was continuously occupied.

"Darhynne, bring me that golden trim. No, the one with the pearls. The pink pearls," added in tones that seemed to imply the other woman was a fool for not knowing immediately which pearl-encrusted trim the seamstress had demanded.

I said nothing, but stood in place as my wedding gown was dropped over my head and pulled this way and that to ensure the best fit. Strangely, the dress was already made, and only needed to be altered, and the trim traded for the one Mistress Allynde, the seamstress, had determined would suit my coloring better. The gown itself was of a soft ivory silk, shot with pink and blue, rather like the inside of a seashell.

My curiosity overcame me, and I found myself emboldened enough to inquire, "Whence came this gown? For it seems as if it was made for someone else."

"That it was," Mistress Allynde returned as she fussed with the hem. "For Lord Mayson's betrothed. But she has no need of it now, poor girl."

"But...wouldn't the gown have been with that other girl's family?" I could see no reason why it would be here at Bellender Rise, as it was the responsibility of the bride's family to supply her wedding dress.

"So it was, but Lord Elwyn had it sent for," the seamstress replied. From the set of her mouth, I could tell she had little wish to answer any more of my questions.

It seemed very strange to me that a family mourning the loss of their daughter would be eager to hand over the gown she should have been married in, especially to have that gown worn by their daughter's replacement. But then I thought, *Yes, it is odd...but Lord Elwyn has the ability to make others do as he bids them. I have no doubt that poor girl's family sent it over without even thinking twice about it, for his lordship would have cast a spell to make them think that nothing about the situation was extraordinary at all.*

After that, I fell silent, and let the two women work on the dress. During that time, I could feel Tarly's eyes upon me, could tell that she also thought something was very strange about the situation, although of course she would not comment with the seamstresses there. I prayed she would leave the subject alone even after they left, for I did not dare tell her the truth that lay behind my sudden engagement to Lord Mayson. I would not put her in such peril.

As luck would have it, almost as soon as they had departed, another servant appeared, saying that his lordship wished to speak to me. So much for allowing me to stay quietly in my room. As I knew I could not demur, I nodded and said, "Will you take me to him?"

"Yes, my lady," the maidservant responded. She looked to be only a year or so older than I, with impish hazel eyes and a cloud of curly brown hair. Surely she could have no idea as to what a villain the lord of the castle truly was.

But as I did not dare tell her the truth, I merely thanked her, and allowed her to lead me from my room and down to the ground floor. She did not take me to the study where I had met with Lord Elwyn the night before, nor to any of the other rooms on that level. Instead, we traversed the long corridor, and at length came to a pair of double doors that opened out onto a loggia with grey flagstones on the ground. What caught my breath, though, were the evenly spaced pillars that held up the roof, and how they were all covered with flowering vines I did not recognize, with pale yellow and pink blooms that lent an intoxicating fragrance to the air. The space was cool, shaded as it was from the sun, and a welcome respite from the warm weather we'd been having.

Lord Mayson stood by one of those pillars, looking down into the gardens below. As soon as he heard us arrive, however, he turned and smiled at me.

"Ah, Iselda," he said, and held out his hands.

All I could do was cross the space between us, and let him take my fingers in his. Immediately afterward, I heard the soft thump of the maid closing the door behind her. I wished I could pull my hand from Mayson's now that we no longer had an audience, but I knew I had to be cautious.

"Mayson," I replied. Wishing to speak of something neutral, I added, "This is a very lovely spot."

"I am glad you like it. I had thought you might prefer someplace cooler and more comfortable. Would you like to sit?"

For the first time I noticed that a carved stone bench stood only a few feet off to his left. Since I knew I could not refuse, I nodded and took my seat there, feeling the cold stone even through the layers of my skirts and petticoats. Or perhaps that chill had come from within.

I cast an oblique glance at Mayson through my eyelashes as he settled himself next to me on the bench. His expression was open and friendly, and seemed no different from the man I had first met at my uncle's home. But how was I to know who the real Mayson Bellender even was? Perhaps I had never seen anything of him, only a puppet controlled by his father.

"Are you settling in well?" he asked.

"Yes, very much so. The view from my room is quite lovely."

"And you enjoyed your breakfast?"

"Yes. It was kind of you to have my favorites sent up."

For just the briefest second, I saw that same flicker of confusion in his dark eyes, the one I had noticed several times previously. At the time, I hadn't thought much of it, but now I realized those odd flashes of befuddlement must have been caused by his waking slightly from his father's spell.

If he was having one of those moments now....

I hesitated. If I said the wrong thing now, then I would let Mayson—and by extension, Lord Elwyn—know that I had guessed something very strange was occurring here. But if the spell had begun to slip, and if I could somehow let Mayson see what had been done to him, then perhaps I could convince him to let me go. After all, Reynar had admitted that Mayson did not wish to marry at all. If he woke up to himself, he would have no reason to do anything else. He did not love me.

I would be free.

"Oh, yes," he said then, speaking quickly as if to cover his hesitation, "I did want you to feel at home your first morning here. I know how much you enjoy a nicely grilled ham steak."

There it was. He could not remember what I liked, because most of the time we had spent together, he had been controlled by his father. "Actually, it was egg and cheese pie," I pointed out.

His expression fell, and he frowned, fine features twisting as he attempted to reconcile what he thought he knew with what he'd actually experienced. "I—"

"It's all right," I said, my tone gentle. I would have to be very cautious here, for I did not know for certain why the spell would be slipping now. Perhaps Lord Elwyn had wished to relax his hold on his son now that he thought our marriage to be a certainty. If that was the case, then I could not bear to let this moment pass without attempting to reach out to the true Mayson Bellender. "Do you—do you feel confused like this often?"

He looked away from me, off through two vine-covered pillars, toward a rose garden that put my aunt's to shame. Still with that frown pulling at his brows, he said, "It is nothing. My father says it is something that has happened to me ever since I had a high fever as a boy." He shifted on the bench so he no longer stared off toward the garden, but faced me, his dark eyes intent. "It will not affect my ability to be a good husband to you."

Despite everything, my heart could not help but be wrung. It was despicable of Lord Elwyn to put his son through this, to make him think as if something was wrong with him, when in actuality the only thing wrong was the pernicious hold the father had over his child.

I reached over and took Mayson's right hand in mine. "I do not think you had a fever, Mayson."

He pulled his hand back as though my touch had scalded him. "Of course I did. What on earth are you talking about, Iselda?"

"I think...." The words trailed off as I debated inwardly whether I should go on. If I stopped here, I could still brush off what I had already said. But if I continued, then I would be crossing a line that could never be uncrossed. Was he truly free enough of his father's influence to understand what I was about to tell him?

No doubt Reynar would have counseled me to stop, would have said that he was sure he could have devised some kind of a plan. But now the wedding was only two days away, and I worried that no such plan would be ready in time. I could end this now...if I was brave enough.

"Mayson," I said, "has your father ever mentioned his powers to you?"

"Powers?" he repeated, brow wrinkling again. "What sort of powers?"

I pulled in a breath, then forced myself to utter the fateful word. "Magic."

He let out a barking sort of laugh before he pushed himself up from the bench, as if he could not bear to sit next to me any longer. "What on earth are you going on about, Iselda? There's no such thing as magic."

"Of course there is," I said calmly. "Otherwise, my sister and my brother-in-law would not now be living in exile. Or do you not believe any of those stories, even though they were the talk of court for years?"

A flicker of doubt showed in Mayson's eyes. "I—I am not sure."

"Do you think I would lie to you about such a thing?"

"I do not think you would lie intentionally, but perhaps you have mistaken some of my father's actions—"

I stared directly into his eyes. To do so was quite uncomfortable for me, as a well-brought-up young lady was not supposed to be that forward, even with the man who was her betrothed. But I could think of no other way to force him to see how deadly serious I was, that this was not some foolish fancy I had dreamed up.

"Have you ever wondered, Mayson, how it is that your father appears so youthful, that he might be your older brother rather than your father?"

"Well, I—some people are naturally well-preserved, I suppose."

Unfortunately, I had thought rather the same thing myself, and so I knew this one argument probably would not hold much water. I pressed ahead, however, saying, "Does your father disappear for long periods of time?"

"Sometimes he must go to Bodenskell on business—"

"Then why does he not take you with him? One would think he would want his heir present so he might learn something of the dealings required to keep this estate running."

Now Mayson looked truly confused. He shook his head, as if to clear it, but I feared more than that would be required to remove the fog from his brain. "I—"

"I doubt very much that he goes to Bodenskell that often," I pressed on. "He goes away so he might train his apprentice, and to cast his spells. One of which was cast on my cousins and my aunt and uncle's ward Janessa, although, thank the gods, they did not suffer any lasting ill effects from his magic."

At that pronouncement, Mayson let out a short, disbelieving bark of a laugh. "Good gods, Iselda, have you listened to yourself? What spell, pray, did he cast?"

"A spell to take a little of their life force and bring it into him," I retorted. "So he might stay as youthful-looking as possible. Everything he does is to make his own life easier. Tell me, Mayson, do you really wish to marry me? Truly?"

A blank and baffled expression passed over Mayson's features. He paused, and scrubbed a hand over his face, as if that would help him think better. "Of course I do."

"I am not so sure about that. You had to stop and ponder the matter for a moment. Surely if you really loved me and wished me to be your wife, you would have said yes immediately."

"Don't be ridiculous, Iselda. It is only that you took me so off guard—"

"That is an excuse. Tell me the truth, Mayson. If that is difficult for you, I can speak first. You were my friend—or at least I thought you were—but I never wished to be your wife. I still do not. You forced this on me, but I do not think that is your fault. I think your father took hold of your mind and made you do it, because he wishes for you to provide him with an heir."

This barrage of words had a singular effect. Mayson took a step backward, eyes widening. He flushed red, and then turned pale as death. One hand went to his throat, and he stood there for a long moment, staring at me as if he had never seen me before. "It is true," he whispered at last. "That is, I do not know how. But it is almost as if I have been standing off to the side, watching as all this occurs, but with no power to stop it."

"That must be the spell," I said sadly. "You could do nothing. Not against magic such as his. But he thinks he has you completely under his control. Let me go now, when he is not paying attention. I will go back to my aunt and uncle, and say that we both realized we had made a mistake, and decided to end the betrothal. I swear I will say nothing of this to anyone. Your father's secret will be safe."

"How very noble of you," came a new voice, and Mayson and I both whirled in fright.

Standing at the other side of the loggia, a mocking light in his eyes, was Lord Elwyn.

❧ Chapter Sixteen ❧

My first instinct was to run, although I knew fleeing would do no good. I still had no clear idea of the true extent of Lord Elwyn's powers, but I feared he must have some spell in his arsenal that would prevent me from getting away.

He moved closer, mouth lifting in an unpleasant smile. "You are quite the clever girl, aren't you, Iselda? To have figured all that out, all on your own?"

I would not betray Reynar, no matter what happened. Surely Lord Elwyn's retaliation would be swift and brutal, should he ever learn of what had passed between his apprentice and myself. Lifting my chin, I replied, "You forget that perhaps I am more open to these sorts of ideas because of having a mage in my own family."

"And you are quite bold, to say such a thing with little care for who might be listening."

"Is there anyone else I should know of?" I inquired, as Mayson looked on, expression aghast. "For I am fairly certain that you made sure there would be no witnesses here."

"Ah, you are right about that." Lord Elwyn glanced over at his son, a look of annoyance twisting his features. "Do shut your mouth, Mayson. You look like a fish on a hook. No, Iselda, that is one more area where you are correct. The servants have been told not to disturb my son and his betrothed, and so they are all busy elsewhere. They are so very diligent about doing my bidding."

"I have little doubt of that. Does it not weary you, to control the minds of everyone around you?"

"Oh, I am not controlling *everyone*," he replied, his voice silky.

And then...it was as though something heavy and dull was pressing against my temples, as if I had a headache coming on. But I knew it was no headache at all, but Lord Elwyn attempting to use his powers on me. Gritting my teeth, I fought back, made myself stare at him as I told my mind that I was the only one with the right to control it. A shudder went through my body, and my vision began to blur. *No.* I would not allow this. He would not enter my mind, my heart, my soul.

This silent conflict lasted for only a few moments. Just as suddenly as it had begun, the pressure eased, and Lord Elwyn smiled.

Why was he smiling? Surely he should be angry that I had managed to fend off his attack.

"It is just as I had thought," he said. "You are very strong, Iselda."

"I—why are you so pleased?"

"Because I had guessed, but I did not know for sure. Your powers are unlike any others I have ever encountered."

"Powers?" Mayson broke in. "What are you talking about? Iselda is just an ordinary girl."

"No, my son, she is not. And if you had any powers of discernment of your own, you would know that." Lord Elwyn sighed then, a sigh I was fairly certain he exaggerated for effect, before he directed his attention back toward me. "But I sensed it when I first met you at your aunt and uncle's home. Of course, you were only a child then. But still, I knew that one day you would be perfect for my son. He must carry some strain of my powers, even if he shows none, and I knew that one day your children would be very great mages."

All of this had my head spinning. Mayson had been perfectly correct when he'd said I was only an ordinary girl. I'd never exhibited any kind of special abilities. Reynar had said he could feel his powers manifesting, and I knew that Tobyn had said much the same thing to my sister. Whereas I—I certainly did not know how to cast a spell. I could not alter my appearance, or disappear from one room and appear in another. The only extraordinary thing I had ever done was withstand Lord Elwyn's attack just a few moments earlier.

"You are mistaken," I said. "I am no one special."

Lord Elwyn's lips thinned. "I am never mistaken. You see, that is one of my other talents...a subtle one, to be sure, but helpful. I can always sense when someone of the old blood is near me, no matter whether they are a full-blown mage or not. I sensed it when I first met you. True, you show no outward abilities, but no one without some kind of powers could have prevented me from taking control of their mind, just as I attempted with you now."

"You—you tried to go into her mind, to force her?" Mayson demanded, taking a step toward his father. His fists knotted with anger, although they remained at his side.

"So very noble, attempting to defend your betrothed," the earl sneered. "Ah, Mayson, you continue to find new ways to disappoint me. Shall I tell her why you had no wish to be married?"

Mayson went pale, dark eyes wide and staring. "You wouldn't dare."

"I think you know now that there is very little I would not dare." Lip still curled, Lord Elwyn turned toward me. "It seems this son of mine, in addition to being entirely lacking in any sort of useful powers, prefers the company of men to that of women. He would never have brought himself to kiss you if he had not been under my control."

To be honest, I did not quite understand what on earth Lord Elwyn was talking about. Prefer the company of men? I had never heard of such a thing. Confused, I looked from father to son, saw how Mayson's jaw was tight with anger. Every line of his form seemed to thrum with rage.

No, Mayson, I thought, wishing with all my might that I possessed the sort of powers which would allow me to speak with him mind to mind. I could only hope he would see the pleading in my face. *You cannot—*

But I did not have time to complete the thought, for in the next moment Mayson had launched himself at his father, his face distorted with rage. What he even intended to do, I had no idea. I only knew that I made an incoherent cry of protest, even as Lord Elwyn lifted a hand. Mayson stopped only a few inches away from his father, rather as if he had run into an invisible wall. And then....

He was flung backward as though he weighed no more than a rag doll. His flailing body slammed into one of the vine-covered pillars, scattering shredded leaves and flower petals everywhere. He slid down to the base of the pillar, where he slumped over onto the ground.

I gasped, then ran to him, dropping to my knees next to his limp form. Even as I reached to take his hand, to see if I could still feel the life beating within his wrist, I knew I would discover the worst. No one could lie with their neck at such an angle and still live.

"You killed him!" I cried. "Your own son!"

Lord Elwyn crossed the space that separated us in a few short strides, then grasped me by the arm and hauled me upward. His fingers bit cruelly into my flesh, but I would not allow myself to wince. What was a little pain, compared to what he had just done to Mayson? "I did kill him. He had proved that he was of very little use to me. But you...." He paused then, cold blue eyes seeming to take in every detail of my countenance. "I think you will do very well. My son was too much of a fool to realize how valuable you are, but I will certainly not make that same mistake. There will still be a wedding two days hence...only you will marry me instead of my son."

I stared up at him in horror. "You would not dare."

"And why wouldn't I? Who is to question me? The servants? Hardly."

"My aunt and uncle—"

"They have no power to stop such a thing. Besides," he added, his tone turning silky, "they are such kind, simple folk. Easy to control. It will be very simple to convince them that this is a far better thing for everyone involved, since you will be a countess now instead of waiting years for me to pass on the title."

"And what of Mayson?" I demanded. "How do you intend to explain his death?"

A negligent lift of his shoulders, although I noticed he kept his gaze fixed on me rather than looking over to the spot where the body of his son lay. "Simple. I will put him on his horse and take him out to the forest. He will be discovered some time later, lying on one of the paths. A spill as he went riding. An unfortunate accident. No one will question such a thing. Just as no one questioned the death of the girl he was first engaged to marry. After seeing you again at your aunt's Midwinter gathering, I knew Mayson's betrothed must be disposed of so he might wed you instead."

I had not thought I could be any more horrified than I already was, but those words made my heart clench. If I could have backed away from him, I would have, but he held me far too tightly. "You killed her?"

"I made certain she would not live, yes. And then I made the suggestion to your aunt and uncle that Mayson should come to stay with you for the summer, to recover from his loss... and perhaps to heal his heart with another. They hoped for a match with Carella, and so they were all too eager to agree." Lord Elwyn shrugged, and something about the indifference in the gesture made my blood run cold. "I even told Mayson that he would be free to indulge his...predilections...once he had fathered a child or two with you. But he did not think that would be honorable, so I had no choice but to control him so he would do as I wished. Just as I had no choice now." If he felt any sorrow or guilt over murdering his son, he certainly showed no sign of it. He merely recited these hideous facts in a neutral tone, hard blue eyes fixed on me the entire time.

Any one of these confessions would have been terrible on its own, but being confronted by them all at once made my stomach lurch with sudden nausea, and my knees felt so weak that I feared my shaky legs would not be sufficient to hold me up. I told myself that I could not afford to lose control now, and made myself focus on the one element in all this that most affected my immediate future. "Do you not think my aunt and uncle will question the father marrying his dead son's betrothed?"

"I will make sure they do not." He let go then, the crushing pressure on my arm gone, although the flesh still throbbed where he had held me fast. "Do you not see, Iselda? There is no contingency I have not thought of, no argument you can make to change the situation. You will be a good, biddable girl, and then...." The words trailed off as he raised his hand to stroke my cheek. Revulsion boiled within me, but I stood my ground and did not flinch. "I think perhaps you will see that being married to me is not quite as terrible as you might imagine."

"No, it will be far worse," I flung at him. "I would rather die than be your wife."

"That would be a tragic waste, I think." Lord Elwyn paused then, and I very much feared he was about to bend down and claim my mouth with his. What I would do then, I had no idea. I had resisted his attempt to take hold of my mind, but in a purely physical contest, I would surely lose.

But, all the gods be thanked, he did not kiss me. He only watched me for a long moment, a small smile playing at the corners of his mouth. At last he said, "I think it best if you go back to your room now. I have much to do."

"I will tell everyone what you have done!" I burst out. "You cannot control my mind, and so you cannot control me!"

The smile vanished. He stepped closer and took me by the arm again—in the same place, so his grip hurt even more cruelly this time. "You will do no such thing, Iselda. I have no wish to hurt you, for you are far too valuable, but at the same time I cannot have you interfering...and you might wish as well to think of your aunt and uncle, and what might happen to them if you were to speak of what has happened here. You should also know that this castle is very old, and the dungeons beneath it are still intact, if somewhat overrun with spiders and rats. Would you rather spend the time until our wedding there, or in the comfortable room I have given you?"

I wished I possessed the courage to tell him to go ahead and lock me up in the dungeon, that I would rather rot down there with the vermin than hold my tongue and tell no one of his guilt. Unfortunately, I knew I would do no such thing. I could not bear to put my aunt and uncle in such jeopardy. Also, even though it pained me to admit to such a weakness, rats terrified me, and always had. And, as he had said, even if I did somehow summon the courage to tell anyone else about what he had done, Lord Elwyn would simply go into their minds and make them believe otherwise.

"I would rather stay in my room," I whispered, hating myself.

"I thought that was what you would say. So come along—I will take you upstairs myself, to make sure you do not get into any mischief."

Wrung with guilt, I allowed him to guide me away from the loggia and into the castle, where we went directly to the stairs and from there up to my room. He paused with me outside the door but did not open it. From within, I could hear Tarly humming tunelessly to herself. No doubt his lordship did not wish for my maid to see him with me.

"Not a word," he said in an undertone. "I know you like having your maid here with you, so do not say anything to her unless you want her sent back from whence she came. Understand?"

"Yes, my lord," I replied. Oh, how I despised the weakness I heard in my own voice! But I knew I could do nothing else, for he had me fairly trapped. Now more than ever I needed Tarly with me, to have her comforting presence nearby when the entire world felt as if it was collapsing all around.

"Good." He let go of my arm, but briefly touched one of the long curls that fell over my shoulder. "Delicious. Yes, you would have been wasted on my son."

I could not help shuddering. Lord Elwyn must have seen, for he smiled again.

"Go in, my dear. I may repulse you now, but I think you may change your mind on our wedding night."

Oh, I could bear no more. I grasped the door handle and turned it, knowing I must get away from him and that horrible mocking smile he wore. He did nothing to stop me, but instead sauntered off down the hallway, no doubt to attend to the next part of his plan...getting rid of Mayson's body.

A sob rose in my throat then, but I choked it back. I knew I must appear to Tarly as if nothing untoward had happened, that I had only spent the last few minutes speaking with my betrothed before I returned to my room.

I closed the door behind me, and she looked up from where she sat by the window, the stocking she'd been darning laid across her lap. She smiled. "Did you have a nice chat with his lordship?"

"Yes," I replied. My voice did not shake. I smiled at her in what I hoped was a pleasant fashion as I went to the mirror and paused in front of it, then fiddled with my hair. My hope was that she would think I was fussing with my curls because they had gotten somewhat disarranged while I was outside. In reality, I needed to see my expression, to make sure my features revealed nothing of the horrors I had just witnessed. And indeed, although there was a certain tightness to my mouth, I could not detect anything terribly untoward. I added, "I think Lord Mayson said he planned to go riding. It is such a fine afternoon."

"Yes, it is," Tarly agreed.

The sourness of bile rose in my throat, and I forced it back. There. I had just done some of Lord Elwyn's dirty work for him. The gods help me.

But in the meantime, I knew I would have to think of something to help myself.

Very late that afternoon, as the day was shading into evening, one of Lord Elwyn's foresters found Mayson's body on a path that wound through the forest. His horse stood nearby, as if keeping watch over his fallen master.

The household became one of mourning, the mirrors draped with dark cloth, the servants all with black armbands to show their grief. Lord Elwyn himself came to bring me the news, looking very sad and dignified. Indeed, he put on such a good act in front of Tarly that I thought he had rather missed his calling, and should have trod the boards down in Bodenskell as one of the king's players.

I wept, and Tarly comforted me, and his lordship said I should remain in my room, so I might mourn in private. For some reason, my maid did not see anything strange about this, although she did venture to say that perhaps I should go back to my aunt and uncle's—a notion Lord Elwyn quashed immediately, telling her that I was certainly in no state to ride, and that I needed time to grieve. These arguments seemed to be effective, for she nodded and said of course, and that she would be here to watch over me.

In a way, I wished I could have been alone, for perhaps then I would have had a better opportunity to think of what I should do next. Trying to be helpful, she hovered, asking if I wanted some tea, or whether I should lie down, or perhaps read a little to try to take my mind away. At last I did lie down and shut my eyes, but that was more so I might have a moment's peace.

I needed Reynar. Where was he? I tried to tell myself that of course he could not appear here in my room in the middle of the day, even wearing one of his magical disguises. No, he would have to wait until the quiet hours of the night. Then he would come to me just as he had the evening before, and we would devise a plan together. In that moment, I did not much care how good that plan might be, only that we must have one. He would take me away, and then we would tell everyone of Lord Elwyn's perfidy.

These thoughts calmed me somewhat. I pretended to sleep, and nibbled at the tray of food Tarly brought up around dinnertime. And after that, I did sleep, but fitfully, starting awake at every sound, certain it must be Reynar come to save me.

Only...he did not. I awakened in the depths of the night and saw the waning moon as it slipped just beyond the window during its journey to the west. Everything was utterly still. I realized I was the only one in the room, and tears of despair stung my eyes. I had no idea where Reynar was or what had happened to him, but clearly he would not be coming to my rescue this night.

And I cried myself to sleep just as the sky began to turn pale grey with the coming of dawn.

The next morning, I did what I could to cure my puffy eyes, dabbing them with cold water. Tarly made no comment about my appearance, for of course what young woman would not weep in the night when she had just lost her betrothed?

Everything I had brought with me was utterly unsuited for mourning, since they were all summery gowns of pale blue or green or pink. Drearily, I told my maid that I did not much care what I wore. With a frown, she brought out the blue and silver dress I had worn at Adalynn's wedding.

"If it is all right, my lady—"

"It's fine," I said. "I suppose blue is a slightly soberer color than green or pink. It will have to do."

She laced me into the dress and then fussed with my hair. I could tell she kept herself busy because she did not know what to say to me. Indeed, I hardly knew what to think. Some of the night's terrors had fled with the coming of morning, but I knew my time was running out. Tomorrow Tarly would put me in the borrowed wedding gown with its pearl trim, and I would be married to Lord Elwyn.

No. I knew that would not happen, just as I knew the sun would rise in the east every morning. And yet...with no word from Reynar, and no one else to help me, how could I possibly secure my freedom?

Someone knocked at the door, and Tarly went to open it. Outside was one of Lord Elwyn's footmen, although I could not recall his name.

Well, I thought drearily, *you will have plenty of time to learn all their names if you do not somehow manage to extricate yourself from this horrible situation.*

"His lordship wishes to see Lady Iselda," the footman said.

"Lady Iselda is not well this morning," Tarly began, but I forestalled her by rising from my chair.

"I will see his lordship," I said calmly. I knew I could not create a scene. The best thing to do was to make Lord Elwyn think he had me beaten, that I was cooperating with him. "We have both suffered a loss. It is only natural that we should meet so we might commiserate."

"Of course, my lady," she replied at once, but I saw the way her brows pulled together, as if she was trying to determine whether some subtext to my words existed, some hidden meaning she could not quite decipher.

Head held high, I went out to meet the footman, who led me downstairs. I could not help but think of the last time I had descended this staircase. Oh, if only I had not goaded Mayson the way I had during our meeting! Perhaps then he would still be alive. Better a sham marriage with him than this travesty which Lord Elwyn wished to foist upon me.

We walked down a long corridor, one hung with forbidding portraits of generations of Bellenders. Or perhaps it was only my own gloomy state of mind that made them seem so brooding, for in general, they were quite handsome men. I refused to think of the earl as one so favored, however, for his evil deeds quite canceled out any beauty that might be seen in his features.

I had never been in this section of the castle before, and I wondered where the footman was taking me. But I did not dare to ask.

We stopped in front of an imposing set of double doors, fashioned from dark oak and carved with patterns of oak leaves and acorns. They were part of the sigil of the Bellender family, and so it did not surprise me to see them here now.

"He is waiting for you, my lady," said the footman as he opened the right-hand door for me.

"Thank you," I murmured, and went in.

The chamber within was quite large, with an enormous fireplace of gold-veined black marble at one end. On this warm summer day, it sat cold and unused, although garlands of roses had been draped over the mantel. I realized that large urns of roses and trailing vines of ivy stood sentinel at the room's four corners, their scent filling the air. Otherwise, the place did not seem to contain much in the way of furniture, save chairs carved of oak with the same leaf-and-acorn motif as on the doors, placed at regular intervals between the mullioned windows. Half of the draperies on those windows were pulled shut, and so the chamber seemed dim and somehow stifling.

Lord Elwyn stood by one of those windows, but he came toward me as soon as the footman shut the door, leaving us alone. His lordship wore somber black, but a heavy gold chain set with the green tourmalines mined in the Daleskeld Hills gleamed from around his neck.

"Lady Iselda."

"Lord Elwyn."

He paused a few feet away from me and smiled as he seemed to inspect me from top to toe. "You are looking very well, my lady. No one would think to look at you that you had just lost your lover a day earlier."

"He was not my lover," I said calmly. "A fact which you knew all too well. What is it you want, Lord Elwyn?"

This question seemed not to discomfit him at all. "You are a very direct young woman, Iselda. I appreciate that. So many girls your age are all simpering and coyness, with not a brain to them."

"If you are attempting to flatter me, you are not doing a very good job of it," I replied. "But that is no matter. I do wish to know why you have brought me down here for this interview."

"Is it flattery to tell you the truth?" he inquired. Again he gave me one of those searching looks, and I felt warm blood rush to my cheeks. Something about his gaze made me feel as if he was trying to determine what I looked like under my gown and chemise, and my flesh positively crawled. "By the way, that color is very becoming to you. I am glad you wore that dress, on this most special of days."

"And what is so special about it, pray?" I attempted to keep my tone cool and almost uninterested, but my heart began to beat faster for all that. Something about this meeting had begun to feel horribly wrong.

"Why, it is the day when I will marry you, Iselda."

Chapter Seventeen

I stared at him, aghast. "You are mad."

"No, I think not." He turned away from me and made a sort of "come here" gesture with his right hand. A door at the far end of the room, one I hadn't noted previously because it was cunningly hidden in the paneling, opened, and an elderly man wearing the grey robes of one of Inyanna's priests emerged.

No. My mind rebelled, even as I realized how neatly Lord Elwyn had trapped me. I had thought I had another day to make some sort of attempt at escape, but he had never planned to give me the leisure of that much time. A hidden ceremony, and then everyone who arrived for the wedding the next day would be presented with the deed already done. The marriage made...and consummated. And no one would question a thing because of the way Lord Elwyn could manipulate all their minds.

Bile rose in my throat. "I will not," I choked out, and took a step backward.

But he had anticipated that maneuver as well, and grasped me by the wrist before I could move any farther away. "Oh, yes, you will," he replied. "You will stand there, and you will repeat the words of the vows. And you will kiss me at the end...and tonight you will share my bed."

Not caring what the approaching priest might think, I sought to wrench my arm from Lord Elwyn's grasp. Unfortunately, my struggles accomplished very little, except to increase his determination. He held on, his grip tightening so much that I gave a gasp of pain.

"This is what happens if you fight me," he said, his voice an ugly rasp. "You might as well bow to the inevitable, my dear Iselda, for there is nothing you can do to stop me, or to prevent this marriage from happening. I won't say I will not enjoy your struggles, for they are rather enticing, but the end result will be the same."

"You're a monster," I retorted, beyond caring what I said. As his lordship had just informed me, there seemed to be little I could do to change the inevitable outcome of this horrible day. I might as well tell him precisely what I thought of him.

"No, I am not. Merely a determined man, no more." He turned toward the priest, who had paused a few feet away. "We are ready, your honor."

Up close, the priest appeared even more aged and decrepit than he had seemed at a distance. His dark eyes were rheumy and tired, and his grey beard reached almost to his waist. It also appeared stained and yellow around the mouth. I wondered where on earth Lord Elwyn had dug up this specimen. But then, I supposed it served his purposes to use a down-on-his-luck priest for this ceremony, someone who had no real connection to the estate and who would disappear after he had done what the earl requested.

The priest glanced over at me. His eyes, which had seemed so distant a few seconds ago, suddenly grew piercing. "And are you ready, my lady?"

"I already said we were," Lord Elwyn responded, irritation clear in his tone.

"I was asking the lady."

"No!" I burst out. "He is forcing me to marry him! He murdered his son and now wishes to make me his wife instead. Please, sir—you must help me!"

"Ah," said the priest. He looked back toward Lord Elwyn. "Is this true?"

"Of course, it's not true. She is a foolish girl beset by foolish fancies. All will be well once we are wed."

"Ah." Another pause. "Well, that is unfortunate. For I do believe her. And I also believe that you should let her go."

And then he seemed to straighten, and grow taller, and in the next instant, it was no longer the tired old priest who stood before us, but Reynar, his silver eyes sparkling with anger.

"You!" Lord Elwyn burst out, even as my heart swelled with relief.

Reynar had not abandoned me. He had only been waiting for the right moment to come and take me away.

"Oh, thank the gods!" I nearly sobbed at the thought of my deliverance, even though I knew I should not be too confident. Not yet. For Reynar was still the apprentice and Lord Elwyn the master, and I truly had no idea how my lover would be able to best the man who had trained him.

"You have nothing to be thankful for," Elwyn snarled, then raised his hand, just as he had with Mayson the day before.

And yet—the effect was not the same, for while Reynar took a few staggering paces backward, he still more or less maintained his ground, and certainly was not flung back against the wall, as no doubt Lord Elwyn had intended.

"Neither—do—you," Reynar panted, and made an odd gesture with his left hand, middle and ring fingers held by his thumb as he seemed to flick something away from him.

An icy unseen wind wrapped around us, breaking Elwyn's grip on my arm. I stumbled away, not sure what had just happened, but very glad that I no longer was the earl's prisoner.

"Ungrateful boy!" Lord Elwyn snarled. "I gave you everything—a home, food on your table, training in magic. And you would take her side? She is mine."

"No," Reynar said calmly. "She is her own. And her heart is hers to give."

"You are a fool," Elwyn replied, jaw clenched. "Do you think I care about her heart? I only care about the sons she will give me, sons whose powers will make yours look as trifling as you yourself are."

"I'd rather die first!" I broke in, but Reynar only shook his head.

"No, my love, there is no need for such sacrifice. You and I will leave his place, and Lord Elwyn will have to get his sons elsewhere."

"You think it is as simple as that?" Again Lord Elwyn raised his hands, and this time the blow was much stronger, knocking Reynar backward a good ten paces. Luckily, the center of the room was empty, and so he did not land on any furniture, only the heavy wool rug. Even so, I let out a cry of worry and began to move forward, only to have Elwyn lunge for me and grasp me by the sleeve. I yanked my arm away, and heard the silk tear.

No matter. The only important thing was that he had not caught me, and I was still free to run to Reynar's side. He had begun to push himself back up to a sitting position when I came to kneel next to him.

"Are you hurt?"

He shook his head, even as I saw him try to hold back a wince of pain. "Not really."

But that brief exchange was all we had time for, as in the next instant Lord Elwyn was beside us as well, his face contorted with fury. From the corner of my eye, I saw him reaching for my arm so he might pull me away, and something within me seemed to snap. No, I would not allow him to manhandle me again in such a fashion. He had lost, even if he did not know it.

For the briefest flash of a second, Reynar's eyes met mine. I seemed to be drowning in a sea of silver, falling into a moonlit rain.

And then his voice in my mind, *We must do this together, Iselda.*

His hand came out to me, and I grasped it. Quicksilver fire rippled through my veins, cold and hot at the same time, flooding through every limb. I had never experienced such a sensation before, and yet I thought I knew what it was.

Magic.

I did not know how to use it. But Reynar did.

Our clasped hands were surrounded by a ball of shimmering light, like the godfire some sailors reported seeing dancing on the open waves. It awoke shimmering reflections in Lord Elwyn's shocked eyes, even as he stumbled backward a pace, clearly uncertain as to what he should do next. Still holding hands, Reynar and I stood. And then he nodded.

Together, we hurled the ball of light at the earl. It hit him and spread out along his arms and down his legs, appearing to cover him in garments of flaring incandescence, even as his limbs jerked in a macabre imitation of some kind of pagan dance. And then the light was gone, and he had fallen to the floor, eyes staring and blank. As I watched, his face began to alter, lines forming at the corners of his eyes, dragging cruel furrows from nose to mouth, while at the same time his hair turned almost as pale as Reynar's own. All those stolen years, returned to him tenfold in but an instant, once his own magic had died with him.

For the longest moment, Reynar and I stood there in silence, staring down at what we had done.

I hated to ask, but knew I must. We had to face what had just happened. A question began to form in my mind. *Did we—*

"Yes," Reynar said aloud, stopping me before I could give mental voice to the words. "We killed him. It was the only way. He would never have let you go."

"How—?" I had to stop there, for I had begun to tremble all over, and my voice shook. My mind did not want to grasp the enormity of what we had just done.

At once Reynar's arms were around me, and he kissed the top of my head as he held me close. "You had the power within you all along, Iselda. You just did not know it was there."

"Why didn't you tell me?" The words sounded far more accusing than I had intended them to, but I did not seem to have a very good grasp on my emotions in that moment.

"Come here, dearest." He led me over to one of the chairs and sat me down, then stood in front of me so he blocked my view of Lord Elwyn's body, slumped on the floor. "I would have told you, at the proper time. Indeed, at first I was not even sure. While it is true that all mage-born can sense one another, my facility for doing so is not as strong as—as my late master's. And what I sensed from you was very different from the power I had always felt within Lord Elwyn. I had to be certain, and it was not until I guessed at his plans that I realized why he desired you so badly for his son."

"His son that he murdered," I said bitterly, for the guilt of that death would weigh on me for years to come. "He said it was because Mayson was a disappointment to him, but now I rather wonder if the main motive for that murder was to arrange things so he could claim me for his own."

"Most likely," Reynar agreed. "And I am sorry that I could not be here to reassure you, but I could not risk being caught by his lordship."

"I understand." And I did. I would never wish to live through another night like the one I had just spent, but better that than to have Reynar come rushing in without a clear plan and risk capture. A sudden thought struck me, and I slanted a glance up at him through my eyelashes. "So where is the real priest?"

"Sleeping it off in Daleskeld Forest," Reynar replied with a grin. "Poor man, he could not resist the temptation of a flask of brandy that a stranger offered him. He will wake up with a headache in a few hours, but should suffer no other ill effects than that."

"I am glad," I said. "But how did you know at all what Lord Elwyn intended?"

"I knew that he planned to marry you to Mayson, and I began making my plans then. But after I heard what had happened to him, I realized my master had no intention of allowing you to return to your aunt. This gift of disguise is a valuable one, for I was able to come and go here in the castle without him even realizing I was about."

"But...." I shook my head as I attempted to put together the pieces of the story. "Lord Elwyn claimed that he could sense anyone who was mage-born. So how did you escape his notice?"

"I can hide that about myself as well, when I take on one of my disguises." A flash of a grin, and he extended his hands to me. I took them and let him pull me upright. "Something I discovered purely by accident, once upon a time. It seemed a useful gift, but I *may* have neglected to inform my master that I had such a skill."

"Well, I am very glad you did."

"As am I." And he drew me toward him, and kissed me swiftly, and said, "But we should go. His lordship informed the household staff that he was not to be disturbed, but his spells will begin to dissipate, now that he is gone."

"Where will we go?" I asked, for indeed, in that moment I could not begin to guess what lay ahead of us. I still could barely grasp the realization that I possessed strange powers, powers which had lain dormant within me for all these years.

"First, to your aunt and uncle. They deserve some sort of explanation. After that...?" His shoulders lifted, and although he still smiled, I thought I detected a hint of worry in his eyes. "I suppose that depends on you."

"North Eredor," I said at once, and an eyebrow went up. I went on quickly, for his expression remained dubious, "Is it not the most logical choice? You can practice magic openly there, and my sister and her husband dwell there as well, in the capital of Tarenmar, and will most certainly give us a warm welcome. We would be part of a family."

"A family," Reynar repeated in musing tones. "I think I should like that."

"Then we must go," I said. "Only...." I paused and gazed at him, at the fall of bright silver hair. He was so very conspicuous.

"My love, you should remember that my appearance is no impediment." And as he spoke, the pale hair was replaced by sooty black, and the silver eyes became dark blue. Lord Elwyn stared back at me, and I gave a little gasp.

"Oh, dear," I said, my voice trembling somewhat. "It is so very convincing. Too convincing, I think."

"Well, my love, rest assured that I will get rid of it as soon as it is safe to do so."

I could not argue with that, and so we exited the chamber and closed and locked the door behind us. Dreadful as he had been, I could not help but be relieved that someone would discover Lord Elwyn's body soon enough, for I did not like the thought of leaving him lying there all alone like that.

But soon I had no room in my thoughts for such concerns, as we went to my suite, and informed a rather astonished Tarly that I would be returning to my aunt and uncle's home after all, and that all my things needed to be packed as quickly as possible. I could not tell what shocked her more—our precipitous departure, or the way Lord Elwyn had accompanied me, and indeed announced his intention to ride with us, rather than sending some of his men along to safeguard our journey home.

At any rate, she worked with dispatch, and within the quarter-hour we were taking my satchels downstairs. There we came across the footman who had guided me to my meeting with Lord Elwyn. The manservant seemed rather surprised that his master would be carrying my bags, but of course he had no reason to think the man standing there in the foyer was anyone except the earl.

So the footman was sent to fetch us some horses, and not so very long afterward we were riding away, with Bellender Rise growing smaller and smaller behind us. Even then, I could not be entirely relieved, for I knew Reynar would have to maintain his disguise until we reached my uncle's estate and Tarly had departed for the servants' quarters. He had said it was difficult to hold the illusion for more than a few hours, and the journey would require almost three.

I sent him an inquiring look, as if to ask that very question, and he gave the faintest of nods. So it seemed he could manage, even if it would put a strain on him.

We rode in silence; I could sense Reynar did not want to waste energy in talking, and I was far too anxious to spend my time in idle conversation. At last, though, the marker indicating the border to my uncle's property appeared next to the roadside, and a few minutes after that, I spied the great grey pile of the castle itself rising from the golden fields which surrounded it.

And soon enough we were riding up to the front steps, and the footmen rushed out to assist us. I could see the surprise in their faces, for my aunt and uncle were supposed to have set out the next morning to attend my wedding, and yet here I was, and with the father of the man everyone thought I was to marry.

I said that his lordship and I would go to the small salon, and if my aunt and uncle could meet us there?

"Of course, my lady," said Jax the footman, who hurried off to fetch them. My word was certainly not law around here, but the servants knew better than to make an earl wait.

"And Tarly," I went on, "you may go ahead and rest. I'll have someone else attend to these bags." In actuality, I hoped that Reynar and I would be on our way soon enough, and so it was best to leave my belongings here in the foyer, so we might gather them up on our way out.

Although I could see speculation in her eyes, she bobbed a curtsey and said, "Of course, my lady," before heading off to the wing of the castle where she shared a room with several of the other maids.

"This way," I told Reynar, and led him to the small salon. I had always liked that room, with its tall windows that overlooked the courtyard, and the hearth of rosy-hued marble. Something about it made me feel safe, and I definitely needed that reassurance now.

Just a few minutes later, my aunt and uncle entered the room. Upon catching sight of me, Aunt Lyselle exclaimed, "Oh, my poor child!" and rushed over, clasping me to her breast.

At the same time, Uncle Danly, much more restrained, said, "Lord Elwyn, we are deeply grieved by your loss. We appreciate your generosity in bringing Iselda home, but—"

"As to that," Reynar cut in, "I fear we by necessity had to perpetuate something of a subterfuge."

And his assumed guise of Lord Elwyn faded away, leaving the Reynar I knew in his place, with his bright hair and fierce eyes, and a simple dark doublet to replace the sumptuous one the "earl" had been wearing.

My uncle let out a shocked oath, and Aunt Lyselle abruptly let go of me so she might bring an astonished hand to her mouth.

"It is all right, Aunt Lyselle," I said quickly. "This is Reynar, who has kept me safe from the earl. And yes, he is a mage, but it seems I might be one, too, and—"

"Wait," Uncle Danly interrupted. That interruption revealed something of his current state of shock, for in general he was all politeness. "What on earth are you talking about, Iselda?"

"It's rather a long story," Reynar said. "So perhaps it would be better if we all sat down."

We did sit, and Reynar and I took turns explaining what had happened, and describing Lord Elwyn's perfidy. My aunt and uncle were alternately shocked and saddened, their eyes growing ever wider as we recounted the tale.

"And so," I said, once we were done...or mostly, at any rate, "it is our intention to ride to North Eredor, and seek out Annora and Tobyn. We shall not be so alone in the world then, and we know we will not have to live in hiding, either."

"Ride off together?" my aunt said, looking quite chagrined. "When you are not married? My dear, that sort of thing simply isn't done."

I did not bother to remind her that my sister had done that very same thing. True, she and Tobyn had been married soon after, but still....

"I would not wish to bring shame to your niece," Reynar said. "At the same time, it is far wiser for us to leave immediately, for as soon as Lord Elwyn's body is discovered, there are those who will want to question Iselda. We cannot afford to waste much time."

"No need for that at all," Uncle Danly put in. "I can have a man here to marry you within the hour. If that is what you both wish, of course."

For a moment, neither Reynar nor I said anything. Our eyes met, and I could not help but see the yearning in his expression. I recognized it, because I felt that same need within my own heart. We would be sealed together forever, and I would have it no other way.

"Oh, yes," we both said at once, and Reynar chuckled.

"Yes," I said firmly. "That is what we both wish."

So my uncle sent for the priest, who came to us in the same small salon and married us there. Perhaps it was not the wedding of my dreams, as I stood next to Reynar with my torn sleeve, he in his garments of plain linen, with no flowers or guests other than my aunt and uncle, but truly none of that mattered so very much, not when I would have Reynar as my husband. Where my cousins and Janessa were during all this, I did not know, but by some stratagem they were kept away.

Afterward, my aunt wept and embraced me, and said she did not know what she would do, now that both her nieces were to live so far from her. I promised I would write if I could, while Uncle Danly shook hands with Reynar, at the same time pressing a small pouch into my husband's hands. I guessed the pouch contained some funds to help us on our way, for Reynar shot me a rather amused glance but said nothing in protest. Truly, we would need the assistance, for while I had the gems Tobyn had sent me, it might be difficult to sell them on our travels.

And then horses were brought for us, and my satchels as well, and not so very long after that we were riding north and west, on the road that would take us to Farendon, and from there to the pass in the Opal Mountains which would at last bring us down into North Eredor. Such a journey could take weeks, although I thought we should be able to travel swiftly, since we had set forth at such an auspicious time of year.

We could not ride so very far that first day, as we had left Mirfeld Hall quite late in the afternoon. But the road brought us down into the village known as Fenwall, where we found a good inn, a place to share a quite excellent dinner of chicken pie, washed down with the local wine. By necessity, Reynar had altered his appearance as soon as we drew close to the town, and wore the same dark hair and eyes and tanned skin that he had used in the very first disguise he had shown me.

When we were alone in our room, however, he let the spell fall away, and it was my Reynar who stood there, so striking and handsome that I went to him at once and put my arms around him, and kissed him again and again, tasting the sweet wine on his lips, and tasting something far sweeter when he drew me over to the bed and lay there with me, and made me his wife in truth, rather than just in name.

Some might say that was where our adventure ended...but I knew it was just beginning.

⌒ Epilogue ⌒

S pring has come again, as it always does. Here in the north, that spring might arrive a little later than what I was used to back in my homeland of Purth, but I do not mind. The northland has its own beauty, with its high, snow-capped mountains and forests of dark fir, and the first pale wildflowers to show their faces with the arrival of the sun.

Annora implied that she and Tobyn were prospering, but I did not realize how prosperous they truly were until Reynar and I arrived in Tarenmar at the end of a weary journey of some six weeks, and saw their grand house of stone, which is located in a fashionable district not so very far from the Mark's palace. And more than that—because the Markess is a mage of some renown herself, Tobyn and my sister are often invited to palace functions, and enjoy a far higher place in society than I might have imagined.

They welcomed us, and gave us a place to live until Reynar and I could acquire our own house. This was not as difficult as it might have been, for as soon as Kadar, the Mark, learned that several new mages had arrived in his land, he gave us a most noble welcome, and provided a home just down the street from where my sister and her husband lived.

I hoped I would belong here...but I what I did not realize was how truly deep that belonging would run. It is a strange thing, to feel so safe, so surrounded by love. My aunt and uncle did their best, but it was not the same as being with one's true family, of not having to hide who you truly are...even if you did not know what that was until very recently.

This is something Reynar and I have come to understand, that the pull we felt toward one another was the old blood speaking within, crying out for its match. There are so few of us now that the chances of a mage-born encountering another who could be their partner in life are very small, and I feel doubly blessed that we ever managed to find each other.

And now the spring has come, and new life is stirring within me. I think of those I left behind, and mourn that I will never see them again. But I do hear from Aunt Lyselle, who writes to the Mark, knowing that he will give her letters to me. So I know that Janessa and Gwyllim were married at Midwinter, and Adalynn and Coryn are also expecting their first child, and Lord Elwyn's death was never explained, and neither was the strange alteration in his appearance. Even so, the estate and the title went to a distant cousin after all the investigations were complete, and the questions and the hubbub eventually died down, just as they always do.

It is a new life here, one which fills me with hope. For perhaps if the Mark and his consort continue their work, the world will begin to understand that magic is not something to be feared, but encouraged and nurtured. There will always be those who seek to abuse it, as Lord Elwyn did, but that is no excuse to turn away from its use, from the many wonders it can bring to mankind.

And perhaps my children will one day live in a world where they do not have to hide who they are, but who can flourish in the light.

I hope this dream will come true, for all my others have.

The End